The Butterfly Circle

a novel

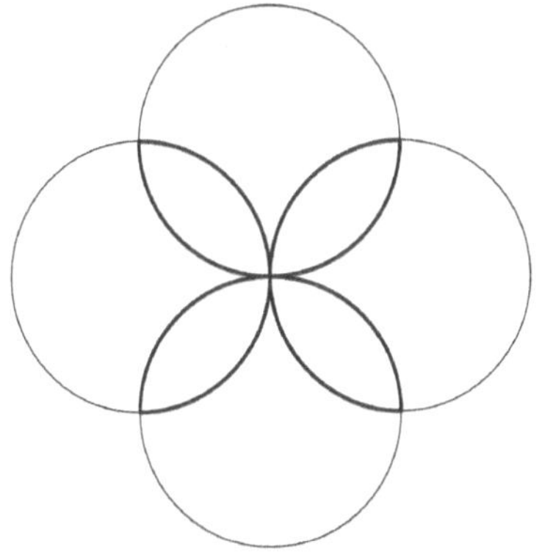

Mary Carroll Leoson

Manta Press, Ltd.
www.mantapress.com

Cover Design by Creative Paramita

First Edition

Dedication

For Ed – Your love gives me the courage to take risks.

For Korinne – I discovered strength rooted in womanhood when I became your mom.

And for my Butterfly Sisters – you know who you are.

We always have the sky.

Chapter 1

June, 1948.

Eliza Kendall– Dandelion Girl

The day before her father sent her to the home for unwed mothers, Eliza sat on top of the hill where she always went to be alone, the warm earth holding her in cupped palms. The hum of nature all around was at once painful silence and a loud roar. It was like the ocean held in a seashell; the sound only emerged when you held it to your ear and paid attention. It was an auditory fantasy, but it was better to be lost in the childlike magic than its explanation. She would give anything to go back to a time before, when life seemed so simple.

The silence beyond the hum of creatures came in the wake of so many losses. She was alone—feeling isolated from friends and family—an abandonment that had no equal. The irony was not lost on her, for it was the love she sought that had brought her to this place.

His eyes appeared in her mind, once so tender. She felt his breath on her neck, the warmth of his hands on her body. A closeness she'd been told was sinful but felt like heaven.

Until it wasn't.

Whatever power had drawn him to her evaporated once the suspect bump in her abdomen appeared. They were like magnets before, drawn to each other with a force that couldn't be denied, until he turned the other way and repelled her with equal force. She kept reaching out for him, for the once tender eyes, the embracing arms that lingered around her like phantoms, but found only emptiness and rumor. She was burned, shunned, shamed.

Like an infection, his disdain spread. Her friends whispered; teachers glanced at her sideways. Her parents looked at her differently—a combination of disappointment and contempt. Like the life growing in her was a vampire, shifting her into a thing of darkness.

She had become unholy.

Stroking the blades of grass with her fingertips, she traveled back in time to the Virgin's Garden, with a statue of the Mother in a blue shroud. Her face was ethereal, an ambiguous silhouette carved in stone, but her love was everywhere— nurturing the life that danced in neat rows. Tulips in bright candy shades, daffodils with buttery centers and petals like a lion's mane. Passionate plum crocuses, lace pink peonies, and pale snowdrops that hung like gentle tears. Her realm was a bouquet of delight.

The reflecting pond at the center of the garden was a wishing well, filled with prayers cast by young girls in ponytails, tartan uniforms, and saddle shoes. The steppingstones were like hopscotch, set wide enough to jump and surrounded by grass to catch girls who fell. And markers were placed around the grove by the feet of the trees—reminders of righteous thinking and the Hail Mary. And if you looked at the garden from the belltower above (she had heard, for she never had been), it was shaped like a rosary. So just being there had to touch you with some part of her grace.

If motherhood was following in Mary's steps, should this not be a blessed act? Eliza's heart had told her this, but the world outside had cast such a shadow it eclipsed all the hope she once had. In her chest was a gaping wound—a place where a cord once attached her to him, and when he left, it ripped away. Now the emptiness poured in, and she was drowning.

As if the pain wasn't enough, she felt like a fool. A fool for loving him, for trusting in the promises of marriage and a life they would build together. She had bought into doing the right thing for all her life. It was the one time she had strayed into temptation—into a passion that bloomed and rooted in her soul. Now the roots invaded sacred places that were only hers; they twisted and turned into a noose of thorned stems and leaves with fangs.

Now she knew the truth. She was no prized rose bush, tamed into a neat row to be admired from afar. She did not belong in the garden. Even in a field of wildflowers, rich with color and vibrance, adventure and freedom, she was but a dandelion. A weed to be plucked. A nuisance that would keep growing and growing until it could no longer be disguised. And in the morning, they would secret her away in a home for those like her.

She waited on the hill as the clouds rolled in, dancing in the wind even as it gained momentum. The rain fell around her in large drops, landing first with gentle plunks, then growing into a barrage of pelting tears. Lightning screamed through the sky before thunder growled in a bass note. She moved with the rhythm, hips swaying like lulling a babe, her sobs muted by the storm's symphony.

She opened her mouth and begged the wind to blow her away as a thousand wishes.

Chapter 2

The immense home was a castle compared to the average Cleveland house. It sat behind a high brick wall with iron grating at the top—to keep people in or out was unclear. Tall towers reached into the sky with jagged crenels and merlons—teeth waiting to bite. The Tudor façade above the portico echoed the medieval tone, taking visitors back to a time of knights and kings. But this was no fairy tale. The home was a shelter for unwed, fallen women to be hidden in shameful shadow.

As the car pulled under the archway lit by a gas lantern, the air seemed to crackle, as if passing to another realm. A man exited the driver's side, leaving the car running, and opened the back passenger door for a small form. The girl, for she was just a girl, emerged reluctantly, shoulders slumped, face cast downward, and did not lift her gaze to the looming building above. She did not feel the eyes upon her.

The man dropped a suitcase at her feet without a glance or an embrace. He returned to his place behind the wheel and sped away, leaving her in a storm of dust that refused to settle. The wind whipped about in a tornado, sweeping leaves and debris around her like Maypole ribbons. Then there was stillness.

The girl sank to her knees, her shoulders shaking with sobs, and the angel in the window was compelled forth.

Rosa knew the girl's pain well, for she had arrived at the home only three months ago in a similar state. On quiet feet, she crept down the dimly lit hall lined with portraits of benefactors to the winding staircase. Peeking over the railing, she listened for movement or whispers. Hearing nothing, she crept down the stairs one by one, keeping her feet on the thick carpet to muffle her steps. She landed on the black and white foyer floor, and moved as quickly as she could across the cool marble, holding her growing belly in an effort to balance.

Rosa swept beneath the oak archway above the vestibule, engraved with *"ultra peccare"*, Latin for 'on the other side of sin'. She rolled her eyes at its message and resisted the urge to spit, then quietly opened the front door. It groaned and squeaked, which she knew it would, but was pleased she had gotten this far without detection. They must not have heard the car pull up outside.

The girl was still crumpled on the driveway, shaking.

"Hello?" said Rosa. As much as she wanted to throw her arms around her and tell her everything was going to be alright, she did not want to startle her.

Two light eyes peered up at her, rimmed with red. Her face looked surprised and wary as she tucked a loose strand of blonde hair behind an ear.

Rosa approached her slowly, reaching out a hand, and said the words with which another had greeted her. "Don't worry," she said. "You're among sisters. I'm Rosa."

The girl's voice was almost a whisper. "Eliza," she said.

Rosa was the most beautiful girl Eliza had ever seen. With her large, dark eyes, delicate nose and short stature, she was right out of a fairy book. The girl's swollen belly was a cantaloupe under the cotton nightgown—a glance into the future that made Eliza shudder. She unconsciously placed her hand on her own abdomen.

"Follow me," said Rosa. While her face was angelic, her voice was unwavering and rich. She reminded Eliza of the popular girls at school, especially the ones with bravado. She wondered if she should trust this girl or if what lie around the corner was teasing and insults—like it often was at school. But there was sincerity in her eyes, and Eliza desperately wanted a friend.

"I know you don't want to be here," Rosa said, her expression somber. "It's not my idea of a holiday either. But you know—" she gestured to her round stomach. "My party invitations seem to be getting lost lately. At least this place has a warm bed and decent food." She stood, waiting.

Eliza bit her lip, the moment stretching out into awkwardness. Her father wasn't coming back. He'd made that clear.

She accepted the outstretched hand.

Rosa's lips turned up into a smile, along with the corners of her eyes. Their deep brown was warm and honest. "You don't have to do this alone."

Something shifted in Eliza, and she took a step forward, into the unknown.

Inside the mansion, it was warm and smelled like cleanser. The light was dim, but still revealed the black-and-white checkered floor and dark wood that lined the walls. As they moved through the entry hall and into the larger reception area, Eliza lifted her eyes to the looming ceiling, where a crystal chandelier hung. The grandeur was foreign and unexpected. It made her feel small and insignificant.

"Stop right there, young ladies." The matronly voice cut through the air with a bite.

Rosa froze, and Eliza almost bumped into her. The dark-haired girl spun to face their accuser.

"Mrs. Miller," Rosa said, with a sweet grin. "I was just coming to find you."

"Indeed," said the older woman, her tone sarcastic and her face unamused. "Rosa, please return to your room. Our new arrival will join you shortly."

Rosa's eyes flicked to Eliza's face, then back to the woman. "Yes, Mrs. Miller." She moved like a graceful deer, her naked feet on tiptoes, her elegant fingers brushing the railing as she climbed the stairs.

Mrs. Miller cocked one eyebrow. "Eliza Kendall, I presume?"

"Yes, ma'am," she said, her voice emerging as a whisper.

"Speak up, child."

"Yes, ma'am." It was too loud this time, rising past the chandelier and echoing back down again. She gulped.

The woman sighed, unimpressed. Eliza shifted uncomfortably under her gaze.

"Very well," said Mrs. Miller. "Let's take an inventory of your things and get you up to bed. Lights-out in an hour so you need to be settled."

Eliza picked up her suitcase to follow the woman, but Mrs. Miller turned with another thought.

"And, Eliza, you will be rooming with Rosa, whom you've just met. But I would offer you some advice to keep your distance." Mrs. Miller pursed her lips. "She has been known to cause… trouble." She tilted her head with the last word, giving it a life of its own.

Eliza was not sure if it was Mrs. Miller's commanding tone or her father's abandonment. Or it could have been the desperate loneliness she'd felt lately, or the terror every time she thought of the baby growing inside her. Or maybe she'd had enough of following the rules and ending up with the short end of the stick, anyway. But something told her she and Rosa were destined to be roommates. And it would not take Eliza long to see the fairy girl was prone to mischief, and she would love her all the more for it.

Chapter 3

Rosa Ricci – The Wild Mare

"You've turned the evil eye on this family."

This was the last thing Rosa heard from Mama as her bedroom door shut between them the night before they sent her away. Her family was always afraid of beings that lurked beyond reach. Her fear hung over them, waiting for its chance to point fingers.

But it was Mama who was suffering—from the cancer that took her body, and her spirit, too. All that was once good and gentle about her was eaten away until there was nothing left but fear and anger. The nurturing Mama that had bandaged Rosa's scraped knees and taught her to measure out baking ingredients was just a memory. This decrepit, bitter monster had taken her place.

Rosa longed for who she had been six months before, but would admit that to no one. Papa was wonderful, but his sadness was steeped in wine and rich foods—the only things that brought him comfort. His sadness and his waistline grew, and she worried he might be next. Her family was dissipating before her eyes.

Matteo was a welcome relief at that time—one that lured Rosa out her bedroom window and down the trellis for secret kisses. His arms were like shelter from the strangeness that had once been such a warm and happy home, filled with laughter and games. For that time, he rescued her—and their clandestine love was exciting! He made her stomach dance with butterflies and her palms sweat with mischief.

And then she realized their light-hearted romance had become something more. Matteo did not run; he did not even take a breath before asking her to marry him. But she was not ready for that life. She had plans—adventures, travel, attending college. Once she was married and had children, those dreams would be lost, especially if he went into the military.

As Rosa withdrew deeper into herself and away from him, Matteo's pleas became more persistent. He took to sitting outside her bedroom window until she threatened to inform Papa. Then he started waiting for her outside of the high school building, following her home until she began walking with others—including boys, which made him furious. Finally, he revealed their secret to Papa, asking for her hand in marriage. And while he granted his blessing, Rosa refused. She would not be Matteo's broken horse.

She was a wild mare, running free without constraints or rules or a man to dictate her destiny. Maybe for the time being she was imprisoned, but as soon as her body was free of this burden, she thought, so would her spirit be.

After a snack of cheese and crackers, Eliza was relegated to her boarding room. She stood before the door, slightly ajar, and knocked. It creaked open with the light pressure of her knuckles, spilling light into the hallway. Rosa looked up from her perch on a twin-sized bed and closed the book on her lap. It was marked "The Bible" on the spine, but Eliza could see another paperback concealed within it.

"Finally," Rosa said. "I thought Mrs. Miller was going to keep you all night."

Eliza stepped slowly into the room, eyeing the three other undisturbed beds with sheets tucked into place.

"She seems… nice," said Eliza, wanting to appear polite.

Rosa grinned and rolled her eyes. "She's not."

Eliza smiled despite herself. "Well, I was trying to be, I guess."

"Nice is what landed us in here, right?" Rosa was not afraid to get to the point.

She was so much like Miss Nancy, the Headmistress' old secretary at St. Ann's—the one who didn't last long but said what she thought even if it drew a sideways glance. It filled Eliza with discomfort, the thought of breaking the rules, but it also secretly intrigued her. If only she could be more like that—honest, frank, unapologetic.

Eliza apologized for everything, just like her mother.

"You can choose whichever one you want," said Rosa, motioning to the empty beds. "They're all up for grabs."

Eliza glanced around, weighing her options, then chose the bed beside Rosa, who nodded.

"Good choice," said Rosa. "That was Faith's bed. She'd be happy you chose it."

"Faith?"

Rosa's smile was sad. "Had her baby last week. Moved to the other side of the house." She said *other side* like it was a different country.

Eliza looked down as if to study the floor, afraid to ask what she wanted to know. "Did she… keep the baby?" Her breath became shaky with emotion in the silence that followed.

"She planned to," said Rosa, sandwiching the question with more silence. It was an answer that deserved a significant pause.

She needed to prick the air with something else— something lighter. "I wonder if we will be joined," said Eliza after a beat.

"From what I've heard, we will be. Both beds should be filled in the next week," said Rosa. "I just hope they're not drips." She raised both eyebrows, then grinned.

Eliza decided then she would not be a drip. This was a chance to be different, for no one knew her here. She would wear a mask of bravado!

At least she would try.

When Eliza woke in the middle of the night, she did not remember where she was. Moonlight crept in through the windows at the far end of the room, suggesting hints of furniture and the other three beds near hers. She drew a shaky breath as she sank back into her own body, leaving the fog of dreams behind. It was then the sense of despair creeped back into her heart.

She studied the ceiling and the shadows of moving leaves

that played there. His eyes came back to her—the eyes that had held hers tenderly and made her heart skip a beat. Shame followed quickly as this memory was replaced with his scornful stare, his bitter laugh as she walked away so he could not see her cry. His promises of love had been such a lie!

The tears brimmed her eyes at the corners and ran down her temples into her hair. They snaked to her ears and onto her pillow, leaving damp puddles and trails of tarnished reputation. And the more she tried to quiet her sobs, the louder they became.

"Hey."

Rosa's whisper was startling and made Eliza choke on her tears. She sat up, preparing to unleash a slew of apologies for waking her, for being rude, for her stupidity and very existence.

Rosa's form sat up in the dark, leaned toward her. "I'm here," she said.

Eliza swallowed her words, which probably would have come out in hiccups and splutters, anyway. The girl's hand reached across the space between them, hung in the air like an invitation. Eliza reached back and closed her fingers around the hand and squeezed. Rosa lightly stroked Eliza's palm with her thumb until she fell asleep.

The next morning, Eliza's eyes were sore and swollen. Her head pounded as she took in the sunlight streaming in through the window, its pure glow beautiful but out of her reach. She rolled over, looking over to Rosa's bed, where her friend sat hunched and deep in thought. Her dark hair hung over her shoulders in long tendrils, the curls at the ends gentle in a way that softened her.

"Morning," said Eliza.

Rosa did not look up. "I thought this was the right thing to do," she said, fumbling with a paper in her hands.

"What do you mean?" asked Eliza, pulling the covers back and sitting up.

"Coming here, giving up the baby," Rosa said. Her long lashes created feathery shadows on her cheeks. They disappeared and reappeared with each blink. "Matteo, my—the father. He's gone." She looked as if she was searching for words, but then handed Eliza an envelope.

The note inside was handwritten in rough penmanship. It read:

Rosa,

I am writing to tell you that I have enlisted in the Army. I am going to basic training tomorrow. By the time you read this, I will be on my way. I hope that when I return, you will have reconsidered—everything.

All my love,
M.

Eliza's brow furrowed. "The Army," she said. She knew little about the military except that the Second World War was over and most of the men had returned home. "What does that mean, exactly? Where did he go?"

Rosa shrugged. "No idea."

"I'm sorry," said Eliza. She wasn't sure what else to say. Rosa had not talked about herself or her boyfriend last night. She had merely comforted Eliza.

"I'm not," said Rosa. And then added, quietly, "Well,

maybe I am." She lay back on her bed, stared up at the shapes the sunlight created on the ceiling. Then she placed her hands on her rounded stomach and rolled onto her side, met Eliza's eyes.

"It's my fault," said Rosa. "He asked me to marry him. Chased me everywhere, practically begged. But I wasn't ready for that, you know? I want to live! See things! Maybe have a career. I don't know… I just know I don't want someone else making decisions for me. And being a military wife. It sounds like a prison sentence. No more options, no more choices. Just go where you're told. And maybe end up with a dead husband."

For Eliza, relating to this was a foreign concept. Marriage was all she ever wanted, ever expected for herself. To have one person forever, and to be a mother. But she never pictured the mother part without the ring, the home, the other half. "So, what is it you *do* want?" Eliza asked.

"See the world. Eat interesting food. Wear a kimono. Walk in the Swiss Alps. Dance under the aurora borealis in Alaska. Take some writing classes. Maybe even teach one day," said Rosa. She took a deep breath.

Rosa had so many plans. Eliza had none but marriage—and that had failed her.

"I never wanted a predictable life, you know?" said Rosa.

Eliza shrugged. "It's all I've ever wanted."

"Really?" Rosa squinched up her nose like she'd smelled something off. "Not me."

"A house in the suburbs," said Eliza. "A handsome man to take care of. I'd nurse the children, keep the home clean, have dinner on the table for when he got home at 5:30."

"Every day?" said Rosa, a horrified expression on her face.

Eliza nodded. "Yep. It sounds like heaven."

"So, why are you here, then? Why don't you just do it? You're almost eighteen, right?"

Eliza looked down, felt her cheeks grow warm. "Almost seventeen… Michael, that's my—" she motioned to her belly. "He's not. I mean, he didn't want… me."

Rosa's face softened. "Oh." She swallowed. "I'm sorry. Here I am going on about how I don't want to be tied down…"

Eliza's smile did a sore job covering her embarrassment. "It's not your fault Michael is a drip."

The knock on the door disturbed the atmosphere, chasing away the deeper thoughts. Rosa stood quickly and went through the motions of making her bed. Eliza followed suit, wondering if they might be in trouble. Was there a mandatory wake-up time?

The door opened to reveal a small woman, older, with sharp features and a bland expression. She wore a black outfit, pressed and neat, but plain. Her graying hair was pulled tightly into a bun as if it kept the rest of her in order. She did not smile. "Breakfast in fifteen minutes," she said, leaving the door open as she walked away.

"Not very friendly, are they?" whispered Eliza, afraid her voice might chase the woman down the hall.

"Mostly judgmental. Very strict, very boring," said Rosa, her tone low. She tucked the remaining covers under her mattress and opened her drawer for a clean set of clothes. "They're all like that, the ward assistants, the nurses. Mrs. Miller, the Headmistress, is the one you really need to watch out for. But they're all her little eyes and ears—so be careful what you say."

"Why do I feel like I'm in kindergarten again?" said Eliza. It's as if she had walked into a funhouse with distorted mirrors.

"In their eyes, we're… misguided," said Rosa as they walked to the bathroom. "And it's their job to fix it. Fix *us*."

Eliza simmered about this as she washed her face and brushed her teeth. On the one hand, *how dare they?* She recalled the bible quote about casting stones—that everyone is a sinner. On the other hand, in the darkest corners of her mind, she worried they might be right.

Chapter 4

Bridget O'Donnell – Irish

Bridget stared into the floor-length mirror in the entrance of the unwed mother's home, its substantial mahogany frame like a door she couldn't open. There was no keyhole, no handle, no hinges. Just a reflection of a girl she didn't recognize. The pale face was cream save for a sprinkling of freckles across the nose. Her green eyes, normally crinkled at the edges with smiles, were cloudy and joyless. Her auburn hair was a tumble of curls, shaped purposefully by the pins from the night before—an elegant mane shrouding a haunted porcelain doll's face.

The black cloak hid her swollen belly, but it could not hide her disgrace. The scarlet lining peaked out from beneath like a screaming secret, too loud to lurk beneath the surface. At least she would remain behind closed doors for the next few months, protecting her good family name and her virtue… what was left of it. At least that's how her parents saw things.

Bridget, on the other hand, wanted to erase this nightmare from happening. But there was no going back.

She shifted her weight from one leg to the other, swaying like a new mum rocking her babe. It felt foreign, like a role she might play. What lines might she might deliver at the beginning of Act I, the spotlight on her and the whole high school watching? But her fantasy melted away in a moment. The curtain had already dropped; her parents had written a new script—one where she disappears into a cocoon and emerges without a ripe womb.

The anger burned her chest with such a flash she expected flames. She was angry at herself, angry at her parents, angry at the world. She dug her fingernails into her palm tighter, tighter, until the pain was bittersweet. And as much as she willed it to spark and consume her in an inferno, the reflection showed only her ashen face, surrendering to this sentence.

"Come, child," said the nurse, not unkindly. Mousy eyes peeked out over wrinkled cheeks at her, and the woman motioned with a bony hand.

Bridget moved to follow her, swallowing her irreverent words. It was one of her worst faults, or so she'd been told. Her mouth threatened to spit out all sorts of filth that, at best, might earn her a chiding and, at worst, a slap. Her eyes bore a hole in the older woman's back until she turned to see the endless portal that emerged behind her. The mirror that once held her reflection had a twin cross the entryway, reflecting back a thousand other mirrors like segments of a worm that dug its way further into darkness. She might have seen it as a warning if she had been patient enough to look closer, but her anger had gotten the better of her yet again.

As she stepped into the mouth of the mansion, she felt a slight shudder, like the walls breathed and the doorknobs watched. But her mother's damning voice echoed in her mind, so she proceeded, leaving the outside world behind.

Eliza and Rosa were working in the garden when the new girl appeared for the first time. Her hair was warm brown in the shade of the mansion, but as she stepped into the sun, it glowed with red. Her face was pleasant, with angular cheeks and bright green eyes the color of limes. She did not seem unfriendly, but she didn't smile either. Rather, she looked at the other girls cautiously while she listened to Nurse Edwards' directions.

"You will be in room two with these girls," said Nurse Edwards. "Room two is the garden room, so you will be charged with tending to the garden daily. That includes caring for the flowers, fruit trees, herbs, and vegetables, then gathering appropriate selections for lunches and dinners, per the cook's requests. Today you can begin with weeding. Rosa can answer any questions you have, as she's been here for several months. Very well—get to it." With that, Nurse Edwards left them to their work.

The girls waved in greetings but kept to their chores. It wasn't until Nurse Edwards disappeared inside that Rosa spoke. She wiped a strand of dark hair from her face and left a trace of dirt there, but didn't bother to wipe it away.

"I'm Rosa and this here is Eliza. What's your name?"

The new girl looked up from her seat on the lawn, where she pulled a weed out from the flowerbed. "Bridget."

"Irish?" Rosa replied.

Bridget sniffed. "What gave it away?" Her tone was sarcastic and challenging.

Eliza held her breath, waiting to see what Rosa would do. She nodded for a moment, sizing up the red-haired girl. "Sassy, too." Her serious face relaxed into a grin. "We'll get along just fine, Irish."

Bridget's stare softened into amusement, and she turned her eyes on Eliza. "What's your story?" she said, looking her up and down.

Eliza faltered and wished she had a clever response, like her friend. "Well, I'm pregnant." As soon as it escaped her lips, she blushed.

Bridget's laugh filled the garden. "No shit," she said.

Eliza's jaw dropped.

She had heard curses before, but always from her father, and usually in the middle of road traffic.

Rosa approached her dramatically, a serious expression on her lovely face. She pulled off her gloves one finger at a time and placed her hand on Eliza's forehead, then spoke in an exaggerated southern accent. "Well, my, my," she said. "You say you're with child? Well, then we'd better get you out of this heat. Bridget, get the girl some water."

As Rosa fawned over her, Eliza couldn't bottle the laughter that began lightly, then bubbled out as giggles. Then her friend stopped with a meaningful pause and lowered her voice and said, "But more importantly, you may need to tell us how this happened." Then she looked at Bridget mischievously, who nodded in agreement.

"Yes, do tell," Bridget said, echoing the southern accent, which was even more convincing than Rosa's.

And though Eliza's face burned red, the thought of sharing the most exciting (and ultimately heart-breaking) thing she had ever done tickled her.

After all, wasn't friendship built on secrets?

Eliza was still learning her way round the mansion, as she spent much of her time in the same three areas—her boarding room quarters, the garden, and the dining room. She was not sure if it was the size of the dining room that limited its capacity (it never seemed full) or if it was done purposefully by the headmistress to limit opportunities for socialization. But each time they breakfasted, lunched, and ate dinner, she and her roommates only saw three or four other young women. And even that was across the hall, in another room. All were still pregnant, though she knew others remained at the house after giving birth; they lived in another wing, but to her knowledge there was only one dining room.

She thought it curious they were kept apart from the others, but perhaps it was because they were tending to their babies—at least those who were keeping them. She was not sure what happened if they were to give them up—how long they would stay, both mothers and children.

Once, when they were on their way back to their boarding room (for they always traveled as a trio or quartet), Eliza glimpsed some of the other girls through a doorway. The door was ajar only for a moment, but it was enough for her to see blonde hair and sad eyes. The hair was like her own. It was a glance into the future, for in several months she would take the other girl's place. But it was the haunting eyes that stuck with her—distant, lonely. Perhaps motherhood was not as she thought it would be.

The image of the girl, who she secretly dubbed "the mirage", stuck with her. She didn't breathe life into it by discussing it with the other girls, but rather kept it to herself. Who was she? What was her story? It felt like seeing through a portal in time, and she struggled to keep that future at bay. What if the mirage was really her—a mirror image of the hollow woman she would become after this? Would the baby take some of her with it? Which part would be stolen, and could she choose? If she could release anything, it would be the yearning for Michael—his eyes, his hands, his voice. But if that's what went with the baby, perhaps it might be doomed to loving an absent father. No—she'd rather keep it than curse a child with emptiness.

"Eliza!" Rosa's voice pulled her out of her own thoughts, and she realized she was just standing in the hallway, staring at the closed door. And as she turned away to follow the other girls up the stairs, she wondered if that door was locked.

Chapter 5

They spent their next two nights in whispers and jokes, making light of their current situation because, well, what else was there to do? The three young women were in the family way, and none seemed to want this situation. None, that was, until they were joined by a fourth. But before her arrival, the tone was one of amusement.

Eliza could not have imagined laughing about this unwanted circumstance in the month prior to her reservation at the home. It had been filled with tears and loneliness and an impending sense of doom that left no hope for her future—only the shame of a tarnished family name and the memory of what she thought was love. Her insides were raw, like a wound that had been picked until it might never heal, and if it did, would leave a crater-sized scar. But with this company, it seemed possible she might be able to do this—that maybe there was some light in the world after all.

One source of their amusement was shadow-play after lights-out. Bridget had sequestered a flashlight, which she called a torch, in the side pocket of her suitcase.

"The old bat missed it during inventory," Bridget said wickedly, when she first revealed it to the girls.

"But why did you pack it?" asked Eliza, a question she meant in earnest.

Bridget and Rosa exchanged a glance with each other, then looked on her with what could have been condescension but felt more like gentle pity. "Well, to sneak out, of course," said Bridget.

Eliza's eyes widened; the thought would never even have occurred to her. "Sneak out? At night?"

"Sweet Liza," said Rosa, who had taken to modifying her name in several ways. "We're going to have to spoil that naivety."

Bridget raised an eyebrow. "How did you ever get past first base?"

The comment went over Eliza's head, and she pursed her lips in frustration.

Bridget shook her head. "You have no idea what I'm talking about, do you?" Then she smiled despite herself and placed a hand on Eliza's. "We'd never be friends outside in the world, you know," she said, "But here we are. And there is something charming about your inexperience."

Rosa nodded. "Agreed," she said, then rolled into another dramatic shift. This time, her accent was English. "So, I challenge you, princess Eliza, oh innocent one, to show us the ugliest face you can." Then she shined the flashlight under her chin and contorted her face into a growl.

Eliza inhaled, filling her lungs and ego with what she hoped would be triumph, and accepted the flashlight. "Very well," she said, propping the light between pillows so it pointed under her chin. She turned her back to the girls while arranging her face in the most disturbing way she knew, one hand over from the top, pulling her nose up like a pig, and the other hand from below, pulling both lower eyelids downward. Then she spun around quickly, placing her face above the light, and snorted.

The girls stared wide-eyed for a moment before they crumpled in a fit of laughter. Eliza continued to snort, moving out of the light and toward them. She came within inches of their faces, up to their ears. She was a swine demon, a grunting specter, intent on terrifying them—or at least entertaining them. Bridget and Rosa squirmed and laughed, giggled and pushed her away, then hid under the covers from the barrage of oinks and snorts.

As their laughter dissipated into sighs, Bridget took her torch and began making shadow puppets on the wall. "Well, Eliza," she said. "Is this what I've been missing out on by avoiding 'good girls'?"

Eliza shrugged. "I'm not all that good," she said in a quiet voice.

"What's that supposed to mean?" said Rosa, her large eyes watching Bridget's shadow puppet bounce along the wall like a rabbit.

Bridget turned to Eliza when she responded with silence. "It sounds like someone has a secret," she said, putting down the flashlight. "I'll tell if you tell."

"Secrets for secrets?" asked Rosa, leaning forward, suddenly more interested.

Eliza shifted uncomfortably, wishing she hadn't said anything. Could she trust these girls? Or would she frighten them off?

"Sworn to silence," said Bridget. "I'll only tell if we take an oath."

Rosa shrugged. "Okay."

Eliza nodded in agreement, more from fear of rejection than anything.

Bridget opened her suitcase and dug through it, then turned around to produce a push pin. "A blood oath," she said. "If we're blood sisters, we have to be loyal."

"I think I did that in elementary school camp?" said Rosa, hinting at annoyance.

Bridget tossed her a fiery glare that softened when she rolled her eyes. "I'm not doing it without the oath."

"Fine," said Rosa, acquiescing with a sigh. She took the pin and pushed it into the side of her thumb without a wince. A small spot of red bloomed there, and she handed it back to Bridget, who poked her pointer finger and inhaled sharply.

"Will it hurt?" said Eliza, abhorring the idea of pricking her own skin.

"Not at all," said Bridget, who moved to hand her the pin. As Eliza reached out, Bridget clasped her wrist and jabbed the pin into the pad of her pinky finger.

"Ow!" exclaimed Eliza, pulling her hand back.

"Sorry," said Bridget, without sounding sorry at all. "I didn't think you'd do it."

"Jesus," said Eliza, then covering her mouth once she realized what she'd said.

Bridget smiled. "Hm. Not so good indeed," she said, then guided the other girls to hold their fingers in the beam of the flashlight. "Now we touch fingers and become of one blood. Then, repeat after me: Blood sisters for life, lest I burn."

"Seriously?" Rosa said, her tone sarcastic.

"Burn?" said Eliza, her nose scrunched.

"Oh, my god, just do it!" Bridget's voice rose, but Rosa squashed it with a "Shhhh!".

The girls' blood blended in the light from the torch, a small smear of red on each of their fingers. Eliza couldn't explain it, but she did feel closer to them as they recited the oath in unison.

"Who's spilling first?" said Rosa, placing her reddened finger in her mouth.

Bridget took a breath, not offering an introduction. "I slept with my math teacher."

The girls stared at her, waiting for a punch line that never came. Then they fired the questions, one by one.

"Do your parents know?" asked Rosa.

Bridget shook her head. "Word spread. Rumors. They heard them. I denied it."

"Are you gonna marry him?" Eliza asked.

Bridget sniffed, then spat, "No. That's not an option."

Eliza hesitated, but she wanted to know. "Why?"

Bridget looked down. Her tone shifted from haughty to vulnerable in an instant. "Because he's already married."

Rosa's eyes grew wide as Bridget teared up. She wiped at them angrily.

"It's okay, I don't care," said Bridget. "I didn't love him. I just… wanted him to want me." She put her hands to her face and left them there.

"We're not judging you, Irish," said Rosa. "Come on, we're all in the same situation."

Bridget dropped her hands to her lap and looked up. "Are you keeping yours, though?"

Rosa looked to Eliza as they both hesitantly shook their heads 'no'.

"That's what I thought," said Bridget.

"You are?" asked Eliza.

"I can't blame you," said Bridget. "It wasn't even my choice, you know. My parents—they're Catholic. 'We're not giving up a baby,' they said—like it was theirs to keep."

"I'm sorry, Bridget," said Eliza.

"Don't do that," said Bridget. "Don't pity me."

"I wasn't—I don't," stammered Eliza, not knowing what to say—how to fix it.

"Just leave it," said Bridget, wiping at her nose. Her expression shifted, and so did her tone. She was done sharing. "Your turn," she said, staring at Eliza.

Eliza felt her face grow warm and was glad for the dim light. "I sometimes know things before they happen." She held her breath, afraid her new friends would withdraw, look at her differently. And they did—but with interest, which was something new.

"What, like… extrasensory perception?" said Bridget. Her eyes narrowed, then she leaned in, wanting to know more.

"You have the sight," said Rosa, nodding with unsurprised confidence.

Bridget turned to Rosa. "You say that like it's normal."

Rosa shrugged. "I mean, in my family, it kind of is. At least my Roma side."

"Roma?" asked Bridget.

"You'd probably say Gypsy—but don't use that word," clarified Rosa.

"And here I thought you were Italian," said Bridget, with a curious smile.

"I am—mostly," said Rosa. "But that's beside the point. Okay, Liza-Lie, tell us about your visions."

Eliza was speechless. As they had bantered back and forth, it had given her a moment to collect her thoughts, to embrace with surprise this seeming acceptance. Yet she was at a loss for words. No one had ever actually asked about them before. The girls at school—the moment they discovered her secret, she was shunned. No—worse than shunned—they labeled her a *witch*. And once the nuns heard about it, they pulled her into the principal's office and given a nasty talking-to. Just thinking about it made her shudder.

"Touched by the devil. Evil within you. Penance required." Those were only a few of the phrases slung at her that day. They'd called her parents in for a meeting to discuss her "inappropriate behavior and lies she told the other children to frighten them."

But they were not lies, and Eliza had never thought of the dreams as evil. She'd even had the audacity to think she was special—until she wasn't. The nuns made that clear. Rather, she was tainted.

"Hey, Kewpie doll," said Bridget, "Snap out of it." She clapped in front of Eliza's face, startling her.

Rosa repeated her question. "Come on. Tell us."

Eliza had never had a more captivated audience before—ever. The girls sat with wide-eyed wonder as she described the countless times she'd had a dream and then woken to see the events play out, just as she had foreseen them. Usually they were inconsequential—a newspaper headline, a specific argument between her parents, a stray cat on her porch that became their family pet. But there were other events, too—more significant ones. Like seeing a particular neighbor stop a child from running out into the street, or hearing a nasty conversation that took place between her friends—about her—behind her back. It was this last one that got her in the most trouble because she had confronted them at school. They couldn't understand how she knew and turned on each other at first, thinking one had confessed to her, but ultimately, they abandoned Eliza, labeling her a witch. Because how else could she possibly know what they'd done if she wasn't a spell-casting conjurer?

And then there were the dreams that had stalked her since as far back as she could remember, when she'd woken drenched in sweat, crying out for her mother. These nightmares—these wicked dreams—felt like something else. Something real. Something sinister.

She was always being stalked by a wolf. Not a gray wolf one might see in the wild, but a large black beast, more immense than any man, with glowing red eyes and a growl that shook the ground. It was common for her to have the dreams when she was upset, and they always disturbed her sense of comfort— both at night and during the day, as if the creature could leap out of the dream and manifest to gobble her whole.

Her mother blamed late-night reading, especially the tale of "Red Riding Hood". She dismissed it as a fantastical imagination and, at one point, worried her daughter was telling lies for attention. This concern became more exaggerated when Eliza was called into the principal's office and reprimanded. But all this had taught the girl was adults cannot be trusted. Or girlfriends. Now boyfriends were to be added to that list with this latest abandonment. So, she had only herself.

But maybe not. That's what Eliza sat pondering as Bridget and Rosa listened to her, urging her to tell them more.

"That is definitely the sight," said Rosa, sounding authoritative. "It's a gift. You should be celebrated in your family, not… punished."

"They're afraid," said Bridget. "Believe me, I know all about how religion instills people with fear. My mother does penance if she says a swear in anger. And God help her if she has to miss mass on Sundays. It's like the wrath of Heaven'll rain down upon our house. She goes twice the following week just to make it up—like a deal with God or something."

Rosa sighed. "Yeah, my mom's like that, too," she said. "Especially now that she's sick. But I remember what she was like before—how my Roma side honors these things."

Eliza had learned to see religion through the Catholic Church, but her feelings about this were complicated. On the one hand, she loved the buildings, with their sacred windows and echoing marble floors. In the church she had grown up in, she felt a sense of peace whenever she sat there in silence. The gardens outside were a sanctuary where she felt the presence of Mother Mary, watching over her and guiding her. In the second grade, the idea of nuns enchanted her, and she thought she might make an excellent one. But then she had felt their judgment, their rejection, pushing her out of those circles because of something she had never asked for in the first place. Both sadness and resentment burned in her.

"It makes me angry," said Eliza.

"Now that I understand," said Bridget, nodding.

Rosa let out a long sigh. "It makes me want to run away," she said, like she was confessing something heavy.

"Me too," said Bridget.

"No, really," said Rosa. "I think I want to leave. After all this." She motioned to her swollen tummy. "I don't want to be here anymore, pretending I fit in with my family and the broken thing they've become. I'd like to be in a caravan, you know— find a band of my people and tell fortunes all day—even if I don't have the sight like Eliza. That's my secret—I want out."

"Maybe they'll take us all," said Eliza.

"Maybe they would," said Bridget.

The silence enveloped them in a shared space as the connection grew among them. Eliza basked in it, feeling its warmth wrap around her in an unexpected blanket. She never wanted to let it go.

"I do have one more secret," confessed Rosa. From within her nightgown, she lifted a chain secured around her neck, at the end of which was an object.

Under the flashlight's glare, they examined the skeleton key. It was dark metal—tarnished and worn, with jagged edges that offered passage to clandestine places. At the top was an intricate marking—four circles joined together.

"It's a Celtic knot," said Bridget. "I know I've seen this before—in a book or maybe embroidered somewhere. What's it for?"

Rosa smiled. "Us. It's for us."

"But where does it lead? What does it unlock?" asked Eliza, her curiosity brimming.

"All sorts of things." Rosa's smile was mischievous. Her dark eyes danced in the torch's light, happy and warm. "But we have to wait for our fourth to arrive. Those are the rules. The butterfly circle needs four girls."

"Butterfly circle," said Bridget, intrigued.

"It's tradition. Those who have come before us have left some messages," said Rosa. "But we have to explore them together. Their rules—not mine."

Chapter 6

Lila Grace Tuinstra – Goody

The time had come for her to go to the unwed mother's home. Lila Grace stood in her bedroom by the window, holding the locket gingerly in her hands. It was a golden oval that opened to reveal his picture, which she had cut out carefully, so it would fit. She opened it one more time to gaze at his handsome face and imagined what they would look like on their wedding day. Her heart raced and her chest swelled with happiness, but she could not let her parents see this—not yet. They were still adjusting to the news of the baby.

When the light rap came at the door, she disguised her smile. "Yes?"

Her mother's face was gentle but disappointed, even though it had been weeks since the situation had come to light. It was annoying. "Collect your things," she said. "Your daddy is waiting downstairs."

Fine, she would play along and follow their rules—until she was free to do otherwise. So, she obediently closed her suitcase, complete with toothbrush and slippers, her best everyday clothing and nightshirts. Then she tucked her locket beneath her modest lavender sweater and headed downstairs to her ride.

Lila Grace's mother waited at the door, her hands folded in prayer, her eyes cast downward. Lila Grace bit her tongue and smiled politely.

"Now, be a good girl and cooperate once you arrive. Be considerate and helpful. Keep your thoughts to yourself and mind the work you're assigned." These were the ridiculous morsels of wisdom her mother bestowed upon Lila Grace as she ushered her off to the home. Her mother hugged her and placed a card in her hand, then closed the door.

As Lila Grace got into the car beside her daddy, she glanced at the card her mother had handed her. It was of the St. Margaret of Cortona—Patron Saint of Unwed Mothers, complete with prayers on the back to save her soul. Such foolishness. She would not be one of those girls—unwed and shamed. This home was a temporary solution until they were properly married. Her mother would see—they would all see. She was going to have exactly what she'd always dreamed of— a handsome husband, a house full of children, and a garden with white lilies so elegant the girls from school would burn with envy. It was what they deserved.

When Lila Grace arrived at the home, she breezed into boarding room two like a princess. Nose in the air, she looked down its rounded protrusion at the other girls, clearly unhappy she had to share their space. They were not too pleased either and it would only be a matter of time before Bridget let her know it.

Eliza's first instinct was to think the best of people before she met them, but Lila Grace's haughty glares perturbed even her. It was hard to decipher her age, for her face held movie star sophistication and her curves were soft, but her manner betrayed her. Few mature women would carry on in similar fashion—at least not out loud.

"You mean to tell me we all sleep here?" she said to Nurse Edwards, who raised an eyebrow.

"Yes," replied the nurse, her tone flat. "You are not away on holiday, Miss Tuinstra."

"But I'm sure my daddy would pay for a private suite," she said in a lower tone, but the girls could still hear.

"Ah, but there are no such accommodations," replied the nurse. "This will have to do. Lights-out at nine thirty sharp. Please be mindful of the rule." With that, she left the room, closing the door behind her.

"That bed's empty," said Eliza, motioning to the tidy mattress closest to the door.

Lila Grace grimaced, but nodded in thanks and then turned her back to unpack. Her suitcase was high quality, with shiny clasp closures and a monogram under the handle. She unpacked a matching nightgown and robe set, pink slippers with shiny bows, and a satin sleep mask. Then she slipped her hands underneath her dark hair at the back of her neck and unclasped the chain that rested there. The locket dangling from it was a golden oval, which she carefully lay on the bedside table.

While Lila Grace stood unpacking her comforts, Bridget moved closer, watching and waiting for her moment to speak. Eliza could see that she was up to no good, for she'd noticed

Bridget always chewed on her lower lip as she was concocting something clever.

"What's in the locket?" Bridget's voice was low and monotone, and her face was awkwardly close to the new girl's.

Lila Grace jumped, glaring at Bridget and stepping away. She shook her head, regaining her composure. "My betrothed," she responded.

Bridget did not try to stifle her laughter. "*My betrothed,*" she mocked dramatically and fanned herself. "Honey, where are you from? High society New York?"

Lila Grace sniffed. "I am from Hunting Valley," she responded, and then added under her breath, "Not that the likes of you would know where that is."

Eliza braced herself, expecting an outburst, but Bridget cocked her head to one side and smiled—and not a nice one. "Maybe they didn't tell you when they checked you into this house of refuge, but glitterati don't matter here. Knocked up means the same thing: downtown, uptown, and as far out in the suburbs as you can drive. So don't pretend you're better than anybody here. It's best you figure that out now than the hard way."

Lila Grace simply stared back at Bridget in a challenge. With rich sarcasm, she said, "The hard way? I imagine that means more terribly boring conversations with you?"

Bridget's eyes narrowed, and she snatched the locket off the table.

"Hey!" started Lila Grace, following the red-haired girl across the room as she jumped up on her bed and opened the locket.

"Let's see this *betrothed,*" said Bridget. She examined the photo as best she could, playing keep-away from the new girl.

"Well, he's not bad looking, I'll say that."

"Of course, he's not," spat Lila Grace, as she jumped onto the bed next to Bridget, who pushed her back.

Lila Grace landed on her rear on the bed, then sat there in shock for a moment. But rather than shrink, she leapt in defense. She grabbed Bridget's pillow and socked her right in the face, then yanked the locket out of her hand before retreating to her part of the room.

Eliza could see Bridget coiling like a snake ready to strike, when Rosa interrupted. "We're all friends here, ladies," she said.

"No, we're not," said Bridget.

Rosa continued, "Until we're given a reason not to be. So, maybe let's ease up tonight before this turns into a *situation*. None of us wants Nurse Edwards back in here tonight."

Rosa held Bridget's gaze evenly, then winked when Lila Grace wasn't looking. "Besides, we have business to attend to this evening," said Rosa, pulling the skeleton key out from beneath the folds of her nightgown.

They waited until fifteen minutes after lights-out, after the night ward assistant had checked their room to ensure all were present and resting. Then, they followed Rosa to the closet in the far corner of the room, Bridget lighting the way with her torch.

As the door creaked open, Eliza's imagination ran wild with possibility. What could be hidden there? Another door? A collection of secrets? The shadows could have held anything in their folds.

Rosa stepped inside, the light slicing through darkness, and slid aside a false panel at the back of the closet. She squatted and retrieved something, then backed away toward them. She turned to reveal a box in her hands—a large jewelry box, it seemed. It was crafted of dark wood. Delicate etchings graced the top panel.

Rosa settled on the floor, in the center of all the beds.

"Light the candle," she said, motioning to her dresser. Bridget picked the holder up, struck a match, and lit the wick. She placed it on the floor beside the box, its warm glow dancing on the engraved shapes that seemed to move.

"So, what does the key do?" Eliza asked, perplexed. She could see no keyhole on the box.

Rosa slid her hand around to the back of the box and moved a wooden leaf to the side. She slid the key into the hole there and turned it.

"They key opens more, but that will have to wait," said Rosa. "You need to earn the right to use it," said Rosa. Her hands rested on the box in protection.

"*We* do?" said Bridget. "What about you?" She took a seat beside Rosa, the girls forming a circle that reminded Eliza of the kindergarten game, Duck, Duck, Goose.

"I've already completed my challenges, that's why I have the key." Rosa's smile was confident without being glib, but her glare silenced Bridget.

"And what if I don't want to play this little game of yours?" asked Lila Grace, her face adorning a haughty pout. But her eyes gave her away. She wanted to know what was inside the box as badly as the rest of them.

Rosa's smile flattened. "Well, I wouldn't suggest you fall

asleep before us, then."

"Now what is that supposed to mean?" said Lila Grace, nostrils flaring. She was a pretty girl, but her temper punctured that. It revealed a kind of ugly that only existed among the proud.

"If you fall asleep before us, we might just dunk your hand in warm water," said Bridget.

"So?" said Lila Grace.

"So, it makes you pee," said Bridget, rolling her eyes. Lila Grace gasped in offense.

Bridget turned to Eliza. "Her naivety's not charming like yours." Her glance swung to Lila Grace. "It's annoying."

"Ladies?" Rosa said. "This is a sacred act. Let's have some decorum, please."

Silence fell among the group.

When Rosa was satisfied, she opened the lid of the dark box. Red velvet lining peeked out from inside, and as soon as the lid was fully open, a tune began to play. The tinkling was soft, though Eliza held her breath, hoping the notes didn't travel down the hall. If luck was on their side, the night ward assistant was already safely tucked away in her bed.

"I know this song," said Bridget, looking uncharacteristically emotional. "My Mama sang this to me as a child." She waited a few beats, closed her eyes. The tune emerged from her like a delicate bird—strange against her tough demeanor.

"Too-ra-loo-ra-loo-ral," she sang. "Too-ra-loo-ra-li, Too-ra-loo-ra-loo-ral, hush now, don't you cry! Too-ra-loo-ra-loo-ral, Too-ra-loo-ra-li, Too-ra-loo-ra-loo-ral, that's an Irish lullaby."

"Wow, Irish," said Rosa. "You can sing."

Bridget shifted under her gaze, her discomfort clear. She cleared her throat. "So, what's in the box?" she asked, redirecting.

"Questions and Commands," said Rosa. "And some answers." She pulled out a slip of paper and read. "If you were a flower, what would you be?"

"A dandelion," said Eliza, without missing a beat.

The girls turned to look at her, perhaps surprised because she was the quietest among them. They waited for more, and the silence hung in the air too long.

"Go on," said Bridget. "Why a dandelion?"

Eliza gulped. "Well… I'd like to be something beautiful." She shrugged, cleared her throat. "But I'm just a weed."

Rosa shook her head. "Well… dandelions have healing properties. And that makes them special."

"Is that from your Roma side?" asked Bridget.

"You're a Gypsy?" Lila Grace spat, incredulous.

"Don't use that word," said Eliza.

"Roma. And proud of it," said Rosa, looking at her with annoyance.

"You know, there are stories in my family about dandelion wine," said Bridget. "From the old country."

"From the fae?" teased Rosa.

"Maybe you're a lion disguised as a flower," said Lila Grace. It was the first time something she said mattered, at least in the other girls' eyes.

"I like that," said Eliza, smiling to herself. "Maybe."

"Well, I'm a rose," said Rosa. "Obviously." She bowed graciously, making fun of herself.

"I guess it makes me a Lily," said Lila Grace.

"And you, Bridget?" ask Eliza. "What kind of flower are

you?"

Bridget thought for a moment. "A snapdragon," she sneered, clapped her hands together loudly, then stifled a laugh as the girls said "Shhhh!" in unison.

Then Rosa held her hands up, asking for demure silence once again. She turned over the slip of paper in her hand. "Answer," she read, "The flower you think you are when you arrive is just part of you. You will discover more on your journey here."

"It's like a fortune tea cake," Lila Grace said, delighted. The others looked at her blankly. "You know, a little cake with a fortune. My daddy brought some back from a trip once."

"So, is this like a fortune-telling game?" asked Eliza.

"Not exactly," said Rosa. "These are questions the other girls asked, the other girls who were here before us. Not just the ones I met—the ones who were here a long time before. We've all added questions to the box. And some answers. And some commands."

"Commands?" asked Bridget.

"Tasks," explained Rosa. "If you don't answer the question, you have to take the command option. You have to complete the task to retain your dignity."

"Well, I think my dignity was gone before I got here," said Bridget, earning a giggle from the other girls. "I mean..." she placed her hands on her slightly rounded stomach. "I did earn an A in that math class, though."

Lila Grace looked at them with a question on her face, but neither Rosa nor Eliza cared to explain. It wasn't their secret to tell.

"We answered your question," said Eliza, pushing ever so gently. She offered an impish smile. "What else is the key to?"

"Well," said Rosa, leaning in, the candlelight shining on her eyes with a twinkle. "I've only been in two of the passages, but… I'm told there are more."

"Secret passages?" asked Bridget. Her mouth puckered with interested.

Rosa nodded. "I don't know for sure, but the other sisters, they said the nurses and ward assistants don't know about them—or the key. Legend has it, this mansion used to be part of the Underground Railroad."

Lila Grace's eyes widened. "You're foolin'." But it was clear she hoped it was true.

"From what I saw, the passages aren't… well kept," said Rosa.

"When can we go?" asked Bridget.

"Now?" asked Eliza.

"We will… when you become part of the Butterfly Circle," explained Rosa.

"What does that mean?" asked Lila Grace.

"You have to earn your place among the sisters," said Rosa. "You have to prove you're worthy."

"By answering the questions and doing the tasks?" asked Bridget. "More of them?"

"Commands," said Rosa, nodding. "They're called commands."

Chapter 7

Eliza had always possessed a grand imagination. Since childhood, her mother had encouraged her to write, fancying her the next Louisa May Alcott or Charlotte Bronte, hoping for romantic tales of courage and family. But while Eliza truly did like to weave stories, she preferred uncanny ones. Those with ghosts and mystery and intrigue. And she knew Louisa May Alcott wrote one or two; she'd found them in the library but could not bring herself to check them out. Her mother said it was unbecoming, reading and writing these stories, so she kept her fancies to herself. She supposed there was only so much room in one's head for such things, though, and they emerged in her dreams with wills of their own.

As Eliza fell into sleep, visions of passageways lingered. She moved through them like a child waiting to be born, always following a faint light ahead but never reaching it. They were cocoon shells stretched out into cylinders, filled with echoes of the past waiting to be discovered. And if she stood still for a moment, she could feel them breathing, contracting and expanding to an unheard beat.

Then she was roused. As the veils of sleep lifted, she wondered who walked the passages, if they ever made it out. Or, if they perished in the walls of the mansion and were left there to rot.

The tapping began behind the wall right above her pillow. *Tap. Tap tap.* The rhythm was like a pattern, perhaps the Morse code Eliza had heard of but did not understand. It could be an animal trapped, trying to claw its way out. But the rhythm was too predictable—not like a scratching or scrambling beast.

She sat up slowly in the darkness, listening to the angry wind howl outside. It whistled through the mansion's tower-teeth, around the stone chimneys and past the Tudor façade, whipping leaves against the windowpanes. And when the tapping had continued for several minutes, she was tempted to answer it.

She traced her finger along the wallpaper—purple lupine with silhouettes of swallows nestled among the buds. As her finger reached the bird's beak, she tapped. Once. Twice. Three times. And then there was a response in the same pattern. Once. Twice. Three times.

Eliza jumped back. She squelched a bellow with a mix of fear and excitement. The tapping resumed in its original pattern, then ceased. In its wake, the wind howled and the other girls breathed slowly in sleep. Eliza inched back toward the wall and reached out to respond, but just as her finger graced the wallpaper, a low growl emerged from the other side.

She shrank back and waited, then struggled to hear. Had she imagined it? Her ears perked up and reached below the whistles and sighs of the girls, beneath the tenor notes of the howling wind, to a bass tone that threatened. There it was—a rumbling vibration that teased the hair on the back of her neck. And then it was gone.

After Eliza had sat, unmoving, for at least a quarter of an

hour, she gathered enough courage to snatch her pillow from the head of the bed and reposition it at the foot. She crawled beneath the covers, upside down in bed, and tucked the sheets tightly around herself. And when it did not seem enough, she pulled the covers over her ears and tried to think of pleasant things. Beams of sunshine. Butterflies in flight. The taste of fresh strawberries. But no matter what trick she used, she kept creeping back to what lurked on the other side of the wall.

When Eliza woke in the morning, she was in a tangle of blankets, head still at the foot of the bed. In the safety of daylight, she stirred, thinking it prudent to shift her body to a more normal position before her roommates rose. But when she rubbed the sleep from her eyes and sat up, she found the damage done to the wall.

Where she had traced the outline of the sparrow last night, was a hole of sorts. Layer upon layer of wallpaper had been peeled away like an onion. The ragged paper plumed in a radial pattern like the petals of a blossom, and at the center, naked plaster and lath wall. And as Eliza inched closer to the protruding scar, she could see a tiny hole in the plaster, like the pupil of an eye.

Her mind raced, searching for a way to hide the damage. Had she done this? Or did something—some *creature*—lurking in the wall do this? But that wasn't even the scariest part. Eliza's insides crawled and her stomach jumped. Perhaps the thing responsible for this disfigurement was not flesh and blood at all.

Eliza jumped when she heard the gasp beside her and

turned to see Bridget staring at the mutilation, mouth agape.

"What did you do to the wall, Dandelion Girl?" she said.

The others were so convinced Eliza had caused the injury in a fit of nightmares that by noon, even she had accepted the likelihood. Though at the back of her mind, the notion supernatural events were possible niggled at her. Unease followed her in whispers through the garden as she tended to pansies and picked lettuce for the dinner meal.

The summer sun was unforgiving, licking Eliza's forehead with its heat. But the cool moisture of the upturned soil in her hands offered a connection to the Earth that always brought her a sense of peace. It took her back to moments with her Aunt Meg, when the older woman was still lingering between adolescent and young lady. Before she began studying nursing at Sisters College, she had been more of a mother to Eliza than her own. At least that's how Eliza remembered it.

There were so many conversations they'd had about the great mysteries of life and what lay beyond in the spiritual realm. Aunt Meg had made Eliza feel safe, accepting the prophetic dreams that often scared her, and seeing them as a gift. Yet they also remained secret from the rest of the family, for she had heard of the way they treated Aunt Meg and her notions about God. For she was interested in the old ways, those of the Great Mother.

But Eliza saw the Great Mother in the Virgin Mary and did not understand why this threatened the rest of her family. It angered them, especially the women, and she found this utterly confusing. It gave birth to a conflict in her that burned still, and rather than pick at it from the inside out, she tried to ignore it, like her own mother had taught her to do.

"Eliza, dear," her mother had said. "One must become disciplined in mind and heart. Swat those thoughts away that tempt you from the gospel, lest you let the devil in."

These chidings were thoughts that echoed through her mind daily, but they had become dimmer since she had entered the home. Though she felt cast aside and shunned by her family, there was a glimmer of freedom this isolation offered as well. It was a small thread now, but if she kept pulling at it, perhaps she could weave it into something more. A shroud of insight, a blanket of hope, a path to follow once freed from this place and released from beneath her mother's thumb.

"Dandelion Girl!" the urgent whisper came from Bridget.

Eliza snapped out of her reverie to find the other girls staring at her. They had ceased all work in the garden and their eyes were wide.

"What's wrong?" Eliza said.

"Don't move," said Rosa, her arms out to the side, as if holding the others back. A gentle smile crept onto her face. "You've got a pair of butterflies on your head."

"What?" Eliza stood without thinking.

The girls pointed to the yellow butterflies as they rose into the air and fluttered above Eliza's crown. She looked up to see the flickering shadows as they engaged in a dance.

"Are they fighting?" asked Lila Grace.

"Or mating?" said Bridget with a smirk.

"Or… both?" mused Rosa, for there was something both romantic and filled with tension about the aerial waltz.

"I think they were swallowtails," said Eliza, shielding her eyes from the sun.

The creatures rose higher and higher into the sky until they were specks against a brilliant blue. They had broken the spell of silence that had existed between the girls since the early morning.

"Eliza," began Rosa, as they turned attention back to the greenery. "Why did you do that to the wall? Was it a dream, like you described the other night?"

Eliza flushed, shook her head. "I don't think I did it," she began, feeling naked and exposed. "I… don't remember though." She looked to the others for input, but they said nothing. "There was a tapping."

Over the course of the next hour, while the girls weeded and tended and watered the garden, they mused about the possibilities. Was it amnesia? They had heard of it before, but knew no one who'd had it for real. Was it a specter that haunted the room? Bridget seemed most fond of this explanation. Was it someone or something stuck in the wall? Lila Grace almost began to cry at this suggestion, but the others assured her that was not the case (even though Rosa winked to say it's not really what she thought).

And then they decided together they would find out—no matter what it took.

Chapter 8

The four girls sat crouched over the candle, which they had opted for instead of the flashlight for its mysterious ambience. They decided if a creature was hiding in the wall, it was more likely to be drawn by firelight than a torch. Eliza said this was ridiculous because any creature is likely to flee from light, no matter the source, but Rosa was steadfast in her thinking and offered evidence of moths and other insects. So, the light remained.

"What if we could coax the information out of you?" said Rosa, the candlelight flickering against her delicate face. Her large brown eyes were full of magic.

"What do you mean?" said Eliza, hesitant.

"Like hypnosis?" said Bridget. "You going to mesmerize it out of her?"

"Not exactly," said Rosa. "It's more like a trance she enters herself. I've seen my Grandmama do it before." The others looked at her with questions in their eyes and she shrugged. "Roma side."

Bridget nodded like that explained it all.

"I don't know about this," said Lila Grace, shaking her head. "It sounds like sorcery to me. Against the Bible. Like devil-worship or something." Her nose scrunched up and her lashes batted with doubt.

Rosa's mouth drew a hard line. "There is no devil worship here, Lila Grace. It's just a cultural difference."

Bridget chimed in. "Yeah, don't be thick, Goody."

"*Goody*?" Lila Grace sneered.

"Two shoes. Goody two shoes. Jesus," Bridget muttered. Then she donned an expression of intrigue. "But just to be clear, I'm not against sorcery."

Lila Grace rolled her eyes. "Don't take the Lord's name in vain."

"No, I get it," said Eliza. "I understand the fear—at least my family's fear. But we didn't invite this problem and we still have to deal with it. I don't want to wake up tomorrow with another hole in the wall—not if there's a way to figure out what happened."

Rosa looked to Lila Grace. "You ready?" And she nodded.

Eliza lay back on her bed, her head beneath the scar in the wall. In the firelight, it seemed to move and shift, shrinking to a blossom, then growing into a medusa with tentacles. Was there something in there? Something that wanted to reach out and bite her?

"Close your eyes," said Rosa, her voice soft and lulling. "Relax every muscle in your body. Start at your head and move your way down to your toes."

Eliza imagined a gentle blue light blanketing her in warmth. It licked the top of her head, caressed her face, and tingled her skin as it consumed her whole body. Her head sank more deeply into the pillow, the blackness behind her lids growing darker and softer. Her breath became slower, deepening into a quiet rhythm that felt like dreams.

Rosa's voice hung just above a whisper. "Remember the tapping. What happened after the tapping?" she said.

Eliza walked through the wall. As she passed through layers of wallpaper, each one felt like a blanket, holding memories both beautiful and terrible. The designs passed over her like intricate lace, their patterns woven with purposeful eyes, always watching. The sparrow she had traced with her finger the night prior pecked at the layers, as if to uncover a mystery with her. It guided her, its shadow form walking the line between life and death. It knew the way, and she would follow. It flapped its wings, peeped its sweet song, though it was muffled, as if it sang through cotton.

And then she emerged into a tunnel, dimly lit by a candle. The walls were made of stone and they wept with dampness and moss. She lifted the candlestick, holding it out before her like a beacon. She heard scampering things behind her and resisted the urge to jump. The sparrow flew before her, weaving back and forth like a pendulum, looking more like a bat than a bird in this dark place.

After what seemed an eternity, the ground sloped upward. Her feet were unsure on the slick stone floor, but it soon became gritty with dirt. The sparrow landed by an opening that offered a faint light. It glowed a pale blue, like the moon. As she drew closer to the mouth of the tunnel, she could see the sparrow resting on a wrought-iron gate as high as her shoulders.

It was worn with age and weather, but remained a substantial barrier, cold beneath Eliza's touch. She imagined that if she swung it open, it would screech and moan in complaint. Her hands did not linger on the metal, for it held sorrow somehow—or maybe held it at bay. Beyond the gate was darkness so deep that she could not see more than a few feet.

The sparrow hopped about, calling Eliza's attention upward, where a crescent moon lit the night sky. The sparrow chirped, its song no longer muffled or sweet. Its squeaks were alarming and growing in urgency. The air began to stir, raising the hairs on her arms. And she couldn't say why, but she felt the need to back up. Back up. Back up!

The growl was low and deep from within the darkness that lay beyond the gate. As the sparrow flew toward the mouth of the tunnel, the creature leapt out from beneath the brush and rammed itself against the gate, gnashing and snarling.

Eliza ran. She ran so fast her toes gripped the earth like claws. She dove into the cave's mouth and tore down the hill, then slid when her feet hit rock. She hit the cave wall with a thud but recovered quickly; she did not stop to examine her hands or her knees. She just kept running—into blackness, for she had left the candle behind.

Eliza sat up with a start. All three girls stared at her, eyes wide.

"Are you alright?" asked Rosa.

"We couldn't wake you up!" said Bridget.

Her heart was racing and her breath coming fast.

"What was it? What made the mark?" asked Lila Grace.

"A bird—a sparrow. It took me through a passage."

"Where did it go?" asked Rosa.

Eliza was still sinking back into her own body. "I don't know—a gate," she said. "I think this place is alive. And it's hungry."

Chapter 9

Throughout the night, the girls jumped at creaks and groans the house made as it settled. They were kept awake by phantom breezes that were likely of imagination. Most of them drifted off in the early hours of the morning. Eliza was the last to fade and fell into dreams of flapping wings and growls that crept under doorways.

The morning sun banished the shadows to their corners and had no patience for girlish notions of magic. Chores did not wait, especially since a new headmistress was to arrive at eleven. It was an unexpected adjustment, but Mrs. Miller had received word her sister in Dayton was ill. They were to arrive promptly for luncheon to meet their new caretaker, and truth be told, they were not sad about it. Mrs. Miller was a sour lemon, as Rosa put it. Nothing could be worse than that, right?

Miss Trill (and it was Miss, for she had never married) boasted a social work credential and she took the business of redirecting young women in peril quite seriously. She had no tolerance for insolence and no empathy for sinners; this is exactly what she said in her 'welcome' speech, so there would be no mistake.

Her face was hardened beyond her 45 years and Eliza wondered what she had been through to make her so. She was not a beautiful woman and not even handsome, but what made her so unseemly was the downward turn of her mouth. Not even her brown eyes held light. They were so dark they consumed her pupils and matched the shade of her charcoal hair. Her skin was pallid, with the slightest hint of yellow in the creases of her neck. She wore neither rouge nor shade on her lips; her eyes were naked as well. The dark circles that hung below them might have disappeared with pan-cake, Eliza thought, but she did not seem to care for such grooming. Her hair was pulled back fiercely into a bun, as if holding her stern expression in place. It made Eliza wonder if she had been a nun, for she had only known such a strict demeanor in the Ursuline Sisters from St. Ann's.

"My goal is to make polite, virtuous young ladies out of you," she said, in an even, unemotional tone. She walked the length of the dining room, her gaze falling outside the windows. "Just because you have been deflowered, does not mean your unrighteous paths are solidified."

The giggle bubbled out of Bridget's mouth without her permission, and she quickly covered it with a cough.

Miss Trill turned sharply and glared at the red-haired girl. "You will learn and practice decorum at all times while on these premises," she said, moving closer to Bridget with each step. She stopped when her face was within an inch of the girl's. "Do I make myself clear?"

Bridget nodded.

Miss Trill straightened, and her voice emerged with a boom. "The correct answer is yes, ma'am!"

Eliza jumped at the sudden yell.

"Yes, ma'am," they parroted back to her.

Once Miss Trill turned her back, though, Bridget stuck out her tongue. Eliza rolled her eyes at the gesture, for elementary school was well behind them. But she admired Bridget's spark, her willingness to thumb her nose at authority. Just the idea of behaving like that made Eliza fidget.

Miss Trill's voice regained its monotone droning at a reasonable volume. "Thus, you four will be working on a special project. In addition to your responsibilities in the garden, you will be helping to restore the chapel."

Lila Grace raised her hand. "Excuse me, Miss Trill? I don't recall seeing a chapel on the property when I toured it with my daddy."

Eliza's brow furrowed. *Tour?* She had merely been told where she was going and dropped off without so much as an introduction.

Miss Trill attempted what might have been a smile, but looked like a grimace. "The old chapel at the back of the property has not been used in some time. It has fallen into disrepair and, as a Christian woman, I find that unacceptable."

Eliza caught Lila Grace fidgeting with her necklace out of the corner of her eye. At first, she thought it was the locket, but at second glance saw it was a cross on a gold chain. Of course, Lila Grace would do something like this to ingratiate herself.

"You will not be asked to lift anything heavy—much of that work is being performed by hired hands. But starting next week, you will tend to the chapel every day, clean the insides and outsides of the building, plant shrubs and flowers, and make it presentable for our Lord and Savior, Jesus Christ."

"Amen," said Lila Grace, as Miss Trill walked out of the room.

Bridget sniffed and said, "Teacher's pet."

Lila Grace cocked her head to one side. "Oh, I think we all know who the *teacher's pet* is in this room."

The insult washed over Bridget like a glass of ice water, and her eyes narrowed. Then she looked at the other two girls to identify the snitch.

"I said nothing," said Rosa, holding her hands in front of herself in explanation.

"Well, don't look at me!" said Eliza, when accusing eyes turned toward her. "I don't spill others' secrets."

"Relax," said Lila Grace, sounding superior. "Neither one of them told me."

Bridget's hands went to her hips. "Well then, how did you know?"

Lila Grace licked her lips and sighed. "My daddy checked into all the girls who are here. You know, to make sure I'm safe."

"Did he tell you to keep your mouth shut, too? Because it's about to get you into trouble," said Bridget.

Lila Grace shuffled, weighing her options. "Look, I—" The words she wanted to say were not familiar. "I don't have girlfriends. I'm… I'm sorry. Sometimes things just pop out of my mouth before I have a chance to think about them."

Bridget examined her, looking for deceit, but finding none. She huffed and relaxed. "I get that. Happens to me, too."

"Can we start over?" asked Lila Grace, looking around at the girls. "All of us?"

Eliza was the first to nod, followed by Rosa. Then Bridget succumbed. "Fine," she said. "But you have to tell us what you know. If you knew that about me, then you've got to know who else is here."

"Oh, I do," said Lila Grace, pointing around the room. "Eliza—good girl in trouble. Rosa—she is trouble, but not the scary kind—just curious, my daddy said. He kind of liked that about you. Bridget—I was told to watch out for you, bein' with older men. He was worried about that."

Bridget glared again.

"I'm sorry, I'm just telling you what he said," said Lila Grace.

"Who else?" asked Rosa.

"Faith Kennedy—another good girl in trouble. Sarah Williams—seems to have some mental stress—I was told to watch out for her as well. Mary Smith—there's some talk a relative might be the father, but you never can believe those rumors. Bette Lewis—family is very wealthy and her daddy's a lawyer. Francis Parker—now this one they said was a rape—a true crime. Louisa Chapman—she has a reputation for entertaining young men—I am to stay far away from her. Maddie Wilbright—her daddy is a doctor, and her parents are going to raise the baby as their child. And Edith White—she was married but divorced—I never actually knew anyone who divorced before."

"And you remembered all this," said Bridget. "Just because your daddy said so."

Lila Grace nodded. "I had to memorize the list. Otherwise, he wouldn't let me come. Pictures, too, for those that were available." She looked to the other girls like it was the most normal thing in the world. "What?"

Bridget swallowed. "Goody, we come from very different worlds."

Lila Grace nodded. "I'm aware." While the comment could have come with bite, it didn't.

As the girls walked back to the garden to continue their chores, Eliza fell into step beside Lila Grace. They walked through the first-floor hallway, their footsteps echoing on the marble floor. The paintings of benefactors loomed over them like gargoyles keeping watch.

"So, you don't you have any friends?" asked Eliza. She never liked the idea of another person's pain. Her mother said she was cursed with too much empathy. "That sounds lonely."

Lila Grace stared ahead, but nodded. "Yeah. Girls can be mean, though. Sometimes, lonely is better."

Eliza thought back to her own experiences with this. In her fifth year at St. Ann's, she had become the target of such pettiness. Eliza and her best friend, Molly, had wonderful overnights and adventures together, riding bicycles and picnicking under trees. But Molly's cousin became jealous, feeling her rightful place had been stolen, for they were all the same age. The cousin convinced Molly that Eliza was not worthy of their time and friendship. It had left Eliza with a deep mistrust of others.

"Yes, they can be." It was all Eliza said, but somehow it was enough.

Chapter 10

When Eliza first laid eyes on the chapel, she felt like she'd walked into a fairyland in England. Part of it was the scenery itself—a stone building with climbing ivy set in the shade of trees—but it was more than that. The air seemed to hum.

It had taken them half an hour to walk to the chapel, which surprised all the girls. They were told it was on the far edge of the plot, but they had no idea the estate was that large. The parcel that faced the Cleveland street was misleading, for it seemed a plot equal to others in the area. But behind the main house and immediate lawn, the property stretched far back into the woods, where it butted against a rock formation.

The air was still there, filled with floating white tufts from the trees and the songs of birds and angels. Sunlight filtered in through branches and leaves, kissing the grass in intricate lace designs.

"This must be what heaven looks like," whispered Eliza, afraid to break the spell.

The girls breathed deeply beside her, all warm and rosy-faced from their walk.

The chapel's façade was a myriad of stone in all shades of gray and brown. At the top was a cutout that framed a bell; it hung still, like it was waiting to sing again. The doors were wooden, a faded grain weathered from the years. They sat on iron hinges that belonged to a castle.

When they pulled open the doors (it took two of them to pry them ajar), it smelled of earth and time. It was in need of cleaning, but the light filtering through the stained glass was warm and inviting. Blue, red, yellow, and green light fell on the altar opposite the door, a simple stone slab that was uneven and charming.

Eliza took a breath in and immediately coughed it back out. "We'll need to dust," she said. Then she sneezed.

It didn't take long for the chapel and its immediate grounds to feel like home. As the girls cleared away overgrown grass, they found steppingstones that led in many directions. And when the afternoon sun felt too much, they took a break, reclining on a mound of clover beneath a giant sugar maple.

The green floor of the woods was cool and inviting. Eliza sipped water from a canteen, then passed it to Rosa. The liquid was refreshing as it slid down her throat, cooling her from the inside. She loosened her laces and pried her feet out of the shoes, then peeled the warm socks off. The breeze was an immediate relief, and the clover felt like satin to her naked toes.

Sitting there in the silence, the girls shared a kind of communion that was at once comforting and familiar. Eliza remembered the bond she'd shared with Molly all those years ago; a safety in her company that made her never want to leave. Like decisions shouldn't be made independently, but always together. Where one went, the other followed.

She watched Bridget pull a buttercup from its stem, twirl it gently between her fingers. Her smile was far away, thinking about other places. She examined the yellow petals and her smile faded. Eliza didn't need to ask, for she knew that shift in feelings. A happy memory followed by pain, by disappointment, usually in someone else.

Bridget redirected her attention and turned to Lila Grace, who lay on the grass beside her. Bridget held the flower beneath her chin and laughed in a soft way Eliza had not heard her do before.

"You like butter," Bridget said. "See?" She motioned to Eliza and Rosa. "It reflects yellow under her chin."

Lila Grace opened her eyes. "Well, yes, I do." Her tone was playful. "I like butter. I like peanut butter. I like apple butter. But most of all, I like butter melted on warm white bread fresh from the oven."

"Mmmmm," sighed Rosa.

"Or butter for chocolate chip cookies," said Eliza, her mouth-watering at the thought.

Lila Grace gasped. "Oh…. Cookies! Yes, that's better than bread."

"Or both. Bread for dinner and cookies for dessert," said Bridget, still watching Lila Grace. She turned away quickly then, fluttering her eyelashes. No one else seemed to notice, but Eliza did.

Bridget caught her eyes, then looked away quickly. "How about a game of hide and seek?" Bridget said.

"What are we, third graders?" said Rosa, though she got up to join.

"Today, we are," said Bridget with a grin. "In this place, maybe we can be."

It was the permission they all needed. After some deliberation about who was "it", Lila Grace counted to 50 and the other girls took a path of steppingstones, each headed in a different direction.

Eliza was still barefoot. That's the way she wanted it, but she carried her shoes with her just in case. The stones were cool in the shade of the trees with moss hugging their edges. Oaks, maples, and sycamores towered overhead, their leaves shifting in the breeze, waving this way and that. The tufts that looked like white cotton bobbed on the air, and stray insects dove between them.

Eliza searched for a good place to turn off the path; if she stuck to the steppingstones, she would be discovered easily. To the left was a wall of rock with a small cave at the base; she considered it but did not want to wake any sleeping thing that might be there. To the right, the trees seemed to go on forever, and she wondered where the mansion's property ended.

She walked tenderly into the brush and stopped to slip her shoes back on. She passed prickly bushes and soft ferns, and junior trees that sprouted at the feet of their forebears. Then she came to a clearing that, while overgrown with vines, had a different look about it than the surrounding woods. A stone sat in the center, round and large, surrounded by a ring of smaller stones.

Curious, she moved to examine the centerpiece, wiping away vines, both old and tired, as well as new and green. She discovered a plaque at the base of the rounded rock, worn with time but still legible. It said: *Harriet Prescott / 1828-1863 / Lost to madness, now redeemed.*

"Harriet Prescott," she whispered. The year 1863 felt like several lifetimes ago. Eliza searched her memory of history—a class in which she seldom paid attention—but recalled the Civil War ended in 1865. *Lost to madness.* The idea shook her.

The tranquil setting in which she stood suddenly felt vulnerable, like she might catch whatever the woman had. *What had she done? Did she rant and rave? Murder someone? Take her own life?*

Tinkles of laughter drifted over the air and between trees to Eliza's ears. Someone had been found and was running to escape being tagged. The laughter became louder as Rosa and Lila Grace bounded toward her and the discovery—one after the other. Just as they breached the stone circle, Lila Grace tagged Rosa and they fell to the ground, giggling.

"Isn't base back the other way?" asked Eliza, catching the fever of laughter from the others.

Rosa shrugged, her cheeks pink and her breath still coming fast. "I guess I got turned 'round."

Lila Grace tilted her head back, carefree, and yelled, "Ollie, Ollie, oxen free!" to let Bridget know it was safe to come out of hiding.

"I suppose we shouldn't be running in our condition," said Rosa, but the joy on her face was clear. Then she added, "Oh, to be a child again." She shook her head.

"I still feel like one," said Eliza. The words were out of her mouth before she realized it. She had meant to keep the thought to herself. There was something about being in the company of these girls, though, that begged her to be herself. But then the vulnerability crept in. "Maybe that sounds foolish," she added, "but it's the truth."

"I don't think it's foolish," said Lila Grace. "Some days I can't wait to grow up. Other days I just want to eat candies and play dress-up and imagine I'm a princess." She flung her head back dramatically.

"Princess Goody?" Bridget appeared in the clearing. "Who's it?"

Eliza pointed to Rosa, who put her hands up in surrender.

"So, what do you think of this?" Eliza said, stepping aside from the large stone.

The girls examined it together.

"Is this a grave?" Lila Grace jumped back, like she'd stepped on someone's toes.

"Why else would there be a stone here?" said Eliza.

"But it's not a headstone, really," said Lila Grace.

"Lost to madness," repeated Bridget, as if echoing their thoughts. "She went insane."

"Or her husband said that's what happened," said Rosa, a skeptical look on her face.

"Now redeemed," read Lila Grace. "Like she's in God's hands now?"

"What if she's the one in the wall?" Bridget gave voice to what they were all thinking but were afraid to say.

It was then they heard the shrill whistle, and their eyes grew wide.

"What on earth?" said Lila Grace, as they all rushed back to the chapel, holding hands and helping each other along.

Chapter 11

The whistle continued in sporadic bursts until they made it out of the woods. The piercing sound invaded Eliza's brain and her hands weren't enough to dull the noise. They were not surprised when they saw Miss Trill with her fists on her hips and a livid scowl on her face, walking the chapel grounds with a silver piece placed to her lips.

When she saw them appear, she did not stop the racket either. She simply motioned for them to come closer. Finally, she ceased.

"That is the sound of your failure to adhere to orders," she reprimanded, a bite in her words. "If you cannot complete simple tasks, what will become of you as women?"

She turned around, looked to the chapel and muttered some words to herself, as if in prayer. When she faced them again, her face was still red with anger, but her tone had softened.

"Your families have entrusted us here to care for you during this time and help you to reflect upon your poor choices. I will not be—" Her voice began to rise, but she regained control quickly. "I will not be made a fool of in my very first week of charge."

Eliza gulped. What exactly did Miss Trill have the power

to do?

"Therefore, you will have another chore added to your list this week before lights-out. You will scrub the latrine and bath for your section of the house. Every night. And I will be checking, mark my words."

With that, she walked away, leaving them feeling like chided children.

The girls were made to scrub the latrines in silence, and while Eliza moved the brush back and forth over the tiled floor, her head was full of notions about Harriet Prescott and her large round stone.

Was it indeed a tombstone? It read like one. It felt like one. But why on the grounds and not in a proper cemetery? Perhaps that's how things were done back then, during Civil War times. Eliza did not know.

What would she have been called? Harriet? Hattie? Hettie? Hennie? She imagined a young woman like herself, young enough to still get into trouble but old enough to know better. She decided on "Hattie" and began to think of her like this.

Hattie Prescott, lost to madness, what drove you mad? The words became a song she repeated in rhythm with her scrubbing. Back and forth, back and forth. The bubbles appeared and popped, disintegrated dirt and scum, and then were washed away with fresh water from Rosa's bucket, for the two worked as a team beside each other. And since Rosa's pregnancy was further along, Eliza refused to let her scrub.

Hattie Prescott, lost to madness, what drove you mad? She moved the brush up, then down, up, then down.

Hattie Prescott, lost to madness, what drove you mad? She paused for Rosa to clear her suds.

Hattie Prescott, lost to madness, what drove you mad? She scrubbed again. Harder, determined to remove a dirt stain that had made its way into the grout. Rosa cleared her suds.

And that's when Eliza saw it.

The face stared back at her from the wet floor, olive eyes rimmed in dark lashes. "Oh!" she exclaimed, then backed away on her knees. Rosa rushed to her side, searching for what made her jump.

"What is it, a spider?" Rosa asked.

But just like that, the face was gone.

"She's shown herself," said Rosa, her dark eyes wide with amazement, and the hint of a smile crept to her lips. They sat in a circle in their boarding room around a candle, its light dancing softly, bouncing off each of their faces.

"I—I've been calling her Hattie, you know, in my mind," said Eliza, the last part fizzling out under her breath as she realized how silly it sounded. But she couldn't deny there was something enchanting about it, seeing the face in the puddle like it was reaching out from the other side.

"Well, whatever you're saying—out loud or to yourself— it's working," said Rosa.

"Working?" said Lila Grace. "When we figure out how to hold the spirit at bay, then it will be *working*."

Rosa sighed. "Lila Grace, it's just a ghost," she said.

"Just a—do you hear yourself?" Lila Grace's voice was rising.

"Shhhhh!" said Bridget. "We don't need any more trouble from Trill."

Lila Grace huffed in tantrum. "I just think you're playing with the dark and it's foolish. Leave the after-death stuff to God."

Eliza heard the surrounding banter, but it was background noise. The hole in the wall called to her as she stared at the flame. Its billowing layered scar sat behind her, tugging for attention. Was she imagining it? She watched Bridget play with the flame, passing her finger through it quickly, like a party trick.

"Would you stop?" said Lila Grace. "You're going to burn yourself."

"It doesn't hurt," began Bridget, continuing the game. Lila Grace reached out and pulled Bridget's hand back, then held onto it like it gave her a sense of control. Bridget did not move to take it away, which Eliza thought was curious.

"I would like some answers," said Eliza. "To know who she was, what happened to her. If the hole in the wall has anything to do with her."

Rosa met her eyes. "I agree, but also…" Her gaze went to Lila Grace. She licked her lips. "Caution would be wise."

Lila Grace smiled, vindicated, and Rosa added quickly: "I'm not saying I think this is evil, or ungodly, or something to be scared of at all. But I have heard of things that can go badly if one doesn't take certain precautions."

"What do you mean?" said Bridget. "Like charms or spells or something? An amulet of protection?"

Rosa shrugged. "Grandmama had her trinkets and believed they offered protection. But one thing I've heard her say about many things—both when reaching into the beyond and just in living—be clear about intention. So, we need to do that."

"I intend to be left alone by ghosts," said Lila Grace, and though she was serious, Bridget and Eliza giggled.

Rosa rolled her eyes. "*We* intend for only good spirits to contact us from the other side." She looked to the ceiling. "Harriet Prescott, are you good?"

The girls waited, for what, they weren't sure.

"Hattie," added Eliza. After a deep breath, she continued. "Hattie Prescott, lost to madness, are you good?"

The flame stretched out before them, growing taller, but otherwise the room was silent.

"We need to give her a way to talk to us," said Rosa, chewing on her lip. "There was a tool Grandmama used. It was like a—" she searched for the words, moving her hands around like they might help her pull the answer out of the air. "Like a… plank with a hole she stuck a pencil in."

"Oh, I think I've seen one of those." Everyone turned at Lila Grace's voice, surprised it was her. "It's a game, right? Mystic hand?"

"Hm." Rosa did not look amused. "It might be sold as a game. But it's really not a game."

Lila Grace's gray eyes were doubtful. "But I know I've seen my mother play it with her friends. She wouldn't touch if she thought she was really talking to ghosts. She's a Christian woman. No, I'm serious. She'd die before going against the Bible. That's just the way it is in my house."

Bridget looked at her and Lila Grace froze under her gaze.

"Maybe you should stop talking," said Bridget gently. "Before you offend someone, Goody."

Lila Grace shrugged in defeat. "Sorry," she whispered. Her eyes studied the floor, embarrassed.

"Our families are different," said Rosa, "And that's alright. My father's side is *very* Catholic. Like goes to mass several times a week and everyone does the sacraments Catholic. And that's fine—for them. But Grandmama had her own ways. And I'm alright with that, too."

The room was silent. Eliza wished for a Grandmama like Rosa's. It wasn't that she disliked her Catholic background. In fact, much of it she loved. It was the judgement part that didn't sit so well with her. She would have liked to know more, discuss more, have a choice in the matter.

"I used to think, growing up," said Eliza, "that if I was raised in the woods by a pack of wolves, there would be no discussion of Jesus or church or sin. And I just kept thinking, well, there has to be more."

"I can understand that," said Bridget. "Like the old ways. The Old Religion from Ireland always spoke to me. I don't know much about it, but I've heard some fairy stories about the land of *Tir na nOg* and the *Tuatha de Danaan*."

"I like how your voices changes when you talk like that," said Lila Grace, finally warming back up. And Bridget's voice did change. She sounded foreign and interesting.

Eliza decided. While goose bumps appeared on her arms when she thought of the face in the puddle and the bird behind the wall, her curiosity trumped caution. "Where can we find one of those—what did you call it? The writing thing."

"Mystic hand," said Lila Grace.

"You leave that to me," said Rosa. "I'll work on it." She

pulled the skeleton key from beneath her nightgown and held it in front of the flame. Behind her, it cast a shadow on the wall—four connected circles that shifted in the firelight. They laced in the center to form yet more shapes—a cross of sorts. Eliza tilted her head, seeing other images placed there.

"Look—there's a butterfly," said Eliza, getting up to trace it for them. But placing her finger in the shadow, but her movement marred the image. It was magic that couldn't be touched.

"Here," said Rosa, beckoning them closer to examine the key itself. "You're right, Eliza. There is a butterfly. It's one of the secrets of the key—the butterfly circle. But we're not supposed to tell. New members need to figure it out."

"So…. we're members now?" asked Lila Grace.

"Does that mean we get to see what the key opens?" asked Bridget, the curiosity wet on her lips.

"A few more questions and commands," Rosa said, moving to the closet to retrieve the box.

When she sat again on the floor, the candle illuminating the box in golden light, Rosa opened the lid. The Irish tune began to play, but this time Bridget did not sing along—she merely hummed. Rosa pulled out another card and read.

"What is your biggest fear?" said Rosa, then looked around the circle.

No one spoke. The flame danced; the house creaked.

Eliza thought. She thought of her parents at home; they were many things good and bad, but she loved them. She was afraid of losing them. She thought of Michael, his warm eyes turned cold. She was afraid of losing him, though she already had. She was afraid of never finding love again. Or of never being loved in the first place by one who held her heart. But more than anything, she was afraid of being trapped—alone as an unwed mother.

"Being a bird in a cage for the rest of my life," said Eliza. Her hands went to her belly, which had grown in its protrusion in the last week.

"You don't want to marry?" asked Lila Grace, surprise clear on her face.

Eliza's throat tightened and she gulped down the tears that threatened. "Yes, I did. I have always… That's not an option for me right now. The father—he isn't what I thought he was. And who else will want me now?" And to her surprise, Lila Grace's eyes welled with the tears Eliza had denied.

"I'm sorry," Lila Grace said in a shaky voice.

Rosa cleared her throat. "I'm afraid of that, too, being stuck in a life I never wanted," she said. "I'm afraid of not being happy. I have a way about me where I seek something out, like it's the most important thing in the world, but once I get it, I don't want it anymore."

"Like what?" asked Lila Grace.

"Everything," said Rosa. "Grades, student body president, newspaper editor… boys." She added the last item with a laugh, but it was almost bitter.

"I'm afraid of losing what I've got," said Lila Grace. "This baby." She rubbed her stomach as she spoke. "My beau. Our future. As long as it continues with my plans, it will be perfect. But all it would take is one thing, one accident, one misstep, and it could all come crashing down."

"It sounds to me like you're lucky," said Eliza. What she wouldn't give for Michael to be supportive. Lila Grace had everything if she had love. The entire world could crumble, and as long as she had love, she'd be alright.

Lila Grace smiled to herself. She took the locket around her neck between two fingers and rubbed it, like a wish.

"Myself," said Bridget, who had been uncharacteristically quiet. Her eyes stayed locked on the candle. "I am afraid of myself."

"Care to elaborate?" asked Rosa.

"No." The declaration was final. "Give me the command instead."

"That's okay," said Rosa. "You answered—"

"Give it!" said Bridget.

Rosa flipped over the card. Eliza could see the top said 'answer' while the bottom said 'command'.

Rosa let out a long sigh. "Go spy on Mrs. Williams."

"But she's not here," said Lila Grace. "Which means…"

"Miss Trill," said Bridget, a look of determination on her face.

Chapter 12

As Bridget disappeared down the dark hall, her chest was full of courage, determined to complete the command she'd been given. She had never been one to back down from a challenge and today wouldn't be that day either. Better this than confessing her deepest fear; she had already done so much to mask it.

And while they might understand—might care for her anyway—she would not risk losing these new friends. Even Lila Grace… especially Lila Grace.

Bridget placed her feet carefully on the wooden planks of the upstairs hallway, creeping as quietly as she could. She hoped Miss Trill would be downstairs, so that she might spy from the stairs, and not already tucked into her room for the night. Then the task would be more daring.

Once she turned the corner to the stairwell, there would be nowhere to hide. She paused, pressed against the wall, and peered around the edge. She quieted her breath, tried to slow her beating heart, and listened.

The voices downstairs were muffled, but she could hear them. It sounded like Miss Trill, and at least one other person. She would have to get closer in order to bring back something to the girls. "Either gossip or an item," Rosa had said. Gossip it would be, then.

Her toe touched the carpet at the center of the staircase and she carefully shifted her weight onto it. One by one, she took the steps until she was about halfway down. The voices were clearer now.

"You understand these situations must be handled delicately." Miss Trill's voice echoed through the foyer from one of the rooms below. "These girls have strayed from the path. They must either find it again and grow into effective mothers, or the alternative. Our goal is to save those children from a life of despair and depravity. Whatever the cost."

"Yes, ma'am." The voice that responded was low and rich, deferential.

"Your duty as a ward assistant," said Miss Trill, "will be to help with any task requested, from administering medication to checking on rooms in the night to other… unsavory activities from time to time."

"Unsavory, ma'am?" asked the voice.

"Cleaning bodily fluids, assisting in procedures, that kind of thing. But it will not be the norm," said Miss Trill.

The muffled sound of a woman screaming interrupted Bridget's train of thought. Was she imagining it? She held her breath. There it was again, like a banshee in another dimension. The scream emanated from a separate wing—the place where the women went during and after labor.

It was the sound of pain that rocked Bridget's insides. Was this what it was like to bring a child into the world?

"I will expect to see you at six am sharp on Monday morning." Miss Trill's voice was surprisingly close, and by the time Bridget scrambled up two stairs, it was too late. She was about to be discovered.

The dark face that appeared in the foyer below was round.

Two brown eyes fixed upon her in surprise, and Bridget froze like a mouse before a cat, ready to pounce. The young woman froze, too, and turned back to toward the other room.

"Ma'am," she said. "Might you show me where the restroom is before I leave?"

Their voices trailed off, back into the darkness of the first floor, and Bridget let out a sigh of relief. Whoever the new ward assistant was, she owed her a favor already.

The relief was still washing over Bridget as she made her way back to the boarding room. As hurried as she was, it would be foolish to run. She crept along the wall, listening for footsteps and the creaking of doors. But what she heard was, once again, a woman's cries.

Bridget knew little of childbirth, save for it would hurt. It was not something her mother discussed with her, which is partly how she ended up in the current predicament. "It will be the hardest thing you ever do," her mother had said of birth in a rare moment of sympathy that lingered between them like a weight. Bridget had been afraid to break the silence for fear her mother would return to a lecture about how ashamed she was, how embarrassed to have a promiscuous and foolish daughter. A Jezebel.

Feelings of anger and shame wafted over Bridget as she recalled her mother's downcast eyes. Before this, she had looked on her daughter with pride. After singing in church, her mother was particularly fond of her, fawning over Bridget and introducing her to friends. But that was a thing of the past. She had no idea what was to become of her after this place. Perhaps they would keep her in a back room of the family home like a secret.

As she approached their boarding room door, her anxiety receded. For now, her excuse for being in the hall might be a bathroom visit. And it was here, as she lingered in the doorway, listening to the woman's cries and imagining her pain, that she heard something else.

The cries sank into sobs. They were not screams of pain or physical strain, but low, moaning wails that spoke to a heartbreak almost unbearable. They were pleading cries, desperate sobs, accompanied by harsh tones. A door down the hall and around the corner opened. The sounds became louder, clearer.

"Cease this nonsense at once," a woman said. "You will do as you're told and work to pay this institution back for the care you received. The baby is gone."

The sobs were guttural now, choking and filled with ache.

The woman continued. "The sooner you let it go and resume normal life, the better it will be for all of us," she said. The door slammed and footsteps grew louder.

Bridget fumbled with the door handle, then snuck inside just before the woman appeared down the hall.

"You look like you've seen a ghost," said Eliza.

"Did you?" asked Lila Grace, reaching out her hands like they might catch some adventure.

Bridget looked at them, her chest filled with fear from what she had just heard.

"Irish?" said Rosa. "What is it?"

"I think they're taking babies," said Bridget. "Without permission."

Try as she might, Eliza could not shake the doom that settled over them in a cloud. It hung on the ceiling like a draped cloth, shutting out the light. It was a familiar feeling— something dangling over her that would drop at any moment and dash out all happiness and hope that lingered inside.

The first time she'd felt it, at least that she could remember, was when she had hid under the dining room table in her childhood home. There was a terrible fight between her parents, with yelling and pounding and crashing. She watched them through the tablecloth lace that hung over the edge, concealing her from her father's wrath.

She couldn't remember words, exactly, but she remembered cowering. His voice was booming, echoing off the walls and into her ears. Her mother's tears were inconsolable as she sat before him, absorbing his fury and squeezing it out of her eyes. Eliza had all of her dolls lined up under the table, too, making sure he could not find them and pop their heads off. She had tucked them under a blanket with the edge folded, just like her mother tucked her in at night.

She drowned out the sounds for the dolls, wrapping them in a nighttime prayer and hoping to lull them to sleep.

She whispered:

> *Now I lay me down to sleep*
> *I pray the Lord my soul to keep*
> *If I should die before I wake*
> *I pray the Lord my soul to take.*

"Liza-lie?" Rosa's voice was soft in the dark.

"Hm?" she breathed, rolling over in her bed to face her friend on the other mattress.

"You awake?" said Rosa.

"Yeah." Eliza studied Rosa's silhouette in the dim room, all shadows in the moonlight from the window. From the side, you couldn't tell she was pregnant at all.

"I know I said we needed to wait to use the key," said Rosa. "There are rules to the sisterhood, but right now… after what Bridget heard…."

"Yeah?" Eliza encouraged her to go on.

"I think we need to break them," said Rosa.

Chapter 13

The following day, Lila Grace was assigned the task of sweeping and dusting the inside of the chapel. She seemed to be the most tolerant of dust, for it was an honor to be the one to wipe down the area of worship. She basked in the peacefulness of the place. The cool stone that echoed back words and footsteps, and the stained glass that splashed color onto the floor in front of the alter, brought her serenity. Every piece of the chapel had been crafted to elevate spirit, all in the name of the Lord.

She imagined God looking down on her, watching her clean his house and being pleased. After all, her middle name was Grace, and she always sought to be in his. Even pregnant out of wedlock. But that would soon change.

As she ran a damp rag over the wooden pews, she thought of her beau and what their future held. Their wedding would be a grand one, filled with flowers and pink ribbons and splendid guests. Her mother would be dressed in a lavender gown and her daddy looking dapper in a tuxedo complete with bowtie. He would walk her down the aisle to the wedding march, then pull back her veil for her husband-to-be. Her beau would look on her with love in his eyes. Were they blue? No, brown. Right? She reached into the recesses of her memory, trying to recall. It was no matter. The details could be filled in later.

Of course, no one would object, though the priest had to ask. They would say their "I do's" and rice would be thrown. They would walk out of the church as husband and wife, with the baby in the arms of her mother. Though they would present the child as her sibling, when enough time had passed, he would join them in a new home. It would be the beginning of their glorious family and only a matter of time before more little feet ran through the house. Four—no, five. Five children would be the best number.

Lila Grace stopped dusting when she reached the alter. She stared at a carving on the front of the wooden base below it. Four circles intertwined.

"Hmm," Lila Grace said to herself, recognizing it as the symbol from Rosa's key.

She ran her fingers over the engraving, tracing the circles. One, two, three, four. She searched for the butterfly Eliza said she saw the night prior, but couldn't see it. What she saw instead was a cross. A holy cross that spoke to her and made her feel safe. The butterfly sisterhood must be holy if its symbol sat in the house of the Lord.

When Lila Grace showed the insignia to the other girls later, they all had something to say about it. It could be a coincidence, offered Bridget, though she did not seem convinced of this fact. What about a clue? That was Eliza's idea, thinking maybe the key was related somehow. And Rosa, she tied it back to the sisterhood.

"When I was given this key to hold for the next circle,"

said Rosa, "Faith told me it symbolized friendship. The sacredness of woman. The great mother."

"The Virgin Mary?" asked Lila Grace, looking delighted.

"Mother Mary, anyway," said Rosa, with a wink. "All women, really. It's a reminder to believe in ourselves and to respect each other."

Bridget huffed. "That's a tall order—if you know some of the girls I do."

"Like Miss Trill?" asked Eliza, her nose wrinkled.

"Even her," said Rosa, with a nod.

They stood in the heart of the chapel in a half-moon, looking at the carving.

"I can't help but think it connects to Ireland—the Celtic knot is so intentional," said Bridget.

"Maybe it does," said Rosa. "I'm not sure. I think lots of women have held the key over the years. I get the sense it's very old."

"Maybe it was Hattie Prescott's," Eliza said, and they all exchanged glances that said more than words could. "Can I hold it?"

Rosa pulled the key out from beneath her shirt. She did not take it from her neck but moved closer to Eliza could handle it.

The key was about the length of her ring finger, a rusty color and heavier than she thought it would be. It was a straight cylinder that turned into a notch at the end. It was simple and beautiful and felt very old, just as Rosa had said. At the top were the connected circles matching the depiction on the alter. Now that she had seen the butterfly, it jumped out at her.

As Eliza turned it over in her hand, she wondered who else had held it. What their stories had been. Their pains and sorrows. Their joys and dreams. *Hattie Prescott, lost to madness, what drove you mad?* She thought silently.

Just then, a bird alighted from the rafters above and flew out the door that was propped open. Eliza jumped, surprised another creature was present with them.

"I didn't even know that was there," said Lila Grace, her hand to her chest.

"Like it was watching us," said Bridget, always a little suspicious.

"Did anyone see what kind it was?" asked Eliza, feeling more and more like Hattie Prescott was making her presence known. "Was it a sparrow?"

When darkness fell, and they were tucked into their rooms after lights-out, the girls huddled around the candle once again.

"We've got to wait until later in the night," said Rosa, "To make sure everyone else is asleep."

"Well," said Bridget, "We do have some other business to attend to. Lila Grace needs to take the blood oath."

Lila Grace's round face scrunched at the notion. "And what is that supposed to mean?"

Bridget produced a pin from behind her back. "Swear you'll be loyal to us—no matter what."

"No matter what," said Lila Grace, nodding her head.

"With your blood," said Rosa. Eliza thought she looked amused. It hadn't been long since they both resisted the idea themselves.

"It's just a little prick," said Eliza. "A formality."

"An initiation of sorts," said Rosa.

"Wait, seriously?" asked Lila Grace. "You want me to—ow!"

Bridget had grabbed her finger and jabbed it, not giving her the option to pull away. Then she poked her own finger and passed the needle to Rosa. When all the girls had a droplet of red resting on their fingers, they touched. Not even Lila Grace argued since the deed was already done.

"Now repeat after me," said Bridget. "Blood sisters for life, lest I burn."

And they did.

When the grandfather clock in the foyer struck midnight, the girls set out on their adventure. They followed in a line behind Rosa, walking in each other's shadows and stepping gently.

Rosa led them down the stairs and across the marble foyer floor, then through the dining room. They passed through a back hallway toward the kitchen, a place most of them had not been. But Rosa knew the way, for she had been there before.

The kitchen stove and utensils took on odd shapes in the dim light, for though Bridget had her torch, they did not want to risk turning it on—not yet. The refrigerator lurked in the corner like a bear and the stove's giant mouth was ready to swallow them whole. Serving spoons and whisks hung from the ceiling like sleeping bats, and the sink was a downspout that might suck them into its hole.

When Rosa stopped at the pantry and opened the latch, the others did not know what to make of it. And when she moved shelving to the side, canned goods and all, to reveal a panel there, Eliza gasped. It opened into the blackest hole she had ever seen, like a doorway into night.

"You want me to go in there?" Lila Grace whispered, her voice a bit too loud with concern.

"Shhh!" Bridget corrected her quickly and yanked at her arm. She pointed to her finger in the hazy gray of filtered moonlight that crept in through the windows, a reminder that Lila Grace was now tethered to them—whatever might befall the group.

And so they proceeded, disappearing into the hole in the wall, with Eliza closing the cupboard door after them.

When Rosa entered the passage, she was flooded with memories of the last butterfly circle and the women who had taken her there for the first time. She was a link in the chain of sisterhood, passing this journey on from one group to the next. Their faces came to her in waves—Faith with her wide blue eyes and laughter that sounded like a cherub. Bette with her perfect curls and messy temper. And Mary—sweet Mary, with a voice like a mouse and a heart larger than all of theirs combined. She wondered where they were now. Still at the home? Back in their lives with new babies? Did they think of her also?

She walked through the cave-like receptacle on the other side of the cabinet and crawled through the opening into the tunnel, looking back to make sure Eliza had closed the door. Three faces stared back at her, eyes large with wonder and a bit of fear. Echoes of her other friends loomed around them as she followed the path they had once walked together.

She held Bridget's torch ahead of them, its light bouncing

off the sides of the tunnel. The rock walls were moist and smelled like earth; the dirt floor was sprinkled with scattering things that ran from the light. She held the beam out, where it bounced off the rounding passage ahead, then dissipated into nothingness.

"What is this place?" asked Lila Grace.

"Yeah, where does it go?" asked Bridget.

"And is it safe?" Eliza's voice was shaky.

"Just follow me," said Rosa, urging them to hush with her finger.

Her feet were sure on the dirt path as they walked to the curve in the tunnel, then located the stairs that took them down another level. The air grew colder, wetter, and more filled with the smell of dirt. She could hear Eliza breathing more quickly now, elevating her nerves.

When they reached the door at the bottom of the stairs, Rosa pulled the skeleton key from between her breasts. It was warm from her skin and slid into the keyhole easily. With a turn, there was a click, then she pushed the heavy door open.

Inside was a small room, about a fourth the size of their boarding room. It was crude and had an uneven stone floor with what looked like the remnants of a pallet against the wall. There were no windows, for they were below ground, but there were three doors leading in other directions. One to the left, one to the right, and one that went straight ahead.

They stood together in the house's womb, where the air tingled. It was a curious place, for what other houses had a basement like this one? But it was more than that—special. For Rosa, it symbolized the secret place where hearts of friends meet, even if walls and miles and families separated them. If the space could talk, share what had taken place there before, what would it say?

"Like I told you, I think it was a part of the Underground Railroad," said Rosa. "At least that's what the other girls told me."

"Wasn't it like 100 years ago?" Lila Grace asked, looking around the floor like something might jump out at her.

"It feels powerful like that," said Eliza, walking the circumference of the room, her hand trailing along the walls in a caress, like a mother stroking a baby's head. "And sad. Lonely."

"These doors—they're situated—" began Eliza.

"Like a cross," said Lila Grace.

"Or a butterfly," said Eliza.

"Hmm…," said Rosa. "I hadn't thought about it like that. Well, this one goes to the other wing of the house." She pointed to the one on the right. "And the other two, I'm not sure. Other parts of the house, I suppose."

"Where does it come up?" Bridget pointed to the door she said led to another part of the house.

"The library," said Rosa.

"We have a library?" asked Lila Grace.

"Not that we'll ever see it," said Bridget, then her face turned into mischief. "Unless we sneak. Right now."

"Done," said Rosa.

As they followed Rosa down the passageway, Eliza noticed a paper in the path, half covered with dirt and tattered on the edges. She and picked it up. It was too dark to read, so she tucked it into the pocket of her bathrobe for later.

The path to the library was almost a mirror of the trek they had just traveled. Up the stone stairs and down a dirt tunnel, then to another cave-like opening with a removable panel. This one led to a tiny room the size of a closet. There was a door, but it appeared to be nailed shut. The only other opening was a low grating where the wall met the floor. The girls squeezed into the small space, which barely left them room to move.

"Where does this door go?" asked Eliza.

"This is as far as I have been. Turn off the light," Rosa whispered, and Bridget, who held the torch, obeyed.

"Why are we squeezing in here like sardines?" asked Lila Grace. "Does it just stop here?"

"There's a panel over here," said Eliza quietly. "But it's sealed." As her eyes adjusted to the dark, Eliza could see a pale light coming in through the grating and could hear voices in serious discussion.

"Shhh…" hushed Bridget as they all strained to hear.

Miss Trill's voice was unmistakable. "If you had any doubt about Miss Smith's ability to become an effective mother, let this be the proof to convince you I was right from the start," she said. "All it takes is examining her records to see the family is questionable. She's a feeble-minded, promiscuous fool who will only nurture the same in her offspring. If that child has any hope, it has just received the gift from us."

Another voice responded quietly, but Eliza couldn't hear what it said.

"And if she doesn't comply, we'll just have to take things to the next level. Let her know there is no place for rebellion in this institution," said Miss Trill. "Check on her once more tonight and then leave her for tomorrow."

Eliza felt Rosa's hand in hers and then it squeezed. She squeezed back for solidarity, but wasn't sure what Rosa was trying to say. Her body was shaking, though, and her breath quivering with emotion.

When Miss Trill had exited the room and turned off the lights, Rosa exhaled audibly.

"What is it?" whispered Eliza.

"I think she was talking about Mary Smith—my friend," she said. "She's not feeble-minded—not at all. She's the nicest girl you'll ever meet." She rubbed at her eyes and Eliza wondered if she was brushing away tears.

"Maybe that's who I heard crying," said Bridget.

"I thought we waited until late because we thought everyone would be asleep," said Lila Grace. "Why is Miss Trill up so late?"

"Maybe something happened," said Rosa. "Something they didn't expect."

"Can we go back now?" whispered Lila Grace, her voice urgent. "I have to pee. And what if they check on our room?"

"Hopefully they won't look that close," said Bridget. "We left those pillows under the blankets for a reason."

As the girls moved to head back the way they had come, the pounding from the other side of the wall was swift and sudden. The thud echoed through the small chamber and into Eliza's chest, making her jump and her heart leap in response. She clenched Rosa's arm, who stood beside her, breathing quickly and trying not to move.

"Damn rats," said Miss Trill. "You have something coming to you!" she said forcefully. "Ida, we'll need to distribute rat poison again. I hear them in the walls."

"Yes, ma'am," responded a voice.

The girls remained frozen for a good fifteen minutes, wanting to run but afraid to move. They had thought Miss Trill was gone before, yet she'd been lurking on the other side of the wall. There was no room for mistakes on their adventure, especially not with the suspect conversation they'd overheard. They must tread carefully.

Chapter 14

As they crawled into their beds for the night, Eliza reached her hand across the space between hers and Rosa's beds. The other girl grabbed it and squeezed gently.

"I want to help Mary," whispered Rosa, "but I'm not sure what to do."

"I know," said Eliza. "But I'm not sure we can do anything until we figure out what's going on."

"She wanted to keep her baby," said Rosa, her voice shaking. "I know that. She wanted it more than anything."

"I'm here," said Eliza, trying to soothe her friend. "I don't know how, but we'll figure this out together."

Eliza clutched Rosa's hand until her sobs subsided and her breathing became gentle. Following Rosa into sleep was tempting, but all Eliza could do was stare at the scar in the wall above her head. It was an invitation to disconnect from her own pain—to disappear into the wallpaper, become a part of it. The house had a story to tell and, afraid as she was, she wanted to listen.

Late into the night, Eliza fell through layers of thoughts into a deep sleep, where forgotten voices and pockets of memory lurked.

The pallet was hard under Hattie's body, and the cold had seeped in so there was no warming up. The air licked her skin with moisture, the hunger in her belly twisted. The room was so dark she felt buried in the earth. She had also used up the last of the matches and the candle was of no use.

Was she just to be left here to starve and waste away, then? Was her captor really so cruel? Was it grief over losing his son that drove him to harm others? Or was it that the war had ravaged his body and left him a slave to his nightly medicine?

She shuddered at the image of this face, at once a reflection of her deceased husband and nothing like it at all. His eyes—a pale sea green with pupils so small they could fit in a needle's eye—held no warmth, no love, no sincerity. They were fixed on the spoils to be gained from her loss. And lost she was to this grave she had designed herself.

When she heard movement on the other side of the door, she shrank from it as far as she could, pressing herself against the moist stone. If she could will herself to die and become the stone itself, she would have done. If she had more strength, she might rush him, push him back, lock him in this hole instead. But there was nothing left inside her to resist. She wanted to become smaller and smaller, sink into the ground. Pile the layers of soil atop her so that he might never touch her again.

The door opened, and she shuttered—her breath no longer in control. Words escaped without permission—no, no, no. The moans were animalistic, yet they came from her.

And then there was a voice. "Hattie?" It was an angel speaking. Was she dead?

"Hattie-Hen?" said the voice. "I've come for you!"

In the corners of her mind, this was familiar. Hattie-Hen. That was her. Her name. Her sister's pet name for her.

"Rebecca?" Hattie said.

The gentle arms surrounded her, pulling her to her feet. She was covered in kisses and tears, then urged to follow— "quickly, quickly, before he wakes."

The candlelight splashed the walls, and she saw they were not alone. The cook—always stern and cool—had come to her rescue after all. She held the key—the glorious key—that would lead them to safety.

Cook Maria unlocked the door to the right of the one that had delivered them and supplied them with a candlestick, matches, and a basket of provisions. "Get thee out," she said. "And never return."

Rebecca took the supplies, the key, and tugged at her sister's arm.

"He will not forgive you for this," said Hattie, looking in warning to the cook.

"Nonsense," she said. "He will not know. He believes I detest you. And tonight, you will die. The servants will bury you in the garden with a stone of remembrance. And when he wakes from his drunken sleep, the deed will already be done."

"Thank you," said Hattie, knowing it was not enough.

"I detest you still," she said. A weak smile appeared at the corner of her lips, then disappeared like it had never been there at all. She ushered them through the door as they made their escape.

When Eliza woke, it took her a moment to come back into her own body. She was far away and steeped in another's mind. Yet, she pried herself away from the safe embrace that part of her did not want to release.

"Eliza, get up," said Lila Grace. "You're going to be late. And no one wants the wrath of Shrill Trill."

Eliza sat up, disoriented in the early morning light streaming through the windows. She rubbed the sleep from her eyes, still not feeling completely lucid. And as she went through her routine of changing clothes and washing her face, she knew Hattie was looking over her shoulder.

After so many tragedies happen on a plot of land, the place can pick up a memory of such things. This is what Eliza thought the home had become—a receptacle of lives—their joys and sorrows, hopes and fears, pleasures and torments. Her mind had merely picked up one thread—that which belonged to Hattie Prescott, lost to madness.

While her hands worked, pulling weeds and pruning rosebushes in the courtyard garden, Eliza turned the events over and over in her thoughts, remembering being stuck in the very room in which she had stood the night prior—the one with the four doors. Maybe a cross, or a butterfly, or a nexus to freedom. Maybe all these things.

If the dream held any truth, Hattie did feel partly mad, but only from the abuse she received at the hand of another. Eliza recalled Rebecca, her sweet and tender embrace, and the protective nature Hattie had over her. Rebecca must have been the younger of the two. And what of the man, the beast who lurked upstairs while she was held below? The one who looked so much like her husband, but then not at all. Had her husband lost his mind? Or was he a brother-in-law? Father-in-law? Cousin? She tried to unravel the knot, find the answers to one hundred questions, yet there was no one to ask.

Eliza kept the ideas to herself for a little while, preserving this intimate connection she had with Hattie. Though it was a window into pain, it allowed her escape from her own. And when she finally did share it, she would propose to the other girls another attempt at self-hypnosis.

Eliza was jarred from her thoughts by a sudden gasp, and when she turned, found Bridget bent at the waist, her hands covering her mouth. She had dropped the spade to the ground and ceased the digging that preceded her muffled cries. Her voice was a strangled lullaby, sharp and off key, as it escaped through the spaces in her fingers.

"What is it?" asked Eliza, as she dropped her own basket of weeds. The others rushed to her side and all she could do was point.

There, in the dirt beneath the dying rosebush she was trying to dig up, was a small round object.

At first, it appeared to be a flower bulb that had not yet bloomed, but the more that was uncovered, it revealed a substantial circle. The white was bone. And more digging revealed it was not a chicken carcass or dog remains, but a human skull. Baby bones.

As the realization dawned on Eliza, she grew dizzy, like the ground shifted beneath her. The heat climbed up her neck and she could not breath. What had been a sanctuary with its flowers and butterflies had now become wicked.

"What is the meaning of this?" Miss Trill spoke harshly as she came upon them in the garden.

Each of the girls was caught in a state of shock and horror. Bridget was on her knees choking back tears and could not rip her eyes from the scene. Rosa tried to comfort her but refused to look upon the bones. Lila Grace held her hands over her ears as if she could block out the world, and all Eliza could do was watch. It was slow motion in her eyes until Miss Trill's gaze fell upon her.

"There's a baby in the roses!" Lila Grace exclaimed, pointing, but keeping her distance.

Miss Trill walked to the place Bridget had been digging and peered down, her expression frozen in apathy. "Hm," was all she said.

"That's all you have to say?" said Lila Grace, uncharacteristically defiant. "That is a child. A *child*. What kind of place is this?" Her sobs broke through her words, her nose beginning to run. She swiped at it angrily, waiting for a response.

"It is upsetting to think that," said Miss Trill, her response unemotional. "But likely a stray dog who came here to die. There's no need to be so dramatic." She motioned with her hands for Bridget and Rosa to back away, and they fell in line beside Eliza. But Lila Grace could not be consoled.

"That is no dog, Miss Trill. That is a baby's skull. Do you hear me?" Outraged, her face grew pinker. "I'm going to call my daddy. He will set this right," Lila Grace said as she stomped toward the door leading to the interior.

"You'll do no such thing," said Miss Trill, grabbing her elbow.

Lila Grace roughly shook her arm, breaking Miss Trill's grasp. "I'm going to be collected. I want to go home."

Miss Trill's slap landed hard on her face. The crack echoed in the courtyard, bouncing off the walls and shocking them all with its violence.

Lila Grace stared at her in surprise and her hand flew to her cheek. Her eyes welled with more tears and her mouth moved, but no sound came out.

"You'll thank me for that in time," said Miss Trill, her face stern. "Hysterical women do little to help their situations and yours is a precarious one. You believe your father will come to rescue you, but I have clear orders on your paperwork to hold you until the child is delivered. He will not come for you until then."

Lila Grace's eyes were wide with disbelief. She shook her head but said nothing.

"I don't think you all appreciate the length to which this institution has agreed to care for you," said Miss Trill, walking back and forth and assuming a lecturing tone. "My role is to ensure you regain your moral standing so that when you leave this place, you will walk the righteous path. It requires discipline, and if you won't hold yourselves to that standard, I will do it for you."

Lila Grace inched closer to the other girls slowly, putting distance between herself and Miss Trill, afraid to incur more wrath.

"Now, I have examined the evidence," said Miss Trill, even though she had not. "And I have determined these remains are that of a dog." She looked directly at Lila Grace, whose gaze went to the ground. "A *dog*. Is that understood?"

"Yes, ma'am," said Eliza, though her insides burned with the truth.

"I can't hear you," said Miss Trill.

"Yes, ma'am," the girls said together.

"Very well. You are dismissed for the afternoon. Have your supper and retire early," said Miss Trill.

The girls shuffled inside, Lila Grace clinging to Bridget, who wrapped her arm tightly around her waist.

"It's alright," whispered Bridget into Lila Grace's ear. "We know the truth."

Chapter 15

Drizzles of rain slipped down the windowpanes, breaking up the light that shone on Lila Grace's face. She stood staring out into the evening, disengaged from them all. She traced the trails of water on the glass with her fingertip, and Eliza could only imagine what she was thinking.

"The longer I'm here, the less safe I feel," said Rosa, finally breaking the silence now that they were alone in their boarding room.

The girls had spent the entire dinner in quiet, for fear they were being spied upon. The house had eyes and ears of its own, and though Eliza was alright with a ghost, she was not so with a malefactress. Miss Trill was a wicked woman, and one in a line of many.

"I don't want to stay here," said Bridget. "But I know my family won't come for me. They don't want to see me until I am rid of this *burden*." She said it with a bitterness Eliza had not heard from her before.

"You don't plan to keep it, then?" asked Eliza. "I thought you said you were going to."

Bridget met her eyes, all of her guard dropped. Eliza remembered the first time she'd met her and how tough she had seemed. There was no armor now.

"I do," Bridget said. She nodded, emotion shaking her lips. "And I don't. If I give it up, I'll be disowned." She shrugged. "But if they'll do that to me, then what kind of a family are they, right?" She sounded confident, but her expression betrayed her insecurity. It was easy to say such things when the real test lay in the future.

"I understand the indecision," said Rosa. "I never wanted this."

"I doubt any of us did," said Eliza.

"I did." Lila Grace's comment came as a surprise, from across the room, though they already knew this about her. She continued to stare out the window, but at least she was speaking. "My beau and baby and me will make three." She hummed and swayed back and forth. "We'll be married and have four more just like this one. A house with a white picket fence. With tulips and roses and irises and…" Her voice trailed off as she listed flowers, becoming mumbles under her breath.

Rosa whispered to the other girls. "Is she alright?"

Bridget bit her lip. "I don't know. She seems really… distant. Like she's half somewhere else," she said in low tones.

"Maybe that's how she reacts to things like this," said Eliza, not knowing how to be helpful. "Just thinking about that baby in the garden," she whispered, "it hurts my heart. How could someone do that?"

"I keep wondering if there are more," said Rosa.

Bridget nodded. "Under every flower? Out in the other parts of the property? There could be bodies buried everywhere."

There was a knock at the door. Nurse Ida opened the door and peered in. "Nine-thirty," she said. "Lights out."

They complied, turning down the lights and preparing

their beds. Bridget coaxed Lila Grace onto her pillow, where she turned away from the other girls. Bridget rubbed her back gently, and Lila Grace's soft mumbles could be heard as she drifted off to sleep. And when her breath came in even, deep tones, it was time for the other girls to get to work.

Eliza lay down on her bed and did as Rosa directed—the same as the time before.

"Close your eyes," Rosa whispered. "Relax every muscle in your body. Start at your head and move your way down to your toes."

Again, Eliza imagined a gentle blue light blanketing her from head to toe. It enveloped her in a warm hug then seeped into her limbs, humming gently, lulling her to the edge of reality.

Rosa's voice coaxed her further. "Look for Hattie," she said. "Ask her what she is trying to tell you."

The tree branches stretched above Eliza's head like skeletal hands, dark against the moon. Grass was soft under her bare feet, slippery, coaxing her to fall. Her breath was visible in the air, but the cold hadn't yet sunken into her bones. Her white cotton nightgown shifted against her legs; the bottom hem muddied from the damp forest floor. The other girls walked beside her, their nightgowns glowing in the moonlight, casting them as angels against the dark woods. They flitted among the fireflies, Bridget's sweet tune lulling them along.

"Too-ra-loo-ra-loo-ral," she sang. "Too-ra-loo-ra-li, Too-ra-loo-ra-loo-ral, hush now, don't you cry! Too-ra-loo-ra-loo-ral, Too-ra-loo-ra-li, Too-ra-loo-ra-loo-ral, that's an Irish lullaby."

They followed a stone wall that stretched along the edge

of the property, like it was keeping them in—or something else out.

"Shhhh," whispered Rosa sharply. The tune stopped.

The land sloped as they left the mansion's silhouette in the distance, the trees growing thicker around them. Sticks crunched under her weight; pine needles poked the bottoms of her feet. Roots reached out to grab her ankles, but she steadied herself with the help of Rosa's outstretched hand. It was warm in hers, though shaking. What were they even looking for?

A soft trickle grew louder as they climbed downward, placing footsteps carefully on mossy rocks. The moon shone on the water's surface, its face rippling in the gentle flow of the stream. Rosa turned toward her, gripped her hand tighter. Breath rose from her mouth, her face a blur of shadows beneath long, dark hair. It spilled down her back like a cloak.

"I've got you," she whispered, coaxing Eliza forward. "We'll do it together." Lila Grace walked behind them with arms outstretched to break a potential fall with Bridget in her shadow, waiting to catch her if needed.

As Eliza examined her companions' frames, her eyes lingered on their bellies—each one rounding more each day. Their white nightgowns clung to the swelling with the breeze, then fell away as the wind changed direction, tousling each girl's hair. They appeared in shades of gray, but she knew their colors well, for she'd brushed the locks, curled them, braided them with love. Rosa's chestnut brown, Bridget's auburn with flecks of gold, and Lila Grace's midnight tresses. Eliza's free hand moved unconsciously to her golden hair, fingers running through the silky strands. She twirled a lock of the mane around a finger, her mind floating. She was so tired but wanted this taste of freedom. The summer night felt like magic.

A knee buckled beneath her, but she caught herself. The hand grasping hers closed tight, pulled her upward. The girl paused, examined Eliza, tilted her head to the side. She was no longer Rosa, but a mousy girl with lighter eyes and pale hair.

"We're almost there, just a little further," she said. "There's no turning back now."

"I don't feel well." The words drifted from Eliza's lips, though she didn't feel them move. The world was spinning and she just wanted to sink. She was drifting away from her own body.

The growl came from behind them, a warning before the pounce. All thoughts of weariness left Eliza and her heart started to pound. Her feet were moving before she had time to think. The fear crawled up Eliza's back and into her throat, but she dared not shout. The girl's hand was slippery in hers and she stared back at Eliza with wide eyes.

"Hattie, run!" Eliza's legs pushed her forward as the girl's urgent whisper cut the night.

She fled down the bank to the creek, splashed through the icy water, dragging her friend with her, screaming. It was coming.

Eliza sat up in the bed, her breath coming quickly. Rosa and Bridget stared at her in the firelight, their faces full of concern.

"What happened?" asked Bridget.

"We were all there at first," said Eliza, the memories slipping away. She tried to put words to them, to catch them before they jumped out of her hands like struggling fish. "The four of us, walking outside. In the woods, maybe. By the chapel? And then you," she said, pointing to Rosa. "Weren't you anymore."

"Who was I?" asked Rosa, hesitantly.

"A girl—smaller. Lighter hair and eyes. You called me 'Hattie'," said Eliza. "I think you were her sister, Rebecca."

"Like—you were them in another life?" asked Bridget, her nose wrinkled. It was clear she did not believe in such things.

Eliza shook her head. "I don't know—I don't think so. It was more like I shifted from thinking about us to them. Or… maybe they shifted me somehow."

"Or maybe you have a great imagination," said Bridget.

Rosa rolled her eyes. "If that's what you think, then why are you helping?" It was the first time in a long while she'd been short with any of them.

Bridget shrugged. "I'm just playing devil's advocate," she said. "Is that wrong?"

Rosa sighed. "No. It's not." She placed her hands on her temples and thought. "Maybe it's time we try the mystic hand. I've been thinking about it and there's a clipboard at the front desk. If we can borrow it for just a bit, it might work."

"How will we get it?" asked Eliza, though she suspected she knew the answer.

"It sounds like another Command challenge," said Bridget, with a mischievous smile. "Let's pull a card. We'll see who's not willing to share this time. And they can retrieve the board."

The box Rosa pulled from the closet was becoming more familiar, like an old friend whose freckles you begin to memorize. Its dark wood exterior was shiny—perhaps walnut, with a sealing of some kind. The top was carved—a complicated flourish of many flowers interwoven with each other. Inside was a bed of red velvet that tickled the fingertips. And the tune it sang had once been foreign to Eliza's ears, but now was one she could hum.

"Tell a secret," said Rosa, holding the slip of paper to the candle. "That no one knows."

Bridget didn't miss a beat. "I didn't even like him," she said. "My teacher. You know—the father." She exhaled like it had been a relief to speak it.

"Was his body weird?" asked Rosa, her eyes narrowing, followed by raised eyebrows.

Bridget laughed. "I think all men have weird bodies."

"You don't like them?" asked Rosa. She feigned dramatic shock, but there seemed to be some sincerity there.

"If I'm honest," said Eliza, "I find them intimidating. Not boys—our age, but older men. They look like my father. I mean… ew." And it was the truth.

"I think they're delicious," confessed Rosa. "That's my secret."

"No, it's not," said Bridget. "That's way too obvious."

"Is it?" Rosa said, innocently.

"Yes!" said Eliza, giggling.

"Give us a *real* secret," said Bridget.

Rosa looked at them coyly. She thought for a minute, twirling her hair between two fingers. Then she decided on something. "I… have a spell book," she said.

Bridget's eyes became round. "As in a book with curses?"

she said, leaning forward.

"Like… hexes?" added Eliza, almost at the same time as her friend.

Rosa let out a light laugh but looked more uncomfortable than amused. "They're not bad spells. They're just things I've collected over the years. Little sayings my Grandmama would share. Ingredients I'd see her use. Some are even prayers I liked from church."

"How delightfully unholy of you," said Bridget. "I think I like you better now."

Rosa rolled her eyes. "Well, I have been told I'm quite charming," she said.

"So, where is it?" asked Eliza. "Here?"

Rosa shook her head. "No. I thought if they found it, I'd be kicked out in two seconds. It's home, hidden in a nice, safe place."

"I have a revenge list," said Lila Grace. For the second time that evening, she caught the others off guard, making Eliza jump. Her voice broke their hushed tones with its harshness.

"Lila Grace, I didn't know you were even awake," said Rosa, her hand on her chest.

"You about made me jump out of my skin!" said Eliza.

"Go on," coaxed Bridget, not seeming the least bit unnerved. "Revenge list sounds interesting."

"I started it freshman year," Lila Grace said, perched on her bed like a gargoyle, her voice flat. "With Macy Gilbert— that wretched, beastly rat." Eliza couldn't see her face well but could hear the edge that crept into her voice. "I'd been friends with all the girls in middle school," continued Lila Grace, "But in high school we merged with other schools and it was a whole new battle for popularity. The boys liked me at first because I was more developed than the other girls—all the other girls. But when Macy Gilbert found out, she spread the rumors, saying I was too heavy. Too round. That I needed to reduce. I guess the boys started to agree with her."

"I would have spread rumors right back," said Rosa. "Did you do anything about it?"

"I would have punched her in the face," added Bridget, before Lila Grace could respond.

"Indeed, I did something about it," said Lila Grace. "And much as I would have liked to punch her, that's not my way."

"So, what did you do?" asked Rosa.

Lila Grace leaned in, her voice slipping into storytelling mode. Her gaze still avoided them. "It was on Halloween. Angela Rich was having a girls' night—a sleepover. I wasn't invited, which also landed her on the list, but we'll talk about that later. I had been friends with Angela for a long time. I knew the layout of her house and I knew when she had sleepovers, they stayed in the living room in sleeping bags. I waited until they all fell asleep, and I snuck in through the back door. It took me a minute to locate Macy, but her blonde hair was lighter and longer than anybody else's. All I had to do was find it in the sea of bodies. And cut it all off."

"You're foolin'," said Eliza, shaking her head, waiting for Lila Grace to laugh. But she didn't.

"I'm dead serious. I was only caught because I held onto that ponytail. I should have put it in the trash, but there was something victorious about having it in between my mattresses. And on Monday, I placed a little braid of it in her locker. The fool broke into tears in the hallway and had to go home for the day. The best part is that, with her new haircut, she looked like a boy. And it wasn't only me who thought so."

Lila Grace's white teeth shone in the dark—a grin against a gray background. A Cheshire cat. Revenge waiting to sink its teeth into the next victim.

The room was silent and all Eliza could do was hold her hair and stroke it, imagining what it would feel like to wake up with it all gone.

"Well," said Rosa. "Remind me not to cross you."

"Wow, Lila Grace. That's vicious. Anyone else on that list?" asked Bridget.

"Oh, yes," Lila Grace said. "And Shrill Trill just landed her name on it."

Eliza raised her eyebrows, caught between never wanting to land on the list herself and understanding why Miss Trill had been added.

"What about Eliza?" said Bridget, and Eliza stiffened. "She hasn't shared a secret yet."

Eliza bit her lip as all eyes turned on her. Her face grew warm under their gazes and she was glad for the candlelight, which she hoped hid her reddened cheeks.

"When I… was *with* Michael. I wasn't sure how to do it," she said. And then she decided to let it come tumbling out. "It was embarrassing and awkward, and I wasn't even sure we *had* done it by the time it was over. And then after he was such a jerk and wouldn't talk to me. And then I was pregnant." She stopped, feeling tears threatening to come. She bit her lip again, determined not to let them. "And then I thought—*that* was *it*? *That* was not worth the price of nine months of feeling like a cow."

When she looked back at them, the other girls—surprisingly—seemed to understand.

"It does get better," said Rosa. "When the boy knows what

he's doing."

"Well, I can't attest to that part, but I do feel like a cow," said Bridget.

They fell into a comfortable silence now that Lila Grace seemed to be getting on. Rosa flipped over the paper. "Answer," she said. "Your secrets can bond you together or tear you apart. Work to find the connection; your friends are all you have here."

Eliza smiled. "I have to say, I didn't think I'd find friends when my father dropped me off here." She looked at Rosa. "But from the first moment with you, I haven't been alone. I feel like we're stronger together."

Rosa smiled. "Best friends," she said, looking around the circle of girls.

"Blood sisters," said Lila Grace. Her face showed weariness, but her eyes were sincere.

"For life," said Bridget. "Now, enough of the sappy stuff. Who's going to go get the clipboard?" She looked around at each of her friends. "We all answered the question, so there's no one who has to perform a command."

"I'll do it," said Lila Grace. "I want to."

There was a bite to her voice that frightened Eliza. She couldn't help but think of the story she'd told and the lengths she might go to secure her revenge. Not that she could blame her for being angry, but Miss Trill had the power right now—over them all. If Lila Grace went too far—if she kicked the hornets' nest—what might Trill do in response?

Chapter 16

Eliza stood at the cracked door with Rosa and Bridget as they watched Lila Grace creep down the hall toward the stairs, on a mission to retrieve the clipboard. Her shapely form disappeared around the corner, and there was only silence. Eliza strained her ears, listening for footsteps or voices or creaking stairs, but there was nothing.

One minute passed, then two. Eliza's breath was so loud in her ears it seemed to drown out the rest of the world. Then she heard a shuffle down the hall, a rustling of fabric.

"That was fast," whispered Rosa.

But the figure that rounded the corner was not Lila Grace. It was rounder, taller, and clad in a housekeeping uniform. The girls shrank back into their room and looked at each other wide-eyed.

"Oh, no," said Eliza. Had Lila Grace seen her? Did she know the coast was not clear?

Before Eliza knew what was happening, Bridget opened the door and stepped out into the hall.

"Oh, hello," she said. Her voice was louder than necessary. "Excuse me, I was just on my way to the restroom."

"Hello," the woman said, surprised at first to see her standing there. "You're not supposed to be out here after lights-out."

Bridget bit her lip. "But I really have to go." She crossed her legs for good measure.

"Very well," the woman sighed. "I'll just wait for you to finish, then. Miss Trill asked me to clean it."

"I will only be a moment," said Bridget, walking with her toward the facilities.

When she emerged moments later, Lila Grace was peering around the corner carefully. Bridget motioned for her to rush, and they both hurried to safety and closed the door.

Lila Grace stifled her giggles under her hand. "That was too much fun!" she said, holding out the clipboard. "I'm glad you spoke to her; I was just ready to round the corner and might have been discovered."

"Quiet," urged Bridget. "Don't get cocky. That's when you start making mistakes."

Lila Grace stared back at her, at them all, her mouth smiling but not her eyes. They were filled with something else. Then the smile receded, leaving only a dark stare that filled Eliza with unease.

"You're welcome," said Bridget, with one eyebrow raised, handing them the clipboard.

Eliza watched Rosa's handiwork as she transformed the clipboard, poking a pencil through the hole in the silver clip at the top. "Now, we just need something to prop it up."

"Maybe we can hold it?" Eliza suggested, but Rosa was unimpressed.

"Lila Grace," said Rosa. "You have curlers, right?"

Lila Grace nodded a confirmation, her face still devoid of emotion.

"May I use two please?" asked Rosa, seemingly not noticing the darkness that had crept over their friend.

Lila Grace produced the curlers quickly from the drawer in her bedside table without a word.

"I think these might work," said Rosa. "Just to prop up the back end while we coax the spirits to write."

"Hattie," said Eliza. "While we coax Hattie to write."

Rosa nodded. "Yes, Hattie. Or whoever else wants to speak."

"I'm not sure that's a wise invitation," said Lila Grace. Her eyes were leery, her expression concerned. It was a strange transformation back to caution—like she was another person entirely.

Eliza watched Lila Grace as she examined Rosa's work, wringing her hands. It was she, after all, who had secured the clipboard, braved the long walk down to the desk and back after hours. Yet that courageous face had disappeared as quickly as it had come—not unlike the vengeful girl who'd snipped her rival's ponytail. The many shades of Lila Grace. Were there more?

Eliza felt eyes upon her and turned to meet Bridget's. She was watching her watch Lila Grace. The cool rush of embarrassment climbed up Eliza's neck and she smiled like she had done nothing questionable. Bridget smiled back, but it didn't quite touch her eyes. Eliza wondered if she suspected her of not trusting their friend. It wasn't quite that—she liked Lila Grace. But she was beginning to wonder about her stability.

It was like an itch she couldn't reach—all the way between

her shoulders. She could stretch and grab, but not eliminate the bothersome tickle that lingered there, egging her on.

"There," said Rosa. She backed away to admire her masterpiece, which, to Eliza, looked questionable. The pencil pointed downward onto a piece of paper, but she predicted the curlers would suffice. She was not one to complain, though, especially when Rosa was trying to help her solve this ghostly riddle.

"Now, let's join hands," guided Rosa. They came together and did as she asked, though Lila Grace remained hesitant.

"Spirits," began Rosa. "We ask you for information. Hattie, we believe you have been trying to tell us something. What do you have to say?"

Rosa released Eliza's hand on the one side and Bridget's hand on the other. She gently placed her hands on the clipboard and closed her eyes. Eliza watched as the pencil began to scrape the paper and wondered if it was merely Rosa moving the object. If so, the results would be nothing more than chicken scratch. Rosa continued this way until one curler rolled out from beneath the board.

Rosa opened her eyes and looked to her friends. "Well, let's see what we have," she said.

They examined the scrawls on the paper, shaky and nonsense at first glance.

"Well, that was a waste of a command," said Lila Grace. It was unclear, though, if she was annoyed or relieved.

"Maybe," said Rosa, turning the paper around and looking at it from different angles. "Maybe not."

"Let me see," said Bridget, taking the paper. She did as Rosa had done, turning it over, even examining the other side. "Wait... I think—" She stopped in mid-sentence and walked to the mirror hanging over the dresser. She held it up to the reflective surface, and they all peered at the image there.

"Do you see it?" said Bridget, her voice hovering above a whisper.

Eliza squinted her eyes, shifted her head, and then the word appeared to her. "Mary," she said.

Lila Grace joined them, pushing Eliza out of the way to get a better look. "Oh, my," she said. "Mary. The Virgin Mother!"

"Or, Mary Smith," said Rosa. "My friend."

"The girl I heard crying," said Bridget.

"Well, we think," said Rosa. Her eyes stayed locked on the mirror. "Thank you, Hattie. It's not what I thought you'd say… but maybe that's what you needed to tell us." Rosa turned to her friends with new purpose. "We've got to reach Mary—somehow. I'm worried."

It seemed to help that they had a new purpose, especially in the wake of the drama with Miss Trill and Lila Grace. The latter was back to herself in the morning, as if nothing had happened. Eliza tossed this over in her mind as they breakfasted and set out for the chapel grounds. She was thankful they wouldn't be in the garden that day; she wondered if she could ever go back there and feel comfortable again. As soon as she conjured an image of what had been a peaceful garden, the baby bones crept into her head. And she couldn't block them out.

White bones once covered in skin—skin of a living, breathing child. One who cooed and cried, reaching for its mother in the dark of the hole in the ground. Or perhaps it had been stillborn, and the grave was meant to be a beautiful place. One filled with petals of all colors that changed with the seasons, in the shade of trees beneath a bright blue sky. Where birds sang and chipmunks scampered and heaven didn't seem too far away.

Yes, this second explanation worked best. The baby deserved heaven. Thinking of a child being treated like trash curdled Eliza's insides like sour milk.

As they made the fifteen-minute trek to the chapel grounds, Eliza walked beside Rosa, with Bridget and Lila Grace just ahead, pinky fingers linked. Bridget's charming voice sang "You Are My Sunshine" as they moved along the now familiar route. They passed over stretches of grass with dandelions and buttercups, then into the shade of trees at the edge of the wood, where the air was cooler and smelled of rich earth.

When they got to the chapel, they separated into their various chores. Bridget was to wash the pews inside while Lila Grace was to scrub the alter. Eliza and Rosa planned to weed the flower beds surrounding the chapel and their aim was to be finished by early afternoon, so they might steal an hour stretched out on the grass in the sunshine. As the girls got to work, Eliza set herself up on the left side of the chapel, with Rosa on the other side of the path leading to the door.

"Where do you think Mary is, exactly?" asked Eliza, glancing at Rosa, whose long brunette hair hung in loose waves, swinging as she bent down to kneel before the flower bed.

"I don't know," said Rosa. "The other side of the house, for sure. But it's hard to say exactly what's over there. It might be a similar layout to our wing, or it might be completely different."

Eliza spoke as she pulled the weeds from the soil, their roots resisting the fight. "The tunnels we went through felt similar in structure," she said. "Maybe they're like mirror images, the two halves of the house."

Rosa nodded, tossing discarded plants into a pile. "I don't know if it's best to use the tunnels… see where they lead. Or just sneak down the hall and hope no one catches us. I mean, the tunnels we've been in only seem to connect to the first floor and lower. She's likely on the second floor."

"Is there any reason we might go there in the day? An errand we could run, or maybe distract Miss Trill so you could sneak up to look for her?" Eliza said.

"Too risky during the day, I think," said Rosa. "It would be horrible to make things worse for her by getting caught." She paused, considering a thought. "I wonder where that nailed door goes—the one behind the library. And I'd like to know where the other two tunnels go—if they're even still viable."

"Viable. As in safe?" asked Eliza. It was foolish, perhaps, but since Rosa had been in the tunnels before with other girls, she'd assumed they were in fact safe.

Rosa shrugged. "I don't know. If they were a part of the Underground Railroad, that was a long time ago. I'd hate to be in one of them if it collapses or one of the doors gets locked."

The thought caught Eliza in a vise. Suddenly she was underground, on the other side of a locked door—like Hattie. The walls seemed to close in on her inside her imagination and her breath quickened. "That's an awful thought," she said, wanting desperately to fill her head with anything else. The claustrophobia was strangling.

"Let's see what the others think," said Rosa. "I'm too emotional about this to make a good decision."

The scream from inside the chapel tore them from their conversation. When they burst through the doors, they found Lila Grace pointing under the pew. "It's a rat—it's huge. It's like the size of a cat!"

"Alive or dead?" asked Rosa.

"Dead," said Lila Grace. She shook her hands out like she'd touched it and was ridding herself of germs.

Eliza peered under the pew, keeping her distance. Flies circled and landed on the grey heap of fur and decaying parts. It dawned on her the musty smell in the air, one not usually inside the chapel, was of death. The air was foul. She had to get out.

Eliza pushed past the other girls and through the door to the fresh air and sunshine. The birds sang their lovely tunes and bees buzzed by like nothing was wrong in the world. The other girls joined her on the step, their faces in various contortions of disgust.

"Well, that was gross," said Bridget, taking a seat on the chapel stairs. Of all of them, Eliza had thought she might be the one to pick it up, examine it like the boys used to do in elementary school. But the corpse horrified even her. "I definitely don't want to clean *that* up."

"I hope it was the only one," said Rosa, her lips stretching into a grimace.

"I doubt it," said Bridget. "Where there's one..." Her voice trailed off in a forgotten comment as her attention redirected behind her. When Eliza turned, she saw the most curious thing.

Lila Grace stood facing the chapel doors, arms crossed, with a devious grin on her face. Her mood had shifted again so quickly it was alarming. One moment she was a shrinking violet, and the next, it was as if she was replaced by another.

Eliza glanced at Rosa, who was now examining Lila Grace as well.

"What?" said Bridget. "Lila Grace?"

"Don't worry," she said, not even glancing at them. "I'll clean it up."

Rosa huffed—partly a laugh, partly in confusion. "But you just—"

Lila Grace turned to her with confidence. "Some things trump fear. I know just where it needs to go."

And with new determination, she plodded back into the chapel with purpose, leaving the three other girls with open mouths.

Chapter 17

Eliza knew it was a bad idea. The risk of getting caught was the first problem, followed by the likelihood Lila Grace would be fingered as the culprit. But nothing she, nor the other girls for that matter, said could dissuade her revenge. And so it was that the evening's plans were interrupted by Lila Grace's plot to get into Miss Trill's bedroom.

But Rosa wasn't ready to give up their efforts entirely. She was convinced they could kill two birds with one stone—further their mission to locate Mary, while also supporting Lila Grace in her endeavor.

"We'll work as teams," said Rosa, using a pencil to sketch a crude map of the house—at least what they knew of it. "Eliza and I will investigate where the nailed door behind the library goes first—and we'll drop off a little present on the way. Meanwhile, Lila Grace and Bridget will navigate to Trill's room and deliver the other little present. Got it?"

"Um…," began Eliza. "Please tell me we don't also have a dead rat to handle?" She was trying her best to rein in her temper. She despised conflict and would avoid it when at all possible—even to the point of being uncomfortable. But there were some things she was not willing to do.

"Don't be silly, Eliza," said Bridget. "We only found one

dead rat.”

Eliza exhaled with relief.

“It’s a live one,” said Lila Grace with a wink, and Eliza thought she might pee her pants.

It wasn’t a live rat, as it turned out. But it wasn’t much better. The little mouse was cute—from across the room. It was soft gray with black eyes. Its ears were large and its tail long, like Eliza had seen in picture books about three blind mice. It’s not that she’d never seen a live mouse before, but they were only glimpses she caught as they scampered from basement hole to hole out of the corner of her eye. She’d never seen one up close before.

Rosa seemed unbothered by the small creature, though, like she’d handled them her whole life. And when Eliza asked about how they’d retrieved it, she said Bridget found a few mousetraps in the garden shed, so she knew they were there. All it took was luring one with the bait and putting a box over it before it sprang the trap. Then she placed it safely in a coffee can with air holes until they were ready to release it. It was like God had been on their side—at least that’s what Lila Grace said.

The tunnel to the library was as Eliza had remembered it— damp, dark, and smelling of the earth. As she as Rosa walked the path, they had Bridget’s flashlight with them as a guide since she and Lila Grace couldn’t use it on their adventure. Eliza stayed in the middle of the tunnel, away from the walls and creepy-crawlies. And as they came closer to the library grating,

Rosa turned off the torch.

A dim light shone in from the grating, as it had before, though there were no voices.

"I hope this isn't a waste of a distraction," whispered Rosa. "It won't help if Trill doesn't see the mouse."

"Don't let it go yet," said Eliza, eyeballing the coffee can Rosa placed on the ground.

"Right," agreed Rosa, then turned to pry the nails out of the door. She'd secured the hammer from the same garden shed where Bridget had trapped the mouse. It was a resource they hadn't recognized for what it was, with a bounty of materials they could plunder.

It was a delicate balance between working quickly and quietly. Though no sound came from the library, they'd fallen into that trap before. So, Rosa pried the nails gently, slowly, and they dropped to the ground one by one. Eliza tried to catch them with her skirt, but missed one or two. Thankfully, they landed with little sound.

What would lie on the other side of the door? She fantasized as each nail came loose. Would it be the back of a closet? The inside of a cupboard? A crawl space beneath stairs? Please let there be no spiders, she thought. She hated spiders.

When it was time to open the door, Eliza held her breath, and hoped it wouldn't groan on the way open. But it objected, its hinges old and tired. The air behind it wafted out in a cool burst, bringing with it a smell Eliza could not place but was less than welcoming.

The tickle on her neck came like a breath, and her hand rose quickly to bat a way any creature that might have landed there. She felt nothing under her palm, but the sensation lingered, its echo sending chills up her spine. She shuddered and peered into what lay beyond the door with Rosa at her side.

It wasn't any of the things she had expected—not another small enclosure or hidden space at all. Instead, they found themselves in a hallway with stairs that went up and down. There was no need to turn the flashlight on because moonlight streamed in through a window at the top of the stairs to the left that wound around a corner and upward. They were no longer concealed by a tunnel.

Eliza searched her memory for the smell. It was of someone sick—not yet of death, but of illness. Disease. Suffering. She met Rosa's eyes, which were filled with amazement and caution.

"Where are we?" she whispered, not expecting an answer but thinking aloud.

Eliza shook her head. "I don't suppose this is a *hidden* staircase?" she asked, already knowing.

Once they were both in the hall, they examined the door from which they had emerged. But it did not look like a door from the other side. Rather, it was a wooden panel that matched others like it, all lining the walls. Truly, a secret door one might only find if they knew it was there.

"Well, I'll be," said Rosa. She pushed the door back gently, closing it most of the way, but making sure it stayed cracked—at least for the moment. Then she crept up the stairs, walking with great caution. She motioned for Eliza to follow.

They walked up one flight, then another. If Eliza's calculations were correct, then they were on the second floor of the home now. There was a door that would likely open onto the second-floor wing of the house they sought, then another flight of stairs leading higher—to a third level.

"We don't have a third floor in our wing," whispered

Rosa, peering up the stairs into the dark.

Eliza shook her head, affirming its absence.

Rosa placed her hand on the doorknob and took a breath. If this opened into a hallway, there was no telling who might be on the other side. She turned it slowly, then pulled, cracking the door a little at a time. Sounds echoed down the corridor, a combination of stern voices and wallowing ones, seeking either cooperation or pity. There was also a baby crying, which tugged at Eliza's heart strings and confused her. The tears were almost in her eyes before she knew it—a sudden and strange rush of emotion.

In the private corners of her heart, Eliza did not want to be a mother. It was a truth she'd become aware of over the last few weeks, to her dismay. She wished no ill will toward the baby in her womb, and in fact, felt protective of it, like she was charged with its care until she delivered it. But beyond that, it was freedom she desired, and this was becoming clearer every day.

When she'd first learned of the pregnancy, she was caught in a tumult of emotion, oscillating between denial and what the "right thing to do" was. This, of course, led her to honesty—something she had always valued and assumed would be respected. She had been wrong about that, though. For honesty had gotten her yelled at, ignored, and cast aside by the one person she wanted more than anything—her Michael. On top of that, her own parents looked at her like she was a stranger—and one who deserved to be shamed no less. Her father grew more bitter every time he looked at her, finally ignoring her altogether—literally refusing to acknowledge she was even in the same room.

Here, at the home for unwed mothers, surrounded by these friends who had nothing but compassion for her circumstance (for they themselves were similarly indisposed), she began to wonder if the rules she'd followed her whole life were wrong. She'd taken for granted she would marry and have children, and they would be her life. She thought of the church and the Bible, which had long been a safe place that held answers, but now felt judgmental and suffocating. Even the nuns she disliked she had been able to separate from her own personal feelings about God—the Father, Son, and Holy Spirit. And the Mother Mary, her confidante in the garden at St. Ann's. But the nuns had disparaged her. The priests had encouraged her father to send her away. What had felt like shelter had become questionable. She wanted out from underneath this imprisoning circumstance. And yet…

The baby's cries made her imagine holding the child. Loving the child. Pulling it to her breast and rocking it to sleep. It filled her with longing and fear and terrible sadness all at the same time.

The cries echoed down the hallway and into her ears, into her heart. Should she, could she, give up her baby? Her knees felt weak as she crouched behind Rosa, peeking around her to see into the hallway beyond.

Rosa shut the door quickly and turned, almost stumbling over Eliza. "Someone's coming," she said, pulling her friend back down the stairs. They rounded the corner just as they heard the door open and footsteps beginning to descend—not far behind them.

When they got to the place in the wall where the panel was slightly ajar, Rosa reached into the crack and pulled hard, allowing just enough room for them to squeeze inside. She pushed Eliza through the opening and hurried through herself, squeezing her larger stomach through the slight space. Then she heaved the panel shut, and they stood together, breathing hard and holding hands.

"Holy Jesus," said Rosa, after the footsteps had passed and disappeared into the space below.

"Well, now we know where it goes," said Eliza.

"Did you hear?" asked Rosa. "I do think it was Mary."

Eliza shook her head, knowing her attention had been scattered. "I heard the baby," was all she could say.

"Yes," said Rosa, and Eliza wondered if it had impacted her the same, pulled on her heartstrings. "Maybe Mary's, maybe someone else's."

At least it was not naked in the garden, left to die under a rosebush.

"Eliza." The whisper was faint but sharp like a bell. And it did not come from Rosa.

Eliza straightened and perked her ears. There was nothing but the sound of her own breath and the shifting of Rosa's clothes as she bent to retrieve the coffee can. The air grew cold around her as she watched Rosa crawl toward the grating and opened the top, allowing the mouse to escape and crawl through the crevice into the library.

"Hattie?" whispered Eliza.

"What?" said Rosa, as she rose to her feet.

"Nothing." Eliza followed as Rosa moved back down the tunnel and toward their boarding room. But she placed her warm hand on the space that had tickled her before, considering it with new meaning. And she wondered if Hattie had been with them the whole time.

Chapter 18

In another part of the house, Lila Grace and Bridget prepared to carry out their own plans while Eliza and Rosa caused their distraction.

In their boarding room, Lila Grace fluffed her pillows, then draped the covers over them, trying her best to mimic her body's outline there. They would satisfy any nurse who might check on them. And as she waited for Bridget to do the same, she took a moment to jot down the name in her journal, adding to her revenge list: *Shrill Trill.*

She stared at the entry there, allowing it to feed her anger. The "ill" part of the words glared back at her like two eyes, daring her to challenge the headmistress' authority. And challenge it, she would—right where it counted. In the woman's own bed. The devious thought was delightful, like a lick of cool ice cream on a hot summer day.

She imagined Miss Trill's sour face as she removed her clothing fit for a nun, her body likely never having been touched by a man. For who would want such a beast? She was neither warm nor beautiful, soft nor sensual. Hers was the face of a hag. And what lay inside was even worse. How dare she lay a hand upon anyone? How *dare* she?

"Almost ready?" said Bridget from across the room. She gave the room a once-over, glancing around at all their beds to ensure the ruse. It had been lights out for almost two hours, so they were working by the light of a lone candle.

"Mmm hmm," said Lila Grace with a smile, disguising the rage in her chest. She did not want it to touch Bridget, or any of the girls. She was saving it with purpose.

As she closed the journal, a slip of paper fell to the floor, folded and yellowed. She picked it up and examined it in the candlelight. It was a newspaper clipping—the horoscope for Gemini from the day she was dropped off at the home. *For the twins, this week holds promise*, it read. *A culmination of a long search is about to yield fruit.*

Yes, thought Lila Grace. This journey would yield the greatest of fruit—their child. And then those girls at school would know—they would see she was better than them. He was bound to her now.

She tucked the clipping back into the journal, considering the sign for Gemini represented a Roman numeral two. It suited her, certainly, beyond the idea she happened to be born in June. The twins—two halves of a whole. It's often how she felt inside, with one part of her leaning toward grace and gentleness, and another like a demon on fire. She showed the world the first face—until it gave her a reason not to. And Trill had earned this wrath; she would never see the softness of Lila Grace again.

"Have we given Eliza and Rosa enough time?" asked Lila Grace.

"I hope so," said Bridget. "They just had to make it to the other side of the house and let the mouse out. Fingers crossed, it distracts Trill and keeps her occupied so we can get this done."

"Yes, fingers crossed," said Lila Grace. She also did the sign of the cross for good measure. She knew Jesus wouldn't be happy with her plan for vengeance—he was all about turning the other cheek. But the older God—the Father—he would surely understand.

They blew out the candle and made their way into the hallway with a full pillowcase, beginning to stink.

Lila Grace remembered where the headmistresses' quarters were from the tour with her daddy. While she couldn't pinpoint exactly which room from memory, she knew the general location. It was on the first floor, tucked back behind the office where they had been taken to sign papers. There was a parlor with couches and tea, elegantly decorated but not too flashy. It was, after all, a charity home.

But Lila Grace was not a charity case. Rather, her daddy was a donor—a large one—and promised to continue to support its mission in the years to come. If they would help him address this predicament with his daughter, of course. The former headmistress, who was part of such conversations, was now gone and in her place, Trill knew nothing of this arrangement—or at least pretended she did not.

In her mind's eye, Lila Grace remembered sitting on one of the parlor couches, leafing through a ladies' magazine. *Better Homes and Gardens*, was it? Yes, that was right. The cover had a white picket fence lining a garden she might copy for her own home one day, complete with brilliant colors and lush greenery. She also recalled there was a recipe for oatmeal chocolate chip cookies. She'd ripped it out slowly, so as not to let anyone hear. She'd tucked it into her pocketbook before her daddy and the headmistress were finished with their conversation on the other side of the room. Lila Grace was a good girl under normal circumstances—polite, demure, respectful. Until something woke the demon.

As the girls snuck through the parlor, glad to find it still lit with no sign of the headmistress, Lila Grace tried not to giggle, and Bridget held her temper. Lila Grace could tell Bridget wanted to have fun, but the threat of trouble in this case was so large it pushed her into caution. For Lila Grace, though, she was letting her fury lead, and revenge always instilled amusement in her. Most people didn't understand this, but she had a feeling Bridget would—she just had to wait for the hammer to drop. It was a shame they would not be there to watch Trill find the thing—a rotting corpse crawling with maggots.

The first door they tried was a closet stuffed with coats and discarded things. They shut that one and moved onto the next one, where they found what they sought. Miss Trill's bedroom was tidy, lit gently by a tabletop lamp. It did not have the elegance of the parlor, but it was not lacking, either.

The bed was twice as large as those the girls slept upon and taller, too. There was a stepstool to climb atop the mattress, as one might imagine a queen would have. Lila Grace's eyes narrowed at this sight, for this nasty woman deserved no such comforts. She brought her mind back to the stinking thing in the sack, then got to work, throwing back the covers at the foot of the bed and dumping the contents there. The most delicious part was Trill would tuck her feet into bed, not knowing what lay sequestered there, waiting to taint her with its smell.

Bridget guarded the door, watching for the woman, as Lila Grace pulled the covers back into place, tucking them in for the queen's return. And when the task was complete, they headed toward the door.

The women's voices approached with little warning, but enough for the girls to sneak back into Miss Trill's bedroom. Lila Grace and Bridget did not linger by the door to spy on the pair, but headed back into the recesses of shadow, and felt their way to a wardrobe door. Once inside, they hid behind dresses and coats, their bodies pressed against each other and their hearts pounding madly.

Lila Grace's heartbeat was in her throat, and she fought to calm her breath. She grasped Bridget's arm until she pinched her back, then loosened her grip, whispering an apology. She felt Bridget's hand cover her mouth and understood. *Shut up you fool*, it seemed to say. Never in all the times she had snuck in or out of a place had anyone caught her. But this might be the end of that story.

Lila Grace decided there that if it came to that—if Trill opened the door and discovered them—she would take all the blame. If she had to, she would jump out first and hope Bridget was not seen. It was her fault they were there, and she wouldn't let Bridget pay for it.

The voices droned on, their tones fluctuating up and down. The words were impossible to make out. Lila Grace only hoped this was not the end of Miss Trill's evening—that she still had other business to attend to—for if she did not, they might be stuck in the wardrobe all night long. Would they try to sneak out once she fell asleep? That was perhaps less risky than waiting until she woke and left the room.

She had begun to strategize, considering alternative plans for escape, when the flurry of activity happened. The voices escalated, one speaking frantically, another seeming to chide her—Lila Grace could guess who that voice belonged to. Then they became more distant, and she thought she heard a door close.

Bridget moved first, cracking the wardrobe door and peering out. The room was empty, as it had been before. They crept toward the entryway, sweat beading on both of their brows, and listened. Hoots and hollers came from down the hall, an excitement likely due to the distraction Rosa and Eliza were to deliver to the library.

Lila Grace met Bridget's eyes, and they were filled with amusement. She knew it—Bridget *did* get it. She smiled back, and they snuck to the parlor door, then back through the downstairs hallway, out of reach from the chaos ensuing in the library.

When they got back to their boarding room, Lila Grace was filled with such excitement she could barely contain it. They'd done it! They'd gotten away with it! She felt like she could fly.

Bridget shut the door behind her and giggled. "Woo!" she said. "That was close!" She lit the candle, her face flushed and her eyes dancing.

"Can you believe we did it?" said Lila Grace, her arms outstretched as she twirled around the floor. The room spun, a daze of a world, like she was a tin top and her colors were blurred into one multifaceted swath of paint. She thought she saw Bridget spinning, too, somewhere in the distorted scene. Their laughter blended, lifting them higher and higher.

When she finally stopped, Lila Grace watched the world continue to rotate, and she fell on her bed like she had when she was a child. The ceiling revolved above her, dancing in the candlelight, and then Bridget was next to her, holding her hand.

"I couldn't have done it without you," Lila Grace said.

"You're my soul sister, helping me win back my pride." Her words came between breaths. She rolled over to kiss her friend on the cheek, but in the confusion of the spinning room and her elevated mind, she missed.

Soft lips brushed gently against hers. They weren't hungry or desperate, seeking to move past this touch to the next. They were patient, warm. And utterly by accident.

Lila Grace pulled back quickly. "I'm sorry," she said, trying to laugh off her embarrassment. "I was aiming for your cheek."

Bridget said nothing but stared back at her, green eyes coming into focus, the world no longer spinning. They lingered on Lila Grace, then she turned away, got up and smoothed her nightshirt. "I hope the others come back soon," she said. "They should know how well their distraction worked."

And though they made conversation, went about preparing for sleep like normal, Lila Grace wondered what had happened there—the shift in the air. It might have been the excitement of the evening, swept up in the triumph of it all. Or it might have been Bridget making sense of the close call followed by her blunder. It might even have been herself—and a stirring deep inside. But whatever had begun in that blurry moment of error could not be undone.

Chapter 19

In the early morning hours, when the sun still hung below the crest of earth and a silver mist blanketed the grounds of the unwed mothers' home, Eliza sat on her bed, staring at the hole in the wall. Sleep had been beyond her reach for most of the night. For each time she closed her eyes, she heard whispers on the wind. They tugged at her hair, breathed on her face, fluttered eyelashes against her cheeks.

Hattie was trying to speak.

The mystic hand sat before her on the bed, crudely propped on Lila Grace's curlers, as Rosa had done. But each time Eliza began to move the improvised planchette, the curlers slipped out. In her frustration, she pulled the pencil from the clipboard and placed its tip to paper. She closed her eyes and moved it, scratching the lead back and forth, up and down. It swirled in her hand, in long sweeps one way, sharp jagged jerks in the other. And when it finally was still, she opened her eyes.

She dare not look—not yet. Her eyes were glued to the bloomed hole, staring at the petals of wallpaper, and seeing them for what they were. Layers of the past—like the lives that existed in that room—for a month or a year, with laughter and tears and stories.

"Hattie Prescott, lost to madness, what drove you mad?" Eliza said. The words escaped her lips in a murmur, low and hushed, like insects on the summer breeze.

Then she looked down.

The drawing at first looked like a child's scribbles. No words, just random lines with texture that wove back and forth across the page. But she turned it anyway, as she had seen Rosa do. She lit the candle, doing her best not to wake the others, and continued examining the sketch, searching for meaning. Then she saw it.

The creature stared back at her through naked trees. The trunks obscured its shape, their bark rough and dense. But there it was, lurking behind the maples, angular eyes fixed on her. If there had been color, they might have been red-orange, a flame reaching out to lick her with heat.

Eliza ripped the page out of the notebook, tearing it to shreds and stuffing the waste in the basket beside the dresser. Then she blew out the candle and crawled into bed, head at the foot so she could keep an eye on the hole. As she lay there, calming her disturbed breath, she felt like a fool. It was a pointless act, tearing up the paper, for it erased nothing. But she wanted it as far away from her as possible. She wanted to break the window the wolf had created to watch her. Yet, even with the drawing gone, she felt the eyes upon her.

It was half an hour before they normally woke that Miss Trill came barreling into the room with two ward assistants and Nurse Ida in tow. There was no knock, no vocal prompt, just a door swinging wide and smashing into the wall.

Eliza sat up, heart racing, eyes alert, trying to make sense of the commotion before her.

Miss Trill's face was contorted in fury. She moved without hesitation to Lila Grace's bedside and yanked the covers back. Lila Grace jerked upright; her gray eyes wide with surprise. She attempted to cover her shift with her arms, aware she was more exposed than the male ward assistants were accustomed to seeing.

"Get up, you little brat. I know what you've been up to," spat Miss Trill, her eyes fierce and focused.

Lila Grace's gaze locked on her aggressor first, then darted around the room. "What?" she said, still trying to get her bearings.

"You've been a wicked young lady, Miss Tuinstra," said Miss Trill, her ferocity waning into something else. "And I've been charged with righting your path. Or did you forget that?" The sticky sweetness with which she delivered these words was bitter and dangerous. A smile spread across her face—a horrid one—a warning. "I will set you right. Clearly, one trip to the madhouse was not enough for you."

"I don't know what you're talking about," said Lila Grace, her voice shaking and her face growing bright red.

Miss Trill said nothing. She only stared back at the girl, who swallowed and looked like she was melting. Miss Trill removed her hand from her pocket and revealed a trinket in her palm.

"I don't understand," said Lila Grace. "What is—" Her hand went to her neck and felt the emptiness there.

Her locket—the one with the photo of her beau—dangled from Miss Trill's finger. She walked closer to the girl, the necklace swinging back and forth like a hypnotist's tool. "You dropped something in my bedroom." The words were barely audible but carried a slap.

Lila Grace bit her lip, her eyes flitting to Bridget's face, then back again to Miss Trill's.

"Was there anyone else you wanted to indicate?" Miss Trill continued her interrogation, glancing around the room. And when Lila Grace shook her head, she added, "Very well."

The ward assistants grabbed Lila Grace by the arms and roughly pulled her to her feet. Her sobs were immediate, and she tried to speak, but it came out as mumbles. They dragged her along before Miss Trill, who slammed the door after one final glance back at the other girls.

The echo of the door rudely put back in its place filled the room. Lila Grace's shouts of defiance disappeared further and further down the hall. Bridget inhaled sharply, then let out a sigh that could only come from tears. When Eliza looked at her, they were brimming over onto her cheeks. She'd not seen the girl cry before.

"What just happened?" said Eliza, still in denial and not completely awake.

"Where are they taking her?" squeaked out Bridget.

"I don't know," said Rosa, her dark eyes round and concerned. "I don't know."

The day was an exercise in mastering one's mind. For Eliza, that meant focusing on the tasks at hand- harvesting lettuce and tomatoes for the evening meal. She picked the items from their beds and Rosa washed them, with Bridget barely going through the motions beside them.

As she pulled lettuce leaves and lay them in a pile for Rosa to collect, she watched Bridget out of the corner of her eye. Her friend had cycled through bouts of weeping at breakfast, then moved into anger by the time they were outside. Now she was tearing clean lettuce into pieces for the salad, placing them in a bowl, each leaf feeling her wrath.

Her lips were tight around her mouth, teeth gritted beneath. She swallowed hard every once in a while, and brushed away an occasional tear, but she was out of words.

"They can only do so much to Lila Grace," said Rosa, as she knelt beside Eliza. Her tones were hushed, so that Bridget could not hear. "But what they *can* do might be enough."

Eliza was afraid to ask, but the question escaped. "Enough for what?"

Rosa's eyebrows lifted. "Scare the daylights out of her. Isolate her from the rest of us for her duration. Call her father and say how horrible she's been… or not tell him at all and just do what they please."

"But either way, she'll make it out of here alive," said Eliza. "It's just a matter of time before our parents come for us." She laughed nervously. "We won't be pregnant forever."

"Well, this is what I know. Mary had her baby weeks ago. And she's still here." Rosa stood and took a collection of lettuce with her.

The notion sat in the pit of Eliza's stomach and she couldn't help but imagine—*what if?* She'd felt abandoned and isolated already, but this new information shifted everything inside her. Panic rose in her belly. Was she trapped? What if this place, this home (if it could be called that), was a prison—maybe one from which they'd never escape? Surely that was impossible. Surely nothing could exist like that here in Ohio.

Eliza gulped down the nausea creeping up her throat.

What if her parents did not come for her? What if she was forced to mother this child she did not want? What if one mistake (and one not particularly memorable either) cost her choice and freedom?

Her mind trailed back to Lila Grace, and she felt selfish in that instant. At least she had the liberty to be standing there, out in the sunshine, listening to the birds singing and feeling the breeze on her face. Where was her friend? What if she never saw her again?

Bridget knelt down beside Eliza then, feigning to collect more leaves, though there were none to gather yet. Eliza had been daydreaming.

"I'm going to look for her tonight—if she's not returned to our boarding room before then," said Bridget.

Eliza nodded. "We'll go with you."

Bridget shook her head. "Maybe you shouldn't. Trill knows we were out of the room last night—or at least Lila Grace was. I expect they'll check on us a lot more now. Might be best if you and Rosa stay put."

"Okay," said Eliza. And she did see the wisdom in this line of thinking, but she also began to strategize. If Trill wouldn't let them move about the house at night, then there had to be another way.

Chapter 20

B ridget's plans were dashed when, after the nurse had checked on them for lights out, they heard the door close, followed by a click. Perhaps they should have expected this measure, but they had not. The girls had been locked in, with no regard for the urinary needs of pregnant women or risks of fire hazards; they had been secured behind bolted doors for the night.

It was this desperation that led the girls down two paths. The first was Bridget's stroke of insight, in which she decided to enlist the help of the ward assistant who had kept her secret weeks ago. She was the only colored woman who worked in the building, to Bridget's knowledge, so she would not be difficult to seek. She also had shown she cared about the women there, or at least cared about not letting Miss Trill discover Bridget on the stairs, and that was honorable.

"She's the only worker who has offered an ounce of kindness since I've been in this place," said Bridget, as they sat around the candle that night. "I know it's taking a risk, but I think we can trust her."

The girl's green eyes pleaded with the others. Her passion moved Eliza, and she nodded.

"I'm not asking either of you to risk it," Bridget continued. "It will be all on me."

"Very well," said Rosa, succumbing to the idea.

So, the plan would unfold the following day, just before lunch.

The second path offering some relief to the girls was all Eliza's doing. It came to her like a flash of knowing in the late-night hours during one of her bouts with insomnia. As she had many times before, she sat in the dim room with only moonbeams and her friends' relaxed breath for company. She stared at the hole in the wall, the bloomed wallpaper, and thought of the window it created in time—in her imagination, anyway.

The moon's rays tricked her eyes, fluctuating with the leaves in the breeze outside the window. The light played on the walls, images ebbing and flowing with the shifting wind. But try as she might to lead her mind down other paths, it kept returning to the hole and the secrets that lay in the house—and buried in its reach. And she wondered. If the bird had reached through her dreams and pecked its way through the wall, there must be a reason. Was it merely to get her attention? It had. Was it a message from Hattie Prescott, reaching out from beyond the grave? They'd chased that thread, too. Or might there be something more to this clue that scarred the space above her bed like an eye without a lid or lashes?

She looked to the other girls in their beds. Rosa's dark hair spilled out across her pillow, her face relaxed and eyes closed in dreams. Bridget was a rising and falling bubble under her covers, with not even an inch of skin or hair revealed. She was still, save for the gentle motion of her breath. Then she looked to the empty bed across from her that once held Lila Grace. Was she somewhere in the home thinking of them, too? Was she tucked in and warm or huddled in a corner without a blanket? Had she been fed? An idea occurred to her that filled her with terror—what if she had been locked in the cave in the passageways? The possibility arose before her logic could snuff it, and it bubbled up through her spine like a warning.

But that was impossible. Miss Trill knew nothing of the passages. She repeated the notion, all the while wondering if it was true. The instinct to reach out and protect Lila Grace grew, and when she thought of her friend in a cold and dark place, scared and alone, she could not stop the tears. She shed them openly, given no choice, and buried her sobs in her pillow so as not to wake the others.

And it was there in the space of her waning tears that an idea grew, egged on by a scratching noise that emerged from the closet, as if a rodent was trying to escape. Her eyes flicked to the closed door—thinking of the place where Rosa kept the secret box of Questions and Commands. Eliza had heard noises coming from the closet before, but they quickly dissipated into the ether, leaving her to wonder if she'd heard anything at all. What if there was a space there? It would never occur to her to examine the closet on her own, as she saw Rosa as its warden, but this idea pecked at her brain and would not let her be.

She lit the candle with one of Rosa's matches and walked toward the closet, not trying to be too quiet, for she would really rather have company. But not even stubbing her toe and grunting in response woke the other girls, so she ventured into the closet alone.

The false panel was lightweight and easy to move. Behind it sat the box they had opened and shared many times, but it was not the box she sought. She got onto her hands and knees, pulled it out, and set it on the floor of the closet. Then she took the candle in her hands and moved it into the hidden space, leaning forward to see what lay within.

She gasped when she saw the hole went further into the wall. It was as she had suspected—a potential entry point for a passageway. The space was slight but seemed to open up beyond her arm's reach. This was worth waking the others, she decided, and turned back to the room to begin a new adventure.

It took a moment for Rosa and Bridget to rub the sleep from their eyes and engage in a meaningful way, but once they realized what Eliza had found, they snapped quickly awake. While Eliza had been concerned Rosa would be upset with her forward behavior, the inquiry did not disturb her friend in the least. In fact, Rosa was annoyed at herself for not thinking to examine it further.

"I can't believe it was here the whole time," said Rosa, shaking her head. She had taken the candle to examine it for herself. Then, she studied each of them, taking stock of their size. "I might be the smallest of us, but this may present a problem." She pointed to her stomach, larger and rounder than either of the other girls' wombs.

"I'll go," said Eliza. "I almost tried it without you, but thought better of it," she said.

"Take the torch," said Bridget. "That candle is not a good idea in there."

Eliza nodded, accepting the flashlight.

"I'll make up a decoy in your bed—just in case they check on us while you're in there," said Rosa.

"Well, one of you had better stay right here," said Eliza. "I don't think I can do this without you as a lifeline."

"I'll be here," said Bridget.

Eliza held the beam before her, illuminating the narrow space between walls. Dust floated through the air, catching the light and moving with her breath. It smelled like her attic back home, with the scent of wood and memories pulling her back to childhood. Long ago, she would venture up there with her mother, explore the boxes that had been stashed away for years, delighting in new discoveries that were forgotten relics of a past she couldn't quite remember. Those days were lovely, tucked safely in the presence of a woman who doted on her. It felt warm for a minute, then slipped into a pain that tugged at her heart. Her mother looked at her now with distance, judgement, strangeness.

Eliza breathed more quickly as the walls narrowed around her. While she could still fit, it required her to take smaller steps and walk carefully. Then she was through the mouth and into a belly that was larger, with air that smelled different—a rodent? She wondered. The thought made her pause, glance around the space for eyes staring back at her or scampering things ready to bite her ankles. But all she found was quiet.

Then her torch landed on a hole in the wall. The familiar hole. The one that kept her awake at night with threats and whispers. Eliza walked to it and peered through. Sure enough, she could see the inside of their boarding room. Had something—someone—been watching them? She shuddered, feeling the air crawl around her. She tapped on the wall lightly, then jumped when there was a tap back.

When Rosa's dark eye appeared in the hole, Eliza almost wet her pants.

"What do you see in there?" Rosa said, whispering louder than she probably should.

Eliza placed her mouth above the hole, certain directing her voice through it would help. "Nothing yet. A passage—but empty," she whispered.

Then she turned around and explored further. The unfinished backs of walls stared at her, crude and ancient. But there was also what appeared to be a panel—perhaps like the one from which she had entered. Would it deliver her into another boarding room? Would anyone be waiting on the other side?

She placed the flashlight on the ground and touched the panel gingerly. She pushed, not so rough as to knock it over, but to see if it would move. The wood shifted under her hands, slightly giving way to whatever lay on the other side. There was only darkness and no sound. She pushed again, harder this time, and it budged more. Finally, she gave it one last shove and the panel fell forward, tapping something on the other side.

Eliza held her breath. She listened. There was no movement, no surprised gasps. She crouched down and ventured forth, taking the torch with her as she pulled her body into the next space. She found herself inside of a closet similar to their own, empty but for a few hangers. She knocked them with her head as she stood, jumping at the unexpected touch and tinkling of metal.

But there was still no stirring on the other side of the door.

Eliza turned off the flashlight and took the cold metal doorknob in her hand. She twisted slowly, careful not to make a sound.

The room was lit only by the moon outside the windows. It offered a pale light, just enough for her to see the four beds, empty and coverless. The room was not occupied. As she walked further into the room, she could see it had similar furniture, but it also had a window seat with large panes that opened outward. The room she shared with the others had rather boring windows that simply slid up and down, but these were those for a love story—a Romeo and Juliet production.

Eliza crept closer, placing a knee on the window seat. It groaned under her weight. The glass looked out onto the back of the house rather than their side-view. The trees, tall and lush, waved in the breeze, and she longed to hear their rustling. Unlatching the window, she pushed it slightly ajar and listened to the tree's song, a gentle lulling that brought with it the hint of rain.

"Eliza." The whisper was so gentle and so sweet she wasn't sure it was real. It seemed to come from the outside, floating among the treetops and up into the clouds.

Eliza gulped. "Hattie," she whispered. "Hattie Prescott."

"Eliza." It was louder this time, and she was sure of it. A soft female voice from another realm.

"What drove you mad?" Eliza asked, feeling the words emerge without her permission.

It wasn't another sound that caught her attention, but a motion at the edge of the grounds. It happened far to her right, almost around the corner of the house, so that she had to lean out the window to get a good view.

The moonlight played on the top of a wall there, and she

saw two women walking hand in hand. They wore old-fashioned dresses—straight down to the ankles—but it was too dark to decipher color. One leaned more on the other, walking unsure, and the stronger girl grabbed her companion's elbow. As she watched their silhouettes move, she realized they were at a gate. It was not something she'd noticed there before, but she'd only seen that part of the grounds for a moment and at a distance. As the women disappeared through the gate, they turned and seemed to look right at her.

Eliza waved. She didn't think about it first, she just did it. One of the girls placed a finger to her lips. "Shhhhhhh…." echoed through the night. It was so far away Eliza should not have been able to hear, yet it traveled to her ears, lingered long after the girls had disappeared, and Eliza wondered if they had even been real.

When the bird hit the glass, Eliza stumbled backward, her heart leaping into her throat. Torn from her reverie, she took a moment to get her bearings. The creature fell onto the floor, motionless, its wings still. In the moments before she turned on the torch to get a better look, she wondered if it was not a bird, but a bat. Wasn't it unusual for birds to fly at night?

She clicked the beam on to examine the beast, glad it was in fact a sparrow and horrified it was hurt. Was it merely stunned or dead? It had hit the windowpane hard. She felt bad for opening the glass in the first place, for it might not have gotten in its way otherwise.

She looked about herself for something to lift it and found a small trash bin. As gently as she could, she scooped the creature up and placed it on the sill outside of the window. Then she said a little prayer for its well-being and decided she'd pushed her luck too much for one night.

Before she returned to the closet and the hidden panel, before she re-entered the mouth in the wall, she had one more question to answer. Just as she had suspected, the main door to this vacant boarding room opened with the turn of a knob.

Eliza smiled, triumphant, knowing she could deliver good news to her friends; even though Miss Trill had bound them to their quarters, they were not, in reality, trapped. And as she glanced back over her shoulder before reentering the closet, the bird was gone.

The garden was hazy the following day for a cloud had engulfed the entire property. The air was cool for summer and the gray air shimmered with droplets that floated freely and licked Eliza's face. It offered a sort of mystical ambiance, though, and it was a welcome change from the sunny skies that, while beautiful, were becoming monotonous. The plants were also in desperate need of water, so the girls had to lug buckets of the stuff around; it was no easy task for a pregnant girl. Eliza wondered if they should even be doing so, but Miss Trill demanded it.

At least the fog hid the sun, protecting the vegetation from losing more precious moisture. It also saved Eliza's skin from turning pink with irritation, as it did on the hottest and brightest days—especially those they spent in the garden for there were few places to seek out shade.

It was when she was tending to the herb garden—the rosemary, dill, and parsley—that she first spotted the caterpillar.

It was striped on the back with black, yellow, and white. It creeped along the parsley, perhaps nibbling at the leaves but she could not tell. No doubt Miss Trill would want her to kill the thing, but this was not in Eliza's nature. So, she watched it with a smile and kept its secret, hoping it would remain hidden from the birds.

It was impossible not to think of the baby bones while she worked; they called to her from beneath the roses. Part of her wanted to exhume them and place them in a proper casket with a marker that celebrated its life, short as it had been. But for now, the red buds would have to be marker enough. She considered the caterpillar again and hoped that in some way the new life this garden yielded—plant and insect—replaced the sorrow with hope, little by little. Hope garden—maybe that's what this place should be called, she thought.

Eliza glanced backward at the rose bushes and smiled to herself at the notion of reclaiming the garden in the names of all the women and children who'd been through the home. Bridget caught her eye, as she lurked in the doorway, waiting for the right time to sneak back inside. Eliza nodded slightly, then looked to Rosa, who nodded as well. They would talk loudly to Bridget as if she was in the shed if Trill or any other authority came around.

Eliza crossed her fingers as Bridget slipped through the door, in search of the ward assistant with brown skin and lovely, kind eyes. At least, that's how Bridget had described her, for Eliza had not laid eyes upon the woman. She only hoped Bridget's sense of her was right—that she could be trusted to help her locate Lila Grace and was not one of Trill's spies.

Bridget walked with purpose down the hall, so if she was stopped by anyone, she might say she was on an errand. She had seen the woman she sought head this way and she couldn't be much further ahead. As she rounded the corner by the kitchen, she held her head high, feigning confidence. And to her surprise, no one stopped to question her, though she passed by two different orderlies along the way.

It was outside the kitchen that she located the woman, who was younger than she had thought from first seeing her that night on the stairs, when she'd ventured below for the Questions and Commands game.

As the woman's eyes raised to meet hers, she paused, faltering. All she would need to do is raise a voice to call Shrill Trill. Bridget would be reprimanded at the least, subjected to isolation at the worst.

"Hello," she said. "I wanted to thank you—for keeping my secret that night, a few weeks ago."

The woman's mouth turned up in a brief smile, and she nodded. "You best not be found here, either," she said.

"I'm Bridget," she said, nodding in agreement. She held out her hand.

The woman hesitated to take Bridget's outstretched hand, looking at her with suspicion.

"I could really get it for being here," continued Bridget, still holding her hand out, "But Shrill Trill—she took one of my friends the other night. I'm here to find her."

The woman smiled at the "Shrill Trill" comment, assuring Bridget they had a common enemy. She finally accepted

Bridget's hand.

"Dorothy—but my friends call me Dot," she said. Then she looked around to make sure they were alone.

"Dot," said Bridget, hoping it was alright for her to address her as a friend. "My friend—Lila Grace—have you seen her?"

Dot shrugged. "There's a few girls on the other side of the house from you. And babies—not as many as you'd think, though. There's one girl they put in a dark room by herself—Miss Trill said no cleaning, no tending to her. I do know she's been fed, though."

Bridget's insides tensed. Alone in a dark room. No cleaning, no tending. What were they doing to Lila Grace? "Where is she? The one you can't tend to?" she asked.

"Other side of the house," said Dot, gesturing with her hands. "Second floor, last door on the left."

Bridget exhaled deeply. She took both of Dot's hands in hers, something she rarely did. "Thank you."

"Bridget? That's your name?" Dot asked, and Bridget nodded. "It's not right what they're doing here. I've only been here a few weeks and I know that much. Women are crying all day. Babies are there, then gone. They don't even get to say goodbye."

It was then they heard footsteps down the hall.

"You best hide," said Dot, opening a closet door Bridget hadn't noticed. "Right now."

The closet was dark and smelled like mothballs, but it was better than being discovered in the hall. The voice she heard from the hall did not sound like Miss Trill, but spoke with authority. She barked orders, and all Dot said in response was "yes, Ma'am" six or so times. Then the voices died down, and

Bridget cracked the door open.

When she saw the coast was clear, she made her way back down to the garden where she would lay plans to seek out Lila Grace.

153

Chapter 21

In the deep hours of the night, after the girls had been locked into their room, Eliza wrapped herself in her bathrobe and pulled on thick socks before her shoes. The air had remained unseasonably cool, and it seeped into the house, into their bones. Close together, Eliza led the girls through the panel in their closet and into the vacant room next door. Then they crept silently out its door, through the hall, and down the stairs to the other passageway they sought, where the cool air bit even more.

Since the night prior, since the vision of the women out of doors, Eliza had thought of little else but revisiting the space below the house where Hattie had been held. That is, if her vision was to be trusted.

The heart of the passage was only a stop on the way to seek out Mary and Lila Grace in the other wing of the house, but Eliza needed to stand in Hattie's footsteps—breathe the same air. Something about that space was different from the rest of the house. It was painful and sad but also rich with memory. She felt it with each heartbeat.

When they reached the main chamber, the place where the passages split into four behind closed doors, there arose a blend of otherworldly tugging and panic. In Eliza's haste to return to the heart of the house, she had forgotten her unconscious reaction, the quickened breath, the rushed heartbeat. And when she thought of Hattie, alone in the dark and locked in this place, it exacerbated those symptoms.

But this was a reaction that belonged to her past self—the shadow that was left behind when she first entered the home for unwed mothers. She had transformed, even if she looked the same in the mirror. Thus, she refused to give into these automatic reactions that vied for control. Determined, she stood in the middle of the room, even though Rosa and Bridget were impatient, and she breathed.

Hattie, she thought, I'm here. I'm listening.

Eliza directed her thoughts, took control of the cascading fear and imagined. The place was a cocoon. She was the caterpillar entering, just like the one from the garden. And when she emerged from this place in the coming months, she would have grown wings. She willed it so.

It was when the girls had reached the top of the stairs and had entered the space behind the library that Eliza put her hands in her pockets, trying to warm them. The crinkling she found on the right side was strange, and it made her pause for a moment. As she stood in the shadows and waited for Rosa to determine the "coast was clear" for opening the door to the hallway, Eliza took the paper from her pocket. She recalled picking it up on another trek through the house—a paper that had caught her eye and she'd intended to examine later. But she had forgotten it in the folds of her wrap, waiting there for the right time to emerge.

She touched Bridget lightly on the arm and located the unlit torch, then brought it to life, illuminating the writing on the page. And her eyes grew wide as she read:

14 August 1863
Dearest Rebecca,

I write to you in the darkest of times, when I fear for my life, but at least not my soul. I wrote you last to inform you of my dear William's death, which left me bitter and tired, longing to follow him to the grave. But in the months that followed, I found new purpose in forwarding travelers on their way through hope to heaven. Not everyone shares our vision, though, dear sister.

William's father has returned after being wounded to collect his estate. A wretched man, indeed. But with me here, he has no rightful claim to it, and that is where a new despair began. He bid me to sign it over to him willingly, which I refused. And now he has locked me in here—a place meant to be refuge is now a dungeon. I pray it will not be my tomb.
Your sister,
Hattie-Hen

In her excitement, Eliza swallowed and spoke at the same time. It wasn't something she normally did, but these were interesting times and the new information was quite the find. The result was a coughing fit she could barely contain.

Rosa turned, looking surprised and worried. Bridget turned off the flashlight, then pounded on her back—more roughly than necessary. When the coughing had subsided, the girls sat together in the ebbing echoes, searching the silence for a hint of voices. Had they been heard? Would they be discovered?

But there was nothing.

Eliza gulped. She did not want to risk speaking, so she simply handed the paper to Rosa. They held the flashlight close and read, offering gasps and raised eyebrows in response.

"Well, Dandelion Girl," whispered Bridget. "Looks like you have the sight after all."

In the hallway at the top of the stairwell, they were to divide into two journeys, with Bridget seeking out Lila Grace, and Eliza with Rosa seeking out Mary. But when they reached this destination and planned to part, a peculiar feeling overcame Eliza. The edges of her vision fizzled out, blackened, made her see as if through a tunnel. Then her knees buckled, and she fell against the wall, catching herself.

"Oh!" whispered Rosa, quickly rushing to her and pulling her back to her feet. Bridget hurried to her side also, looking over her shoulder for anyone approaching, but all was quiet.

"Are you alright?" asked Bridget, her voice barely audible.

Eliza nodded, her vision coming back to normal. "I don't know what happened," she said.

"Maybe too much exercise," said Rosa. They had, after all, just walked up a flight of stairs. "Happens sometimes with pregnancy."

"Maybe you should wait in the passage," said Bridget. She searched Eliza's face with her eyes.

Eliza swallowed, knowing it was wise advice, but not

wanting them to go on without her. She shook her head and acquiesced. "Alright," she said, and as they disappeared down the hall to their separate destinies, she was overcome with a loneliness that made her heart ache.

It was silly, she knew, to feel such a thing, but being the host to another human being was making her prone to all sorts of sensitivities. She had expected emotional turmoil, as everyone knew pregnant women were given to a wide range of moods, but she hadn't expected the feelings to be so real—so potent.

Eliza made her way carefully back down the stairs and crept behind the wall, tucking it carefully back into place like a puzzle piece completing a picture. And then she sat on the floor and leaned against the wall, the flashlight on but dampened by her nightshift. The glow underneath was a muted white light, enough so she could see, but hopefully not enough to call attention to the library grating—the only thing that separated her from anyone that might be there. While she would like to be braver, she was not ready to sit there alone in the dark, like a creature of the night.

Rosa knew how to be stealthy, for sneaking was in her bones. Sneaking downstairs for a secret handful of cookies and glass of milk. Sneaking out the window to Matteo's arms. Sneaking out of gym class and off campus to lie under the spring sky—by herself or with others—it didn't matter, as long as she was free. The worst thing in the world she could imagine was a cage.

Once, when she was younger, her father had taken her to a rodeo to see real live cowboys. That's how he had put it—"real live ones." At first, she had been mesmerized. But when she saw them break the mare, bend its will and calm its wildness, she became fury itself. Her head had grown so hot she thought it caught fire—and if she could have, she would have thrown it at them.

To tame something so wild is surely a sin. If God created the magnificent horse to be free, roaming the sands on the edge of a beach, then so it should be. Who made man the dictator of such things? Surely, they did not have that right. Yet they took it.

She remembered trying to paint this event in her art class—the destruction of a thing's spirit, even as it remained in the physical form. It was a pencil drawing of the mare—her beautiful, elongated face, large eyes, and wispy mane. And behind her, whimsical colors like blowing wind, fleeing from the snare in which she'd been caught. "Tamed" they called her, through a process that required breaking. Until she was broken.

It was this portrait of the wild mare that came to Rosa's mind when she laid eyes, at last, on Mary.

Mary had been a vibrant girl, if sweet and quiet. Her cheeks were always rosy, and her pale green eyes were like fresh grass. Her voice was gentle as a lilting song, and her smile so sincere, with deep dimples in her cheeks. Her frame was small and delicate, like a bird, so much her growing belly might topple her over. When they had moved her from their boarding room the month prior, she had been afraid. And now that Rosa saw her, she was afraid, too.

The door stood open, which was strange in this place with locks and rules. Mary's still form lay on a bed. Her eyes were open, but she did not respond to the tending nurse, even when asked a question. Rosa waited for the nurse to leave, hiding around the corner, then took her chance to slip into the room.

What lay in Mary's place on the stark bed was not much more than a skeleton. Her slight form had never had much padding, but what was left was angular and jaundiced. She did not even look at Rosa, standing there in the doorway. Her eyes were distant and bloodshot, the rims red and raw. She could almost see the broken spirit leaving her, floating away into a colorful sunset where she could run wild and free.

Rosa snuck into the room and kneeled, afraid to break the silence. She took Mary's hand in hers, its coldness surprising. Rosa gulped.

"Mary," she said. "Mare?" She searched her friend's face for some type of recognition.

The pale green irises lifted and rested on her, flickered for a moment. Her lips pursed, and she saw them move, but no sound came out.

"What have they done to you?" As soon as she had said it, Rosa wanted to grab the words back—eat them, bury them, apologize for them. Her throat tightened against her will and all she could do was stare at this shell that was once her friend.

"My baby," said Mary, finally. "Rosa, they took her from me."

So, she did recognize her. That was something.

"Took her?" said Rosa.

Mary shook her head, her face crumpling into such raw emotion, Rosa began to cry, too.

"Stole her," Mary wailed, her voice becoming louder. "I didn't even get to hold..." She swallowed her words and replaced them with sobs.

"Shhhh," soothed Rosa, touching her friend's face and drawing her into an embrace. "We've got to be quiet, Mary."

Mary's form slumped against her, shaking and sobbing deeply at first. Rosa smoothed her hair and began to hum in a way her mother had done for her as a child. And Mary relaxed against her friend. There was no room for words, for none could capture the misery that haunted the girl, and none could convey the sense of compassion that swooned in Rosa's chest. It was a moment for tenderness in touch alone.

And then it was over. Rosa could hear the footsteps down the hall. She released Mary and met her eyes one more time. "I'm with you, my sister," she said, squeezing her hand. Mary nodded—it was all she could do. And Rosa slipped behind the door to hide, waiting for a moment to sneak back out.

When Bridget reached the door in another section of the house, the last one on the left as Dot had described, she tapped gently. She didn't want to knock for fear of making too much noise. She placed her ear to the heavy wood and listened. Shaky breath came in a steady rhythm, as if Lila Grace was past crying and into the aftermath of gasps and shudders.

She tried the handle; it turned, but the door was bolted. Then she tried the key Rosa had given her, to see if it might unlatch the lock. But her effort was in vain. So, she knelt to the floor and placed her lips as close to the crack beneath as she could.

"Lila Grace," she whispered, urgently. "Lila Grace, can you hear me?"

There was movement from within.

"I'm here," came a voice, a little too loudly and with desperation.

"Shhhhh," soothed Bridget.

"Can you get me out?" Lila Grace responded more quietly. Her voice shook and devolved into sobbing.

"Not yet," said Bridget. "I'm trying."

"How did you find me?" Lila Grace said in gasps.

"One of the Ward Assistants," said Bridget. "Are you okay?"

"No. It's dark in here. So dark. There are no windows or anything. I think this is a closet or something," Lila Grace said, sniffling.

Bridget felt powerless, but she didn't want to say so. "This is…." Words were failing her. "Trill needs to be put in her place." She gritted her teeth, feeling a rage building deep within her. But none of that would help Lila Grace now. So, she reached her fingers beneath the door. "Can you reach my hand?"

Lila Grace's fingers brushed hers lightly and then laced with them as best they could. Her sobs relaxed into shaky breaths on the other side.

"I'm scared," Lila Grace said.

"I know," said Bridget. "I'm here." It was all she could say.

They stayed like that for several minutes, sharing the silence, the touch of hands meaning more than any words could. And they breathed, and cried, and felt a little less alone.

The nervous pangs stabbed at Eliza's stomach every so often as she sat in the dark place in the wall, waiting for her friends. They were the ones at risk now, but the chance was worth taking to help their fellow sisters. It was how she thought of the four of them now—herself, Rosa, Bridget, and Lila Grace. And though she did not know Mary, Rosa's fondness for her was enough. She was a sister by extension.

Eliza imagined Lila Grace, alone in the room on the second floor. Was she alone? With other girls? And when would they return her to the only sanctuary they had in this place— their boarding room. After so many nights of secrets and laughter, it held their essence.

This notion made Eliza recall how a place can hold the spirit of someone—the things they feel, the impressions of their lives—in its very surfaces. Like grooves in a record where music is imbued, the walls and the floors soak up the living and hang onto it long after the people are gone. Was there a way for her to read it, to tap more closely into what had come before? She thought of the wallpaper and the bloom in the wall upstairs, so many layers of lives in that room. What was the first one? She wondered. Who had put that layer of wallpaper there? What had it seen?

The thoughts tugged at her, pulled her into a lulling place that swayed between sleeping and waking. She imagined she was on a swing, flying back and forth through the air, like she had so many times as a child. In her memory, the wind tugged at her hair, pressing it against her face, and then back as it kissed her. The motion was familiar, rhythmic. And then she slipped beneath the surface of consciousness to the place where she could see with other eyes.

Eliza floated through the mansion like a cloud, gently moving on a breeze no one else could see. She traveled the hallways, up and down, in and out of rooms—some that she knew, some she did not. But in none of them was she alone. The others did not mind her presence, did nothing more than glance her way when she passed—the blond girl in the white gown with the gentle blue eyes.

And then she was pulled down, down into the tunnels she had explored before. Except this time, there were more. More passageways, twisted and turning, some connecting and some with dead ends. Like a labyrinth beneath the home, a spider and its many legs, designed to trick you. And she found herself in a room. It was small, cold, very dark. There was a black stone there that left dust on her fingertips—coal. She was in a coal room.

Eliza breathed, imagining the soot entering her lungs like smoke. It was something that had scared her since childhood, when their kitchen stove had caught on fire and singed her hair. Her mother had batted at it with a towel, so protective, so worried. In the space of that moment, recalling this imprint from the past, something opened in Eliza—a painful wound that had never scabbed over. The longing for a mother that held her without judgment, loved her with no boundaries. But that mother was gone. And she was alone.

Eliza's eyes fell on the mound of coal. Its blackness velvet and echoing the emptiness in her heart. But her flashlight caught something else, too. Something small and pale. The baby bones peaked out from beneath the rocks like stray blades of grass. They were thin, fragile—castaways from the mothers who should have loved them. Or the nurses who should have saved them. Or the other workers in this house complicit in their deaths.

The emptiness pulled her down, down, into herself. The sadness was a well with no bottom, beneath even these tunnels in the house. Beneath the rock and dirt and pain. Eliza was being sucked down a drain.

The growl emerged from the back of the room, where the shadows were darkest. Eliza snapped to attention as best she could, though her vision was hazy and mind blurry. She was trapped in the pull of this misery, this despair. The growl came again, and though she wanted to run, Eliza stood frozen. With her eyes open, her body was stone.

The wolf was black like the coal, so dark he could have been a starless sky, a pool of ink, except for his ruby eyes that glittered as he moved. Eliza's heart quickened, her body tensing but still immobile, her breath coming in gasps. She hoped—no, she prayed—he did not see her. She was nothing, she was nowhere, she was but a dot on the wall.

But he did see her.

His eyes fixed on her shape, studied her form, and rested on her belly. And his mouth parted to reveal gnashing teeth.

"Eliza...." The deep-throated hiss came in hot breath, slipping past her ears.

When she squeezed her eyes shut, tears escaped from the corners. She could smell him—a mix of sweat and stench and decay. Not human, not animal—something in between.

"Eliza!" Bridget's whisper was urgent.

Eliza woke to her face, worried and peering into her own. She was being shaken, not rough, but enough to stir her awake. Her heart pounded in her chest, aching with the urge to run. And the smell lingered, hung in the air, thick and putrid.

"We need to get back to the room," Bridget said, pulling her by the arm, with Rosa leading them back the way they had come.

Chapter 22

Eliza sat on their boarding room floor, legs crossed, with the light of the candle flickering on her face. The orange flame danced and then stood still, resting in a tall, stretched blaze that disappeared into wispy black smoke. The three of them sat in a circle, tighter than normal, for Lila Grace's absence had created a hole. Their knees almost touched, a Celtic knot of legs connecting one to the other.

Rosa and Bridget had shared about their meetings with the other girls, both visibly upset and not knowing what to do. Eliza had no answers either, and debated whether to share her dream. Had it been a dream?

"It could be us up there," said Bridget. "In the closet; in the room left to rot."

"Maybe it will be," added Rosa.

And the silence hung over them, threatening. Like merely saying this aloud made it possible. But Eliza knew this wasn't true. The moment they had walked through the doors to the home, they had become caged birds.

"She said they took her baby," said Rosa. "Just took it, without letting her so much as hold it."

"*Her*. Hold her," said Bridget.

Rosa shrugged. "I think it helps to keep some distance.

Thinking about it—*her*—as a child is enough to make me sick."

Eliza's own stomach threatened to turn. "You don't think they… hurt the baby. Do you?" All she could see in her mind's eye were the baby bones, tucked under the lumps of coal in the tiny room. Decaying under roses in the garden. Slinking down the drain after being cut to pieces.

Rosa's eyes began to well.

"I'm sorry," said Eliza, fast. "I'm not trying to make things worse. I just… I feel like maybe we need to get out of here. You know—run."

Bridget placed her face in her hands, rubbed it up, then down. She sighed an exhausted breath and licked her lips. "I think my parents will just send me back here. Then it will be even worse," she said.

"Maybe," said Rosa. "Maybe not."

"And I'm not going without Lila Grace," said Bridget, crossing her arms.

"No," said Eliza. "We can't leave her."

"Or Mary," said Rosa.

"Or any of them," said Bridget. "When we go, more will replace us. How many girls have to go through this?"

There was stirring in the hall, just outside the door. Rosa blew the candle out and they all crept back into their beds as quietly as they could.

When the door opened, they were still and silent, feigning sleep. The watcher stood there with the door ajar for a moment, spilling light onto their breathing forms. Then she closed the door, and the lock clicked into place. And although they could have continued their conversation, there was not much more to say that night. They were stuck for now and would have to make plans to solve this complicated riddle.

A bizarre thing happened the following morning. When Eliza woke, the letter she had been holding, touching gently, and imagining Hattie penning its words, was in her mouth. The ball of paper had been chewed and was wet with saliva. The letters were mostly legible, though some had run, but that was the least of her worries.

She couldn't help but feel a lack of control. Had she placed the paper in her mouth? What in the world had possessed her to do that? And if she had not, what kind of apparition had? Surely not Hattie.

When Eliza dressed for the day, she could not shake the feeling of being watched. It was more than eyes upon her, more than someone breathing over her shoulder. She was inhabited, like the thing to be afraid of had crept beneath her very skin and into her mind. And while she should confess it to the others, the feeling of shame was so thick in her throat she could not spit the words out.

That week, the heat of the summer finally settled on the region, filling the home with its heavy breath. The air was so thick it was like moving through water and it was impossible to stay cool—even in the shade. The weight of the air matched the frustration that grew for them all. The absence of Lila Grace hung over them.

Bridget knew she was devolving—into what, she wasn't quite sure. Though she visited Lila Grace nightly, the girl's personality was shifting. The remains of her strong will hung in shreds; she was just on the other side of giving up. It had only been four days and three nights, yet it felt like an eon.

They had been working out at the chapel in the afternoon, but upon their return to the main house, Dot presented herself in the hall. She motioned for Bridget to meet with her in private, and they snuck into the restroom to talk, with Eliza and Rosa hesitating in the garden in case Miss Trill happened by.

"If anyone finds these, you didn't get them from me," said Dot, holding a file in her hands, but not offering them up yet. She gulped and continued. "I need this job to care for my family." She paused, nodding to herself and coming to some silent conclusion. "You need to swear that you'll keep my name out of it. Whatever happens."

Bridget nodded. "I swear." She held the woman's dark eyes, a bond of hopeful trust passing between them. "Thieves are never rogues amongst themselves."

Dot smiled, unsure. "Well, I don't know what that means, but I do think you're a good person."

"Just something my dad used to say—back when he liked me," said Bridget.

"Your friend, the one upstairs," said Dot, "I think she's a good person, too. And Miss Trill is not… so…" With that, she handed Bridget the file and turned to leave.

"Dot?" said Bridget. "Thank you."

The woman nodded and closed the door, leaving Bridget alone with the notes. "Tuinstra, Lila Grace" was written on the tab.

When she opened the folder, she wasn't sure what she'd

find. There was an information form listing Lila Grace's name and address, parents' names and her father's profession. There was a parish listed in a wealthy suburb and a contact name for the head priest there. But it was the papers behind that were more curious.

As she leafed through them quickly, she saw they were copies of records from another institution—one called the Cleveland State Hospital. She had been a patient there a year and a half ago and then again earlier this year. And while some of the pages were typed, there were also handwritten notes that appeared to be from a doctor. Under diagnosis, it read: *MDI - manic depressive insanity.*

Bridget stared at the words on the page until the letters seemed to run together. She felt the rush of sweat on her back and her breath quicken. Was it the heat or was it her nerves? Her heart ached thinking of Lila Grace. What did this mean? Was she… *crazy*?

She shut the folder quickly, as if it might banish the words out of existence, and tucked it into her waistband. Then she commanded herself to regain a sense of calm and headed back out into the garden to join the other girls. But she wasn't ready to share this. Not yet. She needed to come to terms with what it meant.

They would judge Lila Grace, she was sure. Was *she* judging Lila Grace? A flush of embarrassment added to her already tense jaw and tightened shoulder muscles. She chided herself silently and blinked her eyes as she walked out into the garden, holding up her hand to block the sun. She would protect Lila Grace's reputation. It's what she would want if the file was her own. Yes, that's what she would do. It would be their secret; she wouldn't even divulge her knowledge to Lila Grace herself, no matter how badly she wanted to understand it. It was Lila Grace's story to tell, and she should do it on her own terms.

On the fifth day, Lila Grace returned, but she was only a ghost of what she had been. Her eyes were red and puffy, her cheeks sunken in. She would not meet their gazes and would only respond to their questions with head shakes and one-word answers.

Eliza didn't know what to do. She sat across from her on her own bed, glancing at her friend but not wanting to stare. She kept waiting for a moment—an invitation—from Lila Grace to commiserate with her or comfort her. But none came—for any of them. Not even Bridget, who had been her loyal visitor throughout her ordeal.

For now, they all maintained a respectful distance, trying not to crowd her or pressure her to talk. Once Bridget approached her for a hug but Lila Grace quickly shrugged her off. Bridget looked as though she had been stung, her face turning a bright red. And Eliza wanted to comfort her but was afraid of the same treatment.

In the end, it was Rosa who broke the spell. She had a way about her that was gentle but confident and she was able to lure Lila Grace in with a story. She simply asked Eliza for the letter—Hattie's letter, crumbled with bleeding words (though no explanation was given)—and read it aloud. When she had finished the story of the woman in peril, imprisoned in the belly of the house, Lila Grace looked up.

"Like me," she said. "Trapped in a dark place—in this

very house."

Rosa nodded, hopeful. At least this answer was a few words.

The silence hung heavily in the air, but before they could sink back into their individual melancholies, Rosa moved closer to Lila Grace. She sat beside her on the bed, a brush in her hand. And when Lila Grace did not flinch, she reached out to brush her hair.

She stroked the long tresses with care, as a mother might do. And when all of Lila Grace's hair had been straightened, though it was greasy from days without a shower, Rosa began to braid.

Eliza saw her chance to help and took a seat on Lila Grace's other side. She began a braid over the other ear, sliding the ribbons of dark hair between her fingers, weaving them in a delicate plait. They were slippery, but Eliza did not falter. The most important thing was for Lila Grace to feel normal. And this was all they could do.

"I can feel them in the walls," said Lila Grace, relaxing into her friends' care. The seal had been broken and she finally came pouring out. "They whisper. I heard them in the closet."

Eliza was afraid to confirm this, as she did not want to sound crazy, but the whispering had followed her, too.

"And when I hear the babies crying," said Lila Grace, "Sometimes I can't tell when they stop. It's silent, and then I hear them again, but it's like an echo of what it was before. Muted."

There were no tears, for it seemed Lila Grace was beyond them. Eliza wondered what that space was like—to be beyond tears. But then she knew. She remembered the days after her father dropped her off here, the tears no longer providing an outlet or comfort. Rosa had been her refuge then. Her friend in her greatest hour of need. Maybe that space is for sharing, to let the pain become a burden for more shoulders than one.

When the braids were almost complete, Bridget moved carefully to join them. She'd lingered in the background, the hurt on her face from the rebuffed hug still clear. But she swallowed her pride and took a seat on the floor by Lila Grace's feet. Bridget pulled her friend's pink slippers out from underneath the bed—the ones with the shiny bows—and placed them on Lila Grace's feet.

Eliza stared at the slippers—a strange symbol of Lila Grace's old life. They all had them, those things that belonged to the versions of them that existed before the home. Where did those girls go? Maybe they were still crawling around inside them somewhere. Or maybe they had been banished by this rude transition to motherhood, even for those who left with no children. This house was their cocoon, but would they emerge as butterflies or dragons seeking revenge? It made Eliza think of *Beowulf* from Sr. Margaret's English class. Only this time, she related to his adversaries.

Eliza glanced at Lila Grace's face, for she realized the girl had fallen into silence. Lila Grace stared at the slippers on her feet and Eliza wondered if she was thinking the same thing. That the delicate princess shoes no longer fit the girl. She'd grown beyond them.

Lila Grace bent down, ran her fingers over the soft pink satin ribbons. "My daddy bought me these, after I came home last time." She continued to feel the satin, rubbing it like a bottled genie, accessing some distant memory.

"Last time?" asked Bridget. Eliza thought it curious the question came more like a prompt, as if she already knew the answer.

Lila Grace closed her eyes, squeezed them tight. She took a breath. "They sent me to…" she paused, took another breath. "An asylum."

Eliza did not know how to grasp what she was hearing. She'd never known someone who went to an asylum. It was a threat her parents made when she misbehaved. A story told on Halloween or round a campfire in deep summer. A place for "those" people. The ones who'd lost their minds.

Eliza's eyes flicked to Rosa, who was also trying to mask her surprise. They didn't move, didn't breathe. Then Eliza looked to Bridget. She did not falter, she did not glance away. Bridget was the first to place her hands on Lila Grace.

The touch was gentle, supportive, as if to say I'm still here. I know this and I'm still here.

Lila Grace opened her eyes, finally looked at Bridget. They held a gaze for a moment and something passed between them. Eliza didn't know what, but it felt private. She looked away, gave them this moment. And then Rosa took Lila Grace's right hand and Eliza her left. She closed her eyes again and let the tears fall.

These tears were not out of desperation or sadness. They were not in defiance or grief. They were relieved tears, thankful tears, ones that knew she was loved despite her shame.

The girls sat there for a good, long while. Eliza imagined them as a statue, like the Virgin Mary in the garden she loved back at St. Ann. She imagined the Mother watching over them, thoughtful and loving, while the world passed by and people lived their lives. If she could ever be a statue, Eliza might choose this—not a solitary one like a shrine, but a monument to friendship, to sisterhood.

Sitting like this, connected at various points, through hands and hearts and tears, was the root of all things. It was a memory that would burn in her mind for the rest of her life, especially since the next day would be the last she saw Lila Grace for a very long time.

Chapter 23

It had been several days since they'd worked out at the chapel, but it was enough time for the irises to bloom. The purple petals stretched in delicate curves, and as they joined at the center, became butter yellow. Clumps of these blossoms danced together in the breeze on long, slender stems. Their leaves were background choreography, their blades like arms waving to an unseen rhythm.

The morning sun drifted in through the trees like magic, bathing the lawn in golden light. The air was still cool, for the sun had yet to peak, and the shadows were long and enchanted. The four girls walked together in the shade, the glow of morning surrounding them, as they came upon the clearing that led to the chapel.

"Do you think she got away, really?" asked Lila Grace, directing her question to Eliza. There was no need for a name, for Eliza knew she meant Hattie.

Eliza shrugged. "It's what I see in my dreams, but who knows if that's true. I hope it is."

"She was lucky to have a sister," said Rosa. "I think that if I had a sister, I would do anything to protect her."

"Yeah," said Bridget. "If she knew Hattie was being held against her will, she would have come for her."

"But," began Lila Grace. "Maybe she didn't know. I

mean, we have the letter. It was never sent."

The point was valid and disturbing. Eliza shuddered, glancing toward the stone erected in Hattie's memory. It occurred to her then that the namesake had something in common with Lila Grace she hadn't realized before. She recalled the stone's inscription: *Hattie Prescott, lost to madness.* What had Lila Grace thought when she'd seen those words? Did she think of herself as mad? *Was* she—and could she be—lost to it?

"If I was stuck here, held against my will," said Lila Grace, as if she'd sensed Eliza's thoughts. "I'd rather die than let my captor win." Her words were chilling because she had been held against her will, if for only a few days. But in the confines of that small room, she hadn't known how long it would last. None of them had. And in that place of unknowing, one meets parts of the self they've not known before. At least that's how Eliza imagined it to be.

"What do you think you would have done?" asked Eliza. "I mean, if they didn't let you out."

"The first day, I was so angry, I kicked the door, the walls, until I hurt myself," Lila Grace said. "And then it just felt useless. So, I decided to wait until they came to feed me or empty out that bucket."

That bucket. Eliza knew it could only be for one thing. She grimaced, embarrassed for Lila Grace.

"I was gonna kick Trill right in the stomach, and any of her little assistants who came to do her work." Lila Grace's lips were tight as she spoke, her voice bitter. And then she let out a shaky breath. "But when the time finally came, it wasn't Trill. It was a colored woman I'd not seen before. She was gentle. And I was tired. I think she might have brought me food in secret. I got the sense she wasn't supposed to be there."

"Dot," said Bridget. "That must have been Dot. She's the one who told me where to find you."

Lila Grace nodded. "It was after you visited me the first time."

"Sounds like we have a guardian angel," said Rosa.

"Or maybe a couple," said Eliza, pointing to the sky. The pair of monarch butterflies danced around each other in graceful loops, like two halves of a whole. "Makes me think of Hattie and her sister."

"Well, look at that," said Lila Grace.

They watched until they disappeared into the treetops and even after, studying the large white clouds that hung above.

"We always have the sky," said Rosa, and she smiled. She looked far away—lost in reverie. "When my Grandmama had to leave after a visit, I would cry so hard that I would throw up. She would tell me to wait for the sky to get dark and look up at the moon. Even if we were worlds apart, we would be looking at the same sky. So, really, it was a way for us to be together— especially when we felt most alone."

"I love that," said Eliza. "We always have the sky."

That afternoon, after their chores had been done, the girls lingered in the woods around the chapel, reluctant to return to the home. Eliza found herself at Hattie's stone, sitting in quiet contemplation. It wasn't a prayer to her, exactly, for Eliza was not sure human spirits could be prayed to, but it was a moment of reflection, certainly. She whispered Hattie's name, listened for any response, and though she felt a peaceful hum in her heart, she heard nothing but the wind.

When Rosa joined her there, she was silent. They both

watched the shadows play on the rock, sunlight peeking through trees and shifting with the wind. They sat together for a while, the quiet surrounding them in a tranquil pool. And Eliza thought what a strange thing it was to feel so free out of doors, on the same grounds as the home that felt like a prison.

"Maybe we should run," said Eliza, breaking the silence.

"To where?" asked Rosa. "Home?"

The thought was not comforting. Eliza thought of her father, the gruff way he had dropped her off at the institution. "I suppose not," said Eliza, feeling foolish.

"Hey," said Rosa, placing her hand on Eliza's arm. "I understand how you feel. Part of me wants to run, too. Then I argue with myself. I say the same thing—to where? Is there a place that would really help us? Treat us like we matter? Give us a choice about what we really want?"

"Call me silly, but I thought that's why we were here," said Eliza.

"Yeah, me too," said Rosa. "Maybe the best thing to do is just cooperate."

"That seems strange, coming from you," said Eliza, looking to her friend. Her dark eyes showed defeat.

"It's really not like me," she said, huffing a laugh that felt hollow. "But being me hasn't been working out so well. I mean, look what they did to Lila Grace. I know she was angry, but she did bring it upon herself with the rat."

"Can you blame her?" asked Eliza, recalling the slap that day in the courtyard garden.

Rosa shook her head. "Not one bit. But it was stupid."

Eliza sighted. "We tried to talk her out of it," she said, remembering how they had warned her, pleaded with her not to do it. They would have done so with more fervor had they known was Miss Trill was capable of.

Rosa shrugged. "She's stubborn. I know what that's like." She rolled her eyes. "Maybe stubborn's not all it's cracked up to be."

An odd feeling came over Eliza then, as they sat in the dancing shade, breathing in the stone's presence. She felt watched, not quietly observed as by the other girls, but watched. Sought. Like prey being pursued. She turned her head and scanned the trees, first one way, then the other.

"What is it?" said Rosa.

"I don't know," said Eliza. "I think we should head back. Where are the others?"

Rosa didn't ask questions. Perhaps it was her trust for Eliza's intuition or her own superstitious upbringing, but she simply rose and followed Eliza back toward the chapel.

When they approached the clearing, they saw the other girls sitting on the steps to the structure. Lila Grace's back was to them, and Bridget's face was barely visible beyond her. And then Eliza and Rosa stopped in surprise. The pair were locked in a kiss. Not a kiss on the cheek or affection between friends, but a romantic, passionate kiss, with Bridget's hand tucked behind Lila Grace's head.

Eliza's eyes widened. An awed "Oh," escaped her lips, and she was thankful it emerged as a whisper. She looked to Rosa, whose face was also clearly shocked. They stood there together, not wanting to break the bubble that existed around Lila Grace and Bridget.

Eliza had heard of homosexuality before and had no judgment about it, though her parents had a lot to say on the subject. So did her school and her church, calling it a sin that would send people straight to hell. She'd never understood the condemnation, the fire it roused in some people, because she was not really bothered by the idea. In the quiet of her heart, she felt no one should be told what to do or what to believe, but of course, this did not align with her Catholic surroundings. It was one of many things she held inside that did not.

And while all of this was true, Eliza had never encountered a circumstance like this. The notion that any of her friends might be attracted to each other had never really occurred to her. Especially when they were both pregnant, for there was only one way for that to happen.

Eliza and Rosa lingered in the trees. But before they could speak to each other, or share a mere thought about it, Miss Trill's booming voice careened toward them, full of poison.

"Blasphemy!" she shouted. "You dare insult the Lord with this… filth. And on the very steps of His house!" Then she placed a silver whistle to her lips and blew. Its shriek echoed through the property, the high-pitched wail of a banshee, calling in reinforcements.

What followed happened so quickly it left Rosa and Eliza in a dizzy blur. Their friends were grabbed—not kindly—by two male ward assistants and dragged back toward the institution. Miss Trill lingered, glaring around the clearing with narrowed eyes and a bitter frown. She was God's judgment, delivering it like lightning. And she had more to pass around.

"I know you're out there, girls. If you've got any sense, you'll head back to your quarters—now," she turned to walk away, then paused. "And if you're also engaging in ungodly acts, I *will* stamp it out. There is no room for sacrilege here."

And then there was nothing but the call of birds, the buzz of bees. Like it had never happened at all.

Eliza and Rosa crouched together beneath a veil of ferns and bushes, watching Miss Trill disappear over the horizon. Eliza's hands were shaking as she reached out to steady herself, then stand up. Her knees ached from the position they'd held, and she breathed deeply to slow her racing heart.

"I don't—" began Eliza, words failing to capture the shock she felt.

Rosa stood and grabbed Eliza's arm, pulled. They walked in the opposite direction from the home, along the natural rock formations that created a boundary to the property. They passed by Hattie's stone and continued south, looking for a breach in the rock. They came upon a stream, not unlike the one Eliza had seen in her dream, and paused to take a breath.

The rock they sat upon jutted out above the water, and they could see to the other side, where the land sloped upward, into a line of trees. Eliza wondered if they could make it across safely. She remembered a stream from her youth—one that looked gentle until you got into it and were swept up in a current stronger than you.

"Where do you think they've taken them?" asked Eliza. "The closet?"

"I don't know," said Rosa. "Probably not together." She rested her face in her hands as though they offered her comfort.

Eliza wiped at her brow, then asked the question that begged asking. "Did you know?"

Rosa met her eyes. "About how they felt? No. And I don't care. They're our friends. Our sisters. Trill can go to hell."

Despite their circumstances, this misery chasing liberation that would never come, Eliza smiled at Rosa. She nodded her agreement. "What can we do?"

Rosa swallowed. "We can survive, for now. Until we get out, we're at her mercy." She paused, placed her hands on her round stomach. "I mean, we could try to cross that water," she said, gesturing to the stream. "But look at me. I'm eight months pregnant. How far am I really gonna get?"

"It might sound foolish," said Eliza. "But even if we could get away, I'd feel like we were abandoning them. You know?"

Rosa sniffed. "Yeah."

"So, we go back," said Eliza, licking her lips, wishing she had some water. They'd left their provisions at the chapel, afraid to return to the clearing.

"Yes," said Rosa. "But we'll do it together."

They stood, began walking back toward the house, the sun hanging lower in the sky.

"Eliza?" said Rosa. "Promise me something."

"Anything," Eliza said.

"If something happens to me. If I don't get out of here," said Rosa. "Promise me that you will. And you'll tell people about this. We can't let this happen again."

"I promise," said Eliza, and she meant it.

Chapter 24

"You don't deserve to be a mother," said the ward assistant, as he shoved Bridget toward the back of the closet. She stumbled forward, landed on the floor, and looked back to see the door closing.

They had taken to calling it "the closet" because that's what Lila Grace said. And she wasn't wrong. The room was large enough to stretch out in any direction, but small enough to feel like a cell. It was dark except for the light coming in through the crack under the door and the keyhole beneath the knob. Other than that, darkness engulfed Bridget.

She kneeled on the floor where she had fallen, still trying to make sense of everything that had happened. It was at once the most beautiful thing she'd felt, a love returned, despite its threat. And then moments later, the tearing away of her heart.

Trill's severe face. The shriek of the whistle. Rough hands upon her. The look on Lila Grace's face—her sweet grey eyes large with fear. How could she have allowed this to happen to her? She would face this punishment again just to feel that love, but to take Lila Grace down with her was a heart-wrenching penalty. There was nothing in that moment she would not give to save her friend, her love, from whatever they were about to face.

Lila Grace's fearful eyes burned in Bridget's memory and she squeezed her own shut, shoving away the haunting image. She fought to replace it with anything else. Lila Grace's laughter, her soft hair, the moment she began looking at Bridget with desire. The feel of her hand wound tightly in hers.

The ache in Bridget's chest was so great she wondered how her body could contain it. The tears came in waves and between them she found comfort in the back corner of the room, where the walls could hug her more tightly. And she reminded herself that Lila Grace was once trapped in this room, so perhaps some part of her remained. She imagined that was true—like an imprint on the floorboards. Perhaps she had sat right where Bridget was now. She placed her hands on the floor beside her, seeking the covert scent of Lila Grace.

That was when she discovered the grooves in the wooden floorboards. Long indented scratches, wide enough for her nail beds. Her hands froze, and it dawned on her that they could be— might be—remnants of Lila Grace. Marks left there like stamps, and traces of splinters embedded under her fingernails, where the room made a mark on her, too. And she dug deeper, until they pierced her fingertips, so that maybe she could retrieve the bits Lila Grace left behind.

Two ward assistants came that night to the girls' boarding room. Without a knock, they opened the door and went to work, packing Lila Grace's things into bags in a haphazard manner.

"Where are you taking her things?" asked Rosa.

The men didn't respond to Rosa. They didn't even look at

the girls. Eliza sat on her bed, covering her body more with the covers. Their intrusion was rude and surprising.

"Hey!" said Rosa. "I asked where you're taking Lila Grace's things?"

One of the ward assistants paused, looked up. He pursed his lips and placed a finger to them. He shook his head. His eyes were not angry, but held a warning. When they had finished their work, he lingered inside the doorway while the other left.

"Listen," he said in a low tone, "I don't know. I was just told to pack them up and not to say anything to either of you. Trill's not someone to test. Stay to yourself. Fall in line. You don't want to get on her bad side. She's… unpredictable."

With that, he nodded once to each of the girls and took his leave.

The naked bed was strange in the room. It had been stripped of anything that felt like Lila Grace or held her warmth. Eliza stared at it, wishing it away, calling Lila Grace's spirit back to them. But, of course, there was no answer.

"I think this means she's really gone," said Eliza. The urge to surrender was overwhelming. To what, she did not know, but just wanted to give up. Give in. Forfeit the game. She'd keep her head down, conform, do what she was told. There was no other option.

The shoe flew across the room, whizzing past her head and hit the closed door with a loud thump. Eliza jumped, turned to see Rosa with eyes ablaze.

"You bitch!" screamed Rosa at the closed door. "I hate you! Do you hear me? I hate you!"

And the surrender Eliza had been feeling dissipated. It fizzed out like a candle with no more wick. Because she felt this anger, too. There was shame, but the anger was burning more brightly, and feeding on Rosa's passion.

"Shhhh," soothed Eliza. She stood by Rosa, trying to calm her with her presence. Her face was enraged, red and hot.

"How could they—" began Rosa. "Who do they think they are? They say they'll help us and then we just disappear. Like we were never there." Her anger devolved into tears, but her mouth spat fire. She gripped Eliza's hands, tried to regain control, and then let them go.

She paced around the room, walking from door to windows and back again.

"They're not going to get away with this," she said, talking to herself more than Eliza. "I won't let them. They can't just erase her." She wiped angrily at her face, forbidding the tears to keep falling.

And then something stopped her in her tracks. It was something she stepped on, small and blending in with the floor. She bent to examine it and pulled the locket up by its chain.

It was Lila Grace's necklace. They would have known it anywhere. Eliza approached Rosa, who stood there staring at it, shaking her head. Rosa held it out to her, her face stressed, like she was asking for an explanation.

Eliza took the locket, opened it, and found it empty. The picture of the boy who had been there was gone. She looked around the floor for the heart-shaped image, bending onto her knees to locate it.

"She'll want this when she comes back," said Eliza, determined.

"She's not coming back," said Rosa, sitting on the edge of Eliza's bed, quiet submission having replaced the fury. She was all spent out.

Finally, Eliza's hand swiped something that felt different from the floor. She carefully picked up the cut-out face and stood to place it back in its home. But when she flipped it over, almost by accident, she noticed it wasn't a photograph at all. Rather, it had been cut out of a magazine. Typed words graced the other side—an article of sorts.

Eliza drew a shaky breath. She nodded. "What do you make of this?" Eliza said and held out the cut-out to Rosa.

Rosa examined the heart, turning it over and over. Her brow furrowed. "I think Lila Grace's beau was not her beau after all," she said.

"She made him up?" asked Eliza. "But, why?"

Rosa shrugged. "Why do we make anything up? Maybe the truth was worse than the lie."

Eliza and Rosa wanted more than anything to go in search of their friends. And Miss Trill had not attempted to visit them, not even at the dinner table. But she would come, eventually. It seemed too big a risk to leave the room, even after lights out, even after the lock was clicked into place from the outside.

So, they sat in the room with the candle between them. It had not been just the two of them since Eliza's first week. They pulled out the box, but a game of Questions and Commands felt pointless without their friends. Eliza carefully placed Lila Grace's locket, with the cutout tucked back inside, into the box. She considered the mystic hand, touched it gingerly, and thought of Lila Grace. And what of Bridget? Were they coming for her things next? If only they could have known all of this was heading their way. Or maybe she had—she just hadn't known it.

"I saw the wolf the other night when I fell asleep waiting for you and Bridget, when I was in the wall," said Eliza. It's not the first time she's remembered the dream, but it is the first she's mentioned it aloud. "Er—I think I was asleep. Can you dream when you're half awake? Could I have entered a… trance or whatever without trying to?"

Rosa sat up. "The wolf like when you were little? Like you told us about before?" Her tone was cautious, eyes narrowed.

"Um, kind of," said Eliza. "Bigger, and it had red eyes. I don't remember that from when I was little. Back then, it was more of a feeling, knowing that it was a wolf, but this one I saw… in detail."

Rosa's gaze turned away, like she was deep in thought. She gulped. "What if it's not the same?"

Eliza shook her head. "I don't follow. What do you mean?"

"Well, in Romani lore, a *muló* can take the shape of a wolf," said Rosa.

Eliza tried to imitate her accent. "A *muló*?"

Rosa nodded. "A spirit seeking revenge."

"A ghost?" said Eliza. That was no surprise at this point.

"Or a vampire," said Rosa.

Eliza cocked her head to the side and pursed her lips. "Oh, come on. Like Dracula?"

Rosa looked at her with seriousness. "I know it sounds silly with the movies and all, but vampires are no joke to my Grandmama's people."

Eliza's smile was still on her face, waiting for the punchline. But it never came.

"The Romani don't joke about the dead," said Rosa. "Or the undead."

Eliza called the memory back up as best she could, tracing the red eyes in her mind, blood against velvet black fur. "Maybe your Grandmama was just trying to scare you with stories."

It was Rosa's turn to cock her head to the side. She shrugged. "Or maybe vampires aren't what we think. Maybe they're ghosts who want to live again, through other people."

The thought was unnerving. A shiver creeped over Eliza's shoulder. She shuddered.

"Maybe," continued Rosa, "Hattie is angry she got locked in the basement and is trying to get out. Still."

Eliza felt foolish then. In all the time they'd been in the house, in all the time she'd sensed Hattie Prescott, never once had she felt in danger. There were evil things that lurked on the grounds, but Hattie had always seemed like a protective presence—a friend. But what if she had two faces?

She could almost feel the name come to her lips without trying. The kindred spirit was never far away, always breathing, wanting to climb into Eliza's skin. She wrapped the blanket around her, tighter, closer.

"Look, I'm not trying to scare you, Liza Lie," said Rosa. "There's just something about it—the way you said it this time—I think we need to be aware."

"And how do we protect ourselves against it? Garlic and crosses?" Eliza fought the urge to roll her eyes, frustrated at this new threat that felt childish… yet looming.

"Don't believe everything you see in movies," said Rosa.

"Or read in books, right? I read Bram Stoker's *Dracula* for English last year. That Doctor Van Helsing seemed to know a thing or two," said Eliza. She didn't divulge that the novel had given her nightmares for weeks. She didn't want Rosa to know, or anything else that might be listening.

Rosa sighed and Eliza could see on her face this had headed in a direction she had not intended. She stood and walked to the dresser beside her bed, opened the drawer, and searched for something. When she was satisfied, she withdrew a small object.

She sat down on the bed beside Eliza and place it into her hands. The object was the size of a dime and silver like one, too. It had etchings in it she did not recognize.

"This was my Grandmama's," said Rosa. "You can borrow it while you're here. For protection. I'll need it back though, when we leave."

Eliza touched it gingerly, not sure she really wanted to keep it. "Thank you," said Eliza, anyway, though, so as not to be rude.

"Keep it by your bed," said Rosa. "It's supposed to ward off bad dreams. Now, let's get some sleep so we can wake up later—maybe figure out where they took Bridget and Lila Grace."

Eliza obeyed, stretching out on her bed and pulling the covers up under her chin. She looked at the amulet and decided it was worth a try. She tucked the talisman under her pillow— the closer the better, she thought.

"Rosa?" Eliza asked. "Do you think it's Hattie?"

"Do I think she's the *muló?*" said Rosa, as she blew out the candle and climbed into her own bed. "Not really, but who knows? Some bad things happened here. There are likely lots of angry spirits lurking in the corners."

And although Eliza didn't want to give any more attention to spying things that might want to inhabit her body, she glanced at the corners of the room, watching for hints of life—or death. She kept her eyes there until her lids became too heavy to hold sleep at bay.

It was after three in the morning when Eliza woke to Rosa's hushed tones. "Liza, let's go. They just opened the door to check on us. We've got a few hours at least."

Eliza pushed the veils of sleep aside and sat up.

They made their way through the hole in the closet and into the adjacent room, then down the hall and down the stairs to the pantry. Then they followed the tunnels to the wall behind the library and listened at the panel door, waiting to exit into the stairwell. But this is where they hit a roadblock, for the stairwell was occupied.

Two female voices on the other side of the wall stood chatting, and from the smell in the air, smoking cigarettes. Rosa and Eliza placed their ears to the wall, careful not to push too hard and reveal themselves.

"Trill's a nutjob, I tell you," said the first voice. "Right from the Pope himself, if you ask me. Full of Jesus this, and blasphemy that. Lady needs a good shagging—that's what she needs."

Their voices joined in laughter for a moment.

The second voice was lighter. "No man I know would come within two feet of that lady. Probably why she's not married."

"Can you blame 'em?"

They went on for ten minutes exchanging insults about

Miss Trill. The girls had to stifle their laughter a few times. But their patience wore thin and their bodies ached from crouching in the space behind the wall. It was when they were about to turn around and go back the way they had come that the conversation took a turn.

"I feel bad for the girl, though. Not her fault she's short a few marbles," said the woman with the lighter voice.

Rosa grabbed Eliza's hand, tugged her back gently. They returned their ears to the wall.

"Now don't start with that soft talk. It won't help you here. Keep your eyes on the job. If you ask me, probably a good thing she isn't actually pregnant. But she put on a good show. Right down to the belly."

"You know it wasn't a decision, right? She didn't just get really fat. False pregnancy is like your mind makes your body think you're with child."

"Way over my head. That's what they're paid for at the looney bin."

"Hey, you see that new ward assistant, Emily, I think? Laziest person I ever met. I tell you, listen to what happened yesterday and tell me if I'm nuts...."

Their voices trailed off as Rosa and Eliza headed back through the tunnel. It was clear the women weren't going anywhere and this new information required conversation.

When they got back down to the heart of the tunnel, the place where Hattie had been imprisoned, they felt safe to talk. Rosa held the beam of the flashlight between them, crudely illuminating their faces and drawing long shadows across them.

"Looney bin," said Rosa. "Did they send them to a psych ward?"

"Not pregnant?" asked Eliza. "Are they talking about Lila

Grace? Or Bridget? Or somebody else?"

Rosa shook her head. "I don't know. But if I had to guess, I'd say Lila Grace. Just based on what she already told us."

"You mean she's already been? To an asylum, I mean," said Eliza. "That makes sense. But false pregnancy? Is that real?" She was horrified by the notion and somehow felt betrayed. Had one of their friends been lying to them?

"I've heard of it before," said Rosa. "One of my cousins, actually. She had lost two babies to miscarriage and finally when she got pregnant again, she was so happy. But it ran its course and there was no baby. To outsiders, the family said she miscarried again, but I overheard my mother talking to hers and that's not what happened."

Eliza sat with this new information, trying to take it in, when she realized Rosa was leading her through another door, into a new tunnel—one they had not yet explored. "Where are we going?" she asked.

"Now's as a good a time as any to see where this goes, right?" said Rosa. She held out the torch in front of them, lighting the tunnel that looked similar to those they'd explored before. "Can't afford any wasted trips like this at night."

Eliza followed along beside Rosa, hugging herself with her arms like it might help her make sense of things. She wished she'd brought a sweater. "So, whoever it was—Lila Grace, Bridget, or someone else. Does that mean they went into labor and nothing happened? Or what?" said Eliza.

"Your guess is as good as mine," Rosa said.

"And she wasn't just lying to us. She was tricked, too? By her own mind?" asked Eliza.

"Maybe," said Rosa, as they came to a bend in the tunnel. This terrain was something new.

"Is it wrong to wish mine was false?" asked Eliza, her tone quiet, ashamed. She hoped Rosa wouldn't think badly of her for saying it. "My God, to just wake up and have this over with, it sounds like coming out of a nightmare."

"But to be crazy? I don't think so—trust me," said Rosa. Her eyes held a warning, like she'd had experience with an insane person. "I bet if most of us could go back and undo the deed, we would," said Rosa. "I would. Especially if you'd asked me when I first found out." She hesitated.

"Me, too," said Eliza. "I wish I had never met Michael. I wish I'd kept my nose in a book. But then I find myself thinking about him, but it's a fake version of him. I know it is—I saw how he acted after he found out. What he showed me before was a lie. It was a beautiful lie, though."

"If I'm honest," said Rosa, "I've been thinking about Matteo. A lot."

"Was he a liar, too?" said Eliza, the bitterness cutting her tone. It came out sharper than she'd meant it to be.

"No." The answer was almost a whisper. "No, he wasn't. He isn't. It's my fault we're not together. Maybe I'm the liar. Maybe all this is what it took for me to see the truth."

"And?" said Eliza, ashamed of the jealousy she felt.

"Maybe if he asked me again, the answer would be different," Rosa said.

"To marry him?" asked Eliza.

Rosa nodded in the dim light. "I hate thinking about him out there with a bullseye on his back, waiting to be shot. I think I wanted him to give it up. You know, the army. I didn't want to be the wife of a soldier."

"But you do now?" said Eliza.

"I still don't." Rosa said it with a laugh, but didn't seem

to be joking. "But I don't think I want to live the rest of my life without him, either."

They came to another turn in the tunnel and found it resulted in a dead end.

"Well, this is strange," said Rosa. "It just stops. Why would it just stop?"

Eliza fought the claustrophobia closing in around her. Suddenly, her breath came quicker, and she fought the urge to run.

"Wait," said Rosa, examining the wall's edges. "Here, it looks like it ends."

Rosa disappeared into the corner that stood in shadows, the light from the torch revealing a narrow doorway of sorts, obscured by rock. Despite the feelings of panic that had washed over Eliza, she followed her friend into another tunnel, this one cruder and sloping upward. The path became more earthy, less rock and more dirt. It seemed like a large animal's burrow rather than a tunnel carved by human hands.

In the sides of the tunnel walls, she could see roots that stretched out like fingers, seeking water. And then there was a light ahead, gentle and glowing, a beacon in the distance. As the girls walked, their steps synchronous, the air became warmer and filled with the hum of insects.

They had emerged from the mouth of the labyrinth beneath the house, birthed into the night. The waxing moon hung low in the sky, beside stars smattered across a black backdrop, twinkling and numerous.

"No door or gate or anything," said Eliza. It felt strange, a way into the house that was left unguarded. But a rock also obscured this open mouth. It wouldn't be found unless someone—or something—was looking for it.

The girls extinguished the flashlight and proceeded in the gray glow of cushion between night and early morning. Birds already sang despite the early hour, heeding the coming dawn and searching for worms.

Eliza looked back at the house, trying to get her bearings. It loomed in the dark, a massive stone mansion like a castle from a fairy book. The structure came to an unexpected point, disturbing the symmetry of the rectangle most houses assume—like this portion of the building was not part of the rest of the beast. It felt older, looked older, even in the dim glow of the moon. And try as she might, Eliza could not decipher where they were on the property—perhaps because she had never been to that spot before.

Yet, strangely, it felt familiar. A memory tickled at the back of her mind, lulling and inviting, beckoning her to slip into the world of dreams where it lay. She grew dizzy, her feet unsure. Her eyes fell on a plaque embedded into the side of the wall: *Bealdor House*. She touched the carved words, feeling the deep grooves in the stone. The rock seemed to vibrate beneath her fingertips, like it wanted to eat her. She snatched her hand away and took a step backward, struggling to maintain her balance.

A creature—*a bird?*—flew over their heads and she followed its path, the unease of lightheadedness threatening her yet again.

It landed on something beyond the lawn, deep in the shadows of the pines that towered above them, reached up to the sky like claws. Eliza turned to Rosa, who watched the bird as well, and though she was only paces away, felt like she spoke through layers of thick cotton.

"Liza," the word came drawn out, slippery. "Look…" She

pointed at the bird—and what it sat upon—her eyes wide with wonder.

The gate was tall and impressive with wrought iron poles that twisted into curls and spirals. It stretched out on either side, a fence like wings, enveloping the land beyond. Yes, she had been here before—if only in her mind.

A mist hung above the ground beyond the gate, silver dust soaking the moon's rays, holding them down like tethers. A breeze disturbed the branches of deciduous trees in the distance, but the pines stood firm, resting on the whispers of night. "Shhhhhh," they said. "Shhhhhhh."

Eliza walked toward the gate, wanting to touch it—to feel the cool metal under her hands, hear the squeak of the gate open, to let them into what lay beyond. As she approached, she could make out the headstones on the other side, standing guard over the bones below.

"A cemetery," said Rosa, her words drawn out even more than they were before.

Eliza was so tired. If she could lie down for a moment, rest her head. That was all she needed, just a moment.

Yet she didn't want to miss this feeling, either. A smile crept across her face as her worries dissipated into memory. She was not pregnant; she was not unloved. She and Rosa were floating on a cloud, seeing into the future that was gentle and happy. She imagined she could fly over the tops of the trees, stretched out her arms to the side like a bird. If only she could fly.

The breeze against her face was sweet, charming her closer to the gate that stood between her and the dead. It smelled of honey and lemon, like warm tea on a cool morning, steam breathing onto her lips. The delicate liquid pouring into her mouth. It tingled her tongue, so sweet…

The shadow lunged, reaching through the gate with claws. The sound of gnashing teeth was loud in her ears as Eliza stumbled, stunned out of her reverie. She scampered backward, her limbs tearing the earth, her heart pounding in her chest. And then Rosa's arm was pulling her, yanking her back toward the house.

"Run!" Rosa yelped.

And they ran. Across the lawn and into the tunnel's mouth, they ran. Down the tunnel with root fingers and earthy ground, back behind the hidden entrance to the strange tunnel with odd turns, and finally into the belly of the mansion and then its heart—Hattie's room.

They stopped to catch their breath, Rosa holding her stomach, looking behind them. Then she grabbed Eliza's arm, examined the three scratch marks that left blood in their wake. The red lines marked the space between her wrist and elbow. She had not even felt the injury.

"What the hell was that?" squeaked Eliza. The swear felt strange upon her lips. She touched the wounds gingerly. They were not deep, but definitely there. They stung beneath her fingers. Had it been the creature behind the gate or the roots reaching out for her as they ran through the tunnel?

"*That* was a *muló*," said Rosa, her breath coming quickly, her eyes narrowing into the darkness behind them.

Chapter 25

It was early in the morning when the door to the boarding room opened. Two ward assistants delivered Bridget back to her bed then, closed the door behind them.

The early light crept in through the windows in a dull gray glow, clouds obscuring the sun's rays. The air had transitioned to a heavy wetness that leaked in through the cracked window, curled around the girls as they woke from a dreamless sleep.

Bridget sat still on her bed, a gargoyle watching over the edge in protection. Her hair was ratted into knots and her face was dirty.

"Are you alright?" asked Rosa, though it was clear she wasn't.

"What happened?" asked Eliza, after the silence begged for cutting. "Where's Lila Grace?"

"I don't want to talk about it. Not yet," said Bridget, drawing a shaky breath in. "But there is something."

She stood with purpose and walked to the closet. "Light the candle," Bridget said. Bringing the box back into the room, she sat on the floor in their usual place.

She took out the Questions and Commands cards, sifted through them until she found one that pleased her. As she stared at the question there, Eliza noticed her fingers in the firelight;

dried blood kissed the tips, and what looked like dirt slept underneath her nails.

Bridget licked her lips, kept her eyes fixed on the paper, then read: "What is your biggest fear?" Her eyes traveled to the candle, like it gave her courage. "That someone will discover how I really feel—that I like other girls."

"We know, Bridg—" Rosa began.

"No, let me finish," said Bridget, shaking her head. She picked up the other slip of paper she had set aside and read: "Tell a secret no one knows." She exhaled slowly, then began to tell.

"It was last year that the rumors started at school," said Bridget. "Sophie Brentar caught me staring at Elaine White, this shy, sweet girl who never had a mean thing to say about anyone. Sophie's a snake—poison. Always in other people's business. Talking, spreading crap that's always meant to hurt. Well, everyone listened to her. Even Elaine—she'd always been nice to me before. But..." Her voice drifted for a moment as she swallowed her feelings.

"So, I decided to prove everyone they were wrong," said Bridget. "I picked someone they all liked. Mr. Grant—the math teacher. And I showed them… but I got him fired, I got myself kicked out of school, and I got this." She motioned to her belly. "So. Now you know."

She finally looked at them, meeting their eyes for a moment, then looking down, waiting.

"We don't care that you like girls, Bridge," said Rosa. "Isn't that right, Liza?"

Eliza took the cue, not knowing what to say, but trying her best. "You're our friend. No, our sister. And I don't really understand it, but it doesn't change anything."

Eliza looked to Rosa, unsure what to do next. She wasn't

the best with words—at least those spoken aloud in times of conflict. She was much better with a pen. But there was no time for that.

Bridget looked up. She opened her mouth to speak, but then closed it. She nodded her head, smiled weakly. "Lila Grace is gone. They sent her to a psych ward. Said she was hysterical. That's all I know."

She sat for a moment, putting the cards away, closing the top of the box. "I'm tired," Bridget said, then stood and crawled under the covers in her bed. She didn't even take off her shoes.

In the creeping haze of early morning, still in a half-dream, Eliza picked at the bloom in the wall with her finger. She caught the edge of a wallpaper layer beneath her nail and tore it downward in long, jagged strides. She ripped slowly. The sound vibrated through her hands and into her arm. She didn't recall making the decision to do it, but she was standing before the hole, knowing what was needed when she woke.

The top layer held the purple lupine and swallows; the rips set them free. And beneath were strata of yellow, blue, green, and pink—all with worn-out patterns like specters of a once vibrant life. In the morning light, they were muted, faded hints of storylines that ran in circles, repeating forever around the room like Charlotte Perkins Gilman's creeping lady. Eliza recalled the author and her haunting story of the rest cure, and wondered what she might think of this place, this so-called "home" for unwed mothers.

She tore and tore, leaving long steaks hanging in some

places, others ripped clean up to the ceiling now resting on the floor. When Rosa and Bridget woke, they joined her, one at a time. They didn't ask questions or look at her like she had lost her mind. They merely selected other layers to peel away, tearing the memories from their boarding room, sifting through reflections of the girls and women who had come before. They ripped away their tears, their hopes, fears, and dreams, leaving streaks of paper here and there, revealing unnatural creatures that were never meant to procreate. Swallow heads with *fleur de lis* legs. Flowers that grew into gilded swirls. A lion's mane atop a flourished castle tower. A wall of curiosities spreading its wings.

Eliza had pulled a stretch of wallpaper all the way to the floor, hoping it would make it in one piece. But it broke off behind her bed, robbing her of the satisfaction she sought. It was a silly thing, really, but Eliza wanted to see it through—make one clear gash in the pattern to set free any souls stuck there. So, she yanked her bed from its nestling place, crouched down to finish the tear she had started. But when she kneeled down, a strange thing happened.

Under the weight of her knee, the floorboard sagged, then turned on its end. She fell forward, caught herself on the wall, then backed away to explore the problem. She pressed again on the board, the other end tipping upward as it had under her weight. What lay beneath it was what looked like folded papers. She reached in carefully, pulled out the object, and discovered it was bound—a book of sorts. On the front page were the initials H.P.

Eliza's heart leapt with excitement, and she turned to find the other girls staring at her, waiting to examine the discovery.

The crude binding was mere thread, but it held the pages

in place, if loosely. The paper had yellowed with age, the handwriting upon it faded and pale. But it was still legible in most places. The contents were a collection of letters.

Eliza read aloud:

April 23, 1862
My Dearest Hattie,

How I long to see your sweet face in the middle of this violence. I wish I was with you, a thousand miles away from the explosions and frightened men. Yes, frightened, my wife. We try to be brave, to fight for the Union in an honorable way, but the fear never goes to sleep.

And I fear the last words we spoke to one another were not in sweetness. I told you I loved you and I always have. I always will. But I also said some things I regret, and for that I am deeply sorry. You were right to advocate for abolition of this horrific institution, for now that I see it with my own eyes, I cannot bear the thought. It was my father's influence that led me astray and all I can do is to beg your forgiveness. Have pity on this fool of a man who loves you so. I do not deserve you.

Yours,
Michael

"Her husband," said Rosa. "So, she *was* an abolitionist."

"The tunnels must surely be part of the Underground Railroad, like you said," said Eliza, staring at the jagged penmanship, amazed to be holding such confirmation in her hands.

"I wonder how many people made it through this

place," said Bridget. "Maybe even stayed in this room."

"No, this was probably Hattie's room," said Rosa.

"But wouldn't the married couple be downstairs in the quarters Miss Trill uses?" asked Eliza.

"Good point," said Rosa. "Maybe this was a sewing room or dressing room or something. I mean, she had to have spent time here. Why else would the letters be hidden under these floorboards?"

"And," added Bridget. "Who even knows if the whole house was built at the same time? Didn't you say that tunnel you took led to something with a plaque that looked older?"

Eliza nodded, flipped the pages to find more letters—the first portion were from Michael. The script changed toward the end and were signed by Rebecca.

"Listen to this one," Eliza said.

June 17, 1862

My Dearest Hattie,

They've told us to write to you in case we do not return. I fear they are right, for there are so many men falling—either where they are hit or in the tents after. But how do I find the words to send to you that might be my last? How are they not spoken to your face? I will try.

My dear wife, remember me. That's what I ask. Know that I will look down on you from heaven and watch over you daily. Nurture the garden we planned. When the sunflowers bloom in late summer, it is me smiling up at you from beneath the earth, where my bones rest. Yes, bring me home and bury me among the flowers, where our angel child sleeps. And until we meet as a family again, continue your good work with the women there, especially those poor souls to whom you've dedicated your remaining years. You have made me more deserving of salvation by loving me.

    Yours,
    Michael

Eliza's eyes remained on the page as she finished reading, her throat tight with emotion. "To be loved like that…" she said, but her thoughts trailed off into the privacy of her own mind.

"And he did die on the battlefield, right?" said Bridget, breaking the silence. Her voice was quiet, solemn.

Eliza nodded, remembering Hattie's letter to her sister. She closed the book of letters for now, walked to the closet and tucked it safely in the hidden box with the game of Questions and Commands. There would be time to read later, though truth be told, she wanted to read all of them now.

She emerged from the closet to find Rosa and Bridget ready to leave for the day's chores.

"You know we're going to get in trouble for this, right?" asked Bridget, motioning to the scraps of wallpaper still hanging in shreds from the wall. It was a question that needed no overt answer.

Yes, Eliza knew that. But there was something deliciously rebellious about it, and though a pang of fear arose at the thought, there was also daring in her chest. And the daring was starting to grow.

Walking to the chapel was bittersweet that day. Eliza could hear Bridget breathing more deeply and with purpose the closer she drew to the last place she'd seen Lila Grace. It was hallowed ground, but for a very different reason now. Eliza stole a glance at her, wondered what she was thinking, but knew better than to ask.

They'd gotten a later start on the day than usual, and surprisingly, Miss Trill had not sent anyone to check on them. And what that meant, Eliza could not begin to guess. But one thing was for sure—Trill was not done with them. They would not be safe until they were out of the house.

In the time it took to walk to the clearing, dark clouds had crawled across the sky. The sun hid behind gray billows filled with water ready to drop. The wind picked up as the chapel came into view and the first drops fell in large splotches as they ran for shelter.

The sanctuary was dim, its colored windows hazy and its dark grey floor like ash. Eliza kept the door open long enough for Rosa to locate some candles by the alter and bring them to life. They had stashed some matches there for a moment like this—just in case. As the warm yellow glow embraced them, the sky ran with tears, pounding the ground violently. Water slid down the chapel roof, bleeding onto the front stairs in long drizzles. It was beautiful and foreboding at once.

"So much for working outside," said Eliza, though she was secretly happy to be tucked indoors, listening to the rain on the roof. She shut the chapel doors and turned to her friends, who had already gathered by the candles.

"There's something I need to show you," said Bridget. "We shouldn't have kept it secret, but it felt nice to share something with just Lila Grace—even for a little while." She picked up the candle in the pewter holder and walked toward the alter. She passed it and stared at the looming cross that hung there, a reminder this was a place of Christian faith.

Bridget held the candle below the cross, motioned for the other girls to join her. And when they did, when they stood behind the alter beneath the large symbol, the backdrop changed. The wall there no longer seemed solid, but revealed an opening wide enough for a person to squeeze through.

"Where does it go?" asked Rosa.

"I don't know," said Bridget. "We never had a chance to find out."

They shimmied through the opening one by one, with Rosa taking the most time due to the size of her womb. It was a tight fit.

On the other side of the stone opening was a door. There was a lock, but the latch was broken, so they were able to swing the door ajar quite easily. It smelled of rot. Not pleasant, but still interesting.

Bridget held the candle up, revealing an old closet with shelves that held moldy linens, tarnished chalices, and what looked like a round incense burner. The candle's flame flickered, like a breeze gusted past them, and Bridget raised a knowing eyebrow. She pulled the shelves forward, which were not secured to the wall. And there before them was a passage— stone stairs that descended into the darkness below.

"Do you think it leads to the house?" asked Eliza.

"Maybe," said Bridget.

"How did you find this?" asked Rosa.

"Well…," began Bridget, "let's just say we weren't working the whole time when you two were tending to the grounds outside."

Eliza looked away demurely, and Rosa stifled a laugh. "Okay, well, when did you find it?"

"A week ago, I guess," said Bridget. "Just never had the chance to explore it. You know, busy doing other things."

"Okay, okay," said Eliza. "We get it."

"Explore now?" said Rosa, taking the candlestick. It was more of a statement than a question, though. She started down the stair, not waiting for the others to follow. But she'd only descended four steps when the breeze picked up and the light extinguished.

"Darn it," said Rosa, climbing back upward in the dark, her voice coming closer to Eliza. "We'll have to bring the flashlight back instead."

"Next time," said Eliza.

"There may not be a next time for me," said Bridget.

"What do you mean?" asked Eliza.

"I've made up my mind about something," she began, as they moved back out into the main sanctuary, back toward the other candle that sat on the alter. "I know how it's going to sound, but I need to do it."

The girls waited, looking at her expectantly. Rosa motioned for her to continue, but whatever it was she was going to say was not easy.

"I'm going after her," said Bridget.

"What?" said Eliza.

"How?" asked Rosa.

"I'm going to make them think I'm crazy," said Bridget. And it did sound crazy, but she didn't laugh. She didn't crack a smile or bat an eye.

"Again, how?" asked Rosa, her eyes narrowing with skepticism.

"I haven't decided exactly, but I'm going to act out—you know, in a way that makes it seem like I've lost it," said Bridget.

Eliza couldn't bottle the worry as it bubbled up from inside and spilled out of her mouth. "That sounds insane."

"That's the point," said Bridget with a sarcastic grin.

"I mean, it sounds dangerous," said Eliza. "How do you even know it will work? And if it works, will they take you to the same place as Lila Grace? And if they do, will you even *see* her?" Eliza's fear was getting the best of her.

Bridget took her gently by the shoulders. "I have to do this, Eliza." Her eyes held a seriousness that said what her words could not.

"But what if they hurt you?" said Eliza.

"If I don't try, I'll regret it for the rest of my life," said Bridget.

"What about the baby?" asked Rosa, her voice sad.

Bridget took her hands from Eliza and crossed her arms. She took a deep breath. "I think it will be better without me. I… I never wanted this. I'd be a horrible mother. It deserves a family that wants it. And I… I deserve to have love. Finally, real love," said Bridget. "But leave it to me to fall for the crazy girl."

The joke was poorly timed, but cut the tension.

"Okay," said Rosa. "If that's what you need to do. You have my support."

"I think it's a horrible idea. Dangerous. Foolish," said Eliza. She squeezed her eyes closed. "But I do want you to be happy. And I know what it's like to regret. So…"

Bridget nodded. "Tonight. I'm doing it tonight."

Chapter 26

They sat at the dinner table in silence. It was how Miss Trill liked meals to be. She was not there, as she did not eat with the girls, but her eyes and ears were. Tonight, it was Millie, a large woman who always smelled of cigarette smoke, and Janet, a quiet ward assistant who usually kept to herself. They watched as the girls ate their spaghetti, gossiping in the corner.

As Eliza spooned some of the food into her mouth, it was difficult not to think of Lila Grace. This meal had been her favorite, though she complained there were no meatballs in the dish. As the red sauce and noodles mixed on her tongue, even the taste brought back Lila Grace's smiling face. It must be worse for Bridget, who sat very still, focusing on each bite like it might be her last.

A nervous pang grew in the pit of Eliza's stomach as Bridget's isolation continued. She watched as her friend used a fork to stab the noodles, wind them in a circle, then scoop them into her mouth. She chewed; eyes fixed on a spot far away from the dining room table. Rosa looked up once in a while, meeting Eliza's eyes and searching for Bridget's, but their Irish companion was in her own head. She was far away, maybe gathering the courage to go through with the ruse. Eliza and Rosa were waiting for the pin to drop.

The moment came when they were almost finished with the meal, as Millie removed the serving dish from the center of the table.

Bridget reached out and grabbed her wrist, refused to let go.

"Hey," said Millie, yanking at her arm, a surprised look on her face. The grasp held fast.

"I'm not done," said Bridget.

"Rolls are done, young lady. Humans are *finished*," said Millie, her face becoming more contorted. "Now let go."

"I'm not *finished*." Bridget cut her words like venom. "You cow," she added for good measure. Her fingers became whiter, squeezed the woman's wrist harder.

Millie sharply broke Bridget's grip and yanked the serving dish off the table. And before Eliza could process what she saw, Bridget was leaping across the table toward the woman, fork in hand. "I said I'm not *finished*!" she screamed, the pitch of her voice higher than Eliza knew it could go.

The silver utensil sank into the woman's fleshy arm, drawing three drops of blood to the surface. Her voice rose into a holler that rang up to the dining room ceiling and out the doors. Millie looked to her colleague, Janet, who cowered in the corner, covering her head from Bridget's attack. But Bridget only had eyes for Millie.

The larger woman smacked the fork away, but when Bridget lost her weapon, she sank her hand into the meal they had been eating and tossed it at her rival. A clump of noodles slapped her in the face, tarnishing her bright red cheeks with red sauce.

Beside her, Rosa let a laugh escape and then tightly clamped her hand over her mouth, not wanting to be thought an accomplice. And Eliza had to admit it was a spectacle alright, but her worry would not let humor creep in.

"Help!" shouted Millie, her face a contorted wreck of fury. "Help—in dining room!" she spat, lunging at Bridget again. And when she'd taken the smaller girl down, wrestling her to the floor despite her pregnant belly, Bridget continued to fight. Her last jab was a string of fresh spit that landed squarely between Millie's eyes.

By the time the other ward assistants entered the room, Millie was almost sitting atop Bridget's legs to keep her from struggling.

"What is going on here?" asked Miss Trill with a look of disdain as the scene came into her view.

"She attacked me," said Millie. "Like a maniac! Couldn't get her to calm down for nothin." Her face was still red, her breaths coming in huffs.

Bridget cocked her head at Miss Trill. "I was still hungry."

Miss Trill pursed her lips and spoke with sarcasm. "Well, were you going to eat Millie here?"

"I'd rather eat you," Bridget said. The words were sharp and held no jest. Then she opened her mouth, snapped her teeth shut. The sound of the bite was loud. It echoed in the room as everyone stared at the performance. Then Bridget tilted her head back, opened her mouth and let out a laugh that was so wretched, so haunting, Eliza wondered if she really was insane.

Rosa spoke then. "She—she hasn't seemed right these past few days. Muttering to herself, saying she sees things—people." Rosa cleared her throat. "Right, Liza?"

Rosa looked at her then, asking for her support with her gaze, her tone a hopeful one. Eliza looked to Bridget, both arms now held by ward assistants. And though she was silent, her face pleaded.

"Yes," said Eliza, swallowing her better judgement, her opposition to this whole ordeal. "You should see what she's done to the wallpaper in our room."

And for a moment, the tight corners of Bridget's mouth turned upward. Then the hint of a smile was gone.

Eliza and Rosa were charged with cleaning the mess in the dining room, with hawk-eyed Millie barking orders. It was a small price to pay, though, for Bridget's freedom. That's what Eliza kept telling herself as she peeled stray noodles off the wall, placing them in a container for disposal.

By the time they reached their boarding room, the two girls were exhausted. Eliza had spent the last hour trying to focus on the fact this is what Bridget wanted, but she couldn't help but think of different scenarios—things that might happen to her friend now—each one more horrific than the last.

Eliza had a talent for this, working herself up in her own mind despite what was actually happening. *Such a powerful imagination*, her father said of her as a child, back in the days when he still looked upon her fondly. But it often did more harm than good, twisting her stomach into cramps and sending pangs of fear through her chest. And on the worst days, she'd fall asleep with balled hands and woke to her own clenched teeth.

Be strong, Brave Bridget, she thought, sending a quiet prayer on the wind after her friend. Then she squeezed her eyes closed, banishing the thoughts that threatened to overtake her, of Bridget being struck, being shut in a room, being tied to a bed.

"What's this?" said Rosa, pulling Eliza out of her tortured imagination. Rosa had turned down her bed covers and was retrieving a long, slender item from her pillow.

As she made her discovery, Eliza pulled her shift over her head, almost too tired to be curious. Almost.

"Well, what is it?" asked Eliza, pulling back her own covers, wondering if she'd be able to read more of Hattie's letters before falling asleep. She was about to climb upon her own mattress, when her eyes fell upon a similar item nestled against her pillow.

The braid was auburn, a long and slender plait, tied at both ends with simple string. Eliza picked it up, ran her fingers down the length of the hair. And she recalled Bridget's story about the women who would bless loved ones with braids of hair as they went to war.

Eliza looked up to find Rosa looking at her. "She cut her hair," was all Rosa could muster. Eliza nodded, looked to the second empty bed that now haunted the space Bridget once was. The only other thing that remained was her black cloak, folded delicately on the end of the bed. Eliza moved to the wrap, touched it gingerly, ran her fingers along the red lining that hid beneath the folds of fabric.

"She'd want you to have it," said Rosa, watching.

It was a bittersweet gift. "Maybe I'll just keep it safe for her," said Eliza, "until she returns." But they both knew that was not likely to happen. She placed the cloak in her drawer, then lit the candle, turned down the lights, and retrieved Hattie's book of letters.

"I hope she's alright," said Eliza. The words hung in the air with no answer. She tucked the braid beneath her pillow, where it nestled beside the amulet from Rosa's Grandmama. And she read. While Rosa fell into a deep sleep, breathing quietly and still holding Bridget's braid, Eliza communed with Hattie.

April 8, 1863
Dear Hattie Hen,

Thinking about you all the way in Ohio with me here in New York feels as though you are oceans away. How I miss your laughter and silly jokes. It has been 12 months since mother and I saw you off on your journey back to Ohio, and if I knew then how much I would miss you, I might have packed myself on the train as well. Mother is handling your absence, but misses father terribly.

I must confess that I made a dreadful discovery today. I found a butterfly wing (enclosed) on our bench by the back stream and felt it was a bad omen. I do not write this to scare you, my sister, but to ask that you remain vigilant in guarding your own safety. You are a brave girl, too brave at times, too quick to put yourself in harm's way to protect others. I admire this about you and hope I cultivate this quality in myself.

Please write soon to let me know you are safe and sound. My dreams have me full of fear this week, so your words would be reassuring.

Sending you all my love,
Your sister, Rebecca.

April 15, 1863
Dear Hattie Hen,

It has been seven days since my last letter and my spirits are falling. I understand you are the lady of the household and have an important mission to complete, but please write to let me know you are safe. The sooner you can send word, the sooner my heart will be put at rest.

Mother is doing well, staying busy with her sewing circle. She does peck at me to find a husband, but that should not surprise you. Yet I do not wish to have my wings clipped. Not yet (maybe not ever?). I wish to see the world, to have a grand adventure all my own.

My sister, at night when I lay down to sleep, I find myself staring up at the ceiling, hoping the Lord will carry my thoughts to you. I know He hears me, but I fear you do not. Send word soon.

Sending you all my love,
Your sister, Rebecca.

May 1, 1863
Dearest Hattie Hen,

A fortnight has come and gone, and there is only silence. The post carries no letter to relieve my worry. I implore you to please send word to let us know you are safe. Surely it cannot be that the war has ventured so far north? My mind weaves grand tales about all the things that could have befallen you and it tortures me on the hour, day and night.

Mother asks about you and I make up stories of what might have happened to your letters. I know she does not believe me, but I think we are hesitant to breathe life into our fears, to speak them aloud, so as not to cause them to manifest.

William Manifeld (I know you recall him) has become rather persistent in coming for visits, though I try to thwart his affections. I care little for his deceitful charm, though he has mother wrapped around his finger. He is handsome enough, I will not deny it. But there is darkness in his eyes, also. And I do not want to be held in his grasp.

Once again, my sister, please write. I fear that if I do not hear from you, I will have no choice but to seek you out.

Sending you all my love and praying for your safety,
Your sister, Rebecca.

It was after this last letter that sleep took hold of Eliza, pulling her into the veils of dreams, and opening her other eyes.

They ran as fast as they could in the state she was in. Hattie's skirts concealed the rounding belly that was evidence of her father-in-law's abuse, but Rebecca knew she withheld something. Many things, if truth be told, but Hattie would rather bury them deep within herself than burden her dear sister.

"Has he starved you for so long, my sister?" Rebecca asked, her hand resting on Hattie's arm to catch her if needed.

"Bec, please don't ask me," said Hattie, feeling for the first time what it felt like to seek freedom through her own tunnels. "I do not wish to lie to you. The truth is too terrible to speak."

Rebecca did not push her further, but walked beside her, transitioning from running to walking, and pausing when needed.

"And these passages," said Rebecca, "this was no small task to complete. Surely you did not do this on your own?"

"No. My benefactor supplied both funds and help," said

Hattie, paying attention to planting her feet on the earth with purpose. She dare not lose her footing in this rush.

"And your benefactor... was not your husband." Rebecca's tone was leading.

Hattie paused and stared at her sister in seriousness over the candle. She hoped her expression was received with the weight she intended. "We must never speak of it. I am the conductor here and I bear the responsibility. I will take the name to my grave."

Rebecca let out a nervous laugh as they continued. "Well, you've never kept a secret from me before, my Hen. I trust it is for a good reason."

Hattie let the silence be her answer.

The sides of the tunnels seemed to close in on them, and Hattie questioned their integrity. What if they had not been shored up well? What if the earth moved and they were lost in its womb forever? Her breath quickened, and she said a silent prayer to deliver her from the descending cloud of fear.

"How did you get here?" Hattie asked, trying to distract herself from the reality of their plight. "How did you come to save me?"

"You'd be proud of me, sister," said Rebecca, and then added quickly, "Though perhaps critical of my bravado."

"I do not doubt it," said Hattie. "But Rebecca, whatever brought you to me, know that I am thankful." It was a task to speak in between breaths, as they stumbled through the black hole, with only a mere candle to light their way. And what of them if it burned out?

"When I did not hear from you for three weeks, I laid plans," Hattie said. "And when it reached one month and two weeks from your last letter, I put them into action. I left mother

a note and took a carriage to the train in New York. That carried me a good while, and then I paid carriages to transport me between train stations."

"My goodness, what a grown-up thing for my little sister to do. And with no companion?" asked Hattie.

Rebecca shook her head in the dim light of the candle. "Oh, Hattie Hen, don't be angry with me. I did what I thought I must."

Hattie smiled to herself, despite their circumstances. "I cannot be cross with you, dear sister, for saving my life."

Rebecca stopped in her tracks and looked at her sister. "Do you mean to say that he aimed to kill you?"

"Indeed," said Hattie. "There is no question. He got what he wanted from me. I have no doubt I was left in that room to waste away."

The words rang so true that they caused a shiver to course through her body. It urged her feet to move faster, as if the devilish man breathed down her neck. She recalled this feeling from previous encounters and the memory woke nausea in her stomach.

"A light ahead!" said Rebecca. "Do you see?"

"Yes, dear Bec," said Hattie. "The next stop. We're out from under the house. There are matches above; it would be wise to retrieve them. We have only one more and we have a long way to go in the dark." She paused, drew a breath for courage. "But for just for a moment. We cannot linger."

As they emerged from the stairs into the chapel, Hattie could see moonlight streaming in through the stained-glass windows. The colors were muted, bathing the sanctuary in an eerie glow.

"It's beautiful," whispered Rebecca, her voice disturbing

the silence, causing something to scatter.

"Hush," said Hattie. And she placed her hand on her sister's arm in warning. It could be a mouse, a racoon, or another critter making its home in the stone structure, but it could be far worse, too.

Hattie strained to hear movement or voices or breathing in the silence, but there was nothing. She ventured slowly into the sanctuary and out to the alter, motioning for her sister to stay behind, the candle extinguished for the time being.

The air in the chapel was heavy, filled with a foreboding that sank into Hattie's bones and lingered. An owl hooted outside the window, making her jump, begging her to move on before it was too late. She located a box of matches on the alter and pocketed them. And as she turned to pull her sister back down the stairs and beneath the ground, she heard the scream.

It sailed over the land in an echo, and at first Hattie was unsure it had happened at all. But then it emerged again, clear though distant, the sound of terror.

Her heart jumped and her body moved forward without a conscious decision. He was awake. He knew. And he was hurting someone. Cook Maria? A pang of guilt stabbed Hattie's chest as she yanked her sister rudely down the stairs and paused only to light the candle, shielding its flame from the air that threatened to leave them in darkness. Now they only had five matches left.

Chapter 27

When Eliza looked in the mirror above the dresser the next morning, the dark circles beneath her eyes were clear evidence of poor sleep. Her head pounded like she was on the verge of illness, and her ears rang like someone had screamed into them. She placed her hands on her temples and sat back down on her bed, glad for the looming clouds outside the windows that obscured the early morning sun. Images of Hattie and Rebecca swam through her mind.

"Are you alright?" asked Rosa, as she glanced at her friend while brushing her hair. "You look ill."

Eliza nodded, closed her eyes. This was going to be a difficult day, not only because of physical malady, but also the holes now left in their circle. She contemplated pulling out the planchette to ask it for information about her friends, but there was little time to do this. They would be missed at breakfast.

But when Rosa moved to open the door, something curious happened. The nob turned but did not release the lock. No one had come to let them out.

She looked at Eliza, her brow furrowed with confusion.

"Did they forget to unlock the door this morning?" asked Eliza, her own words ringing in her head.

"Forgot," said Rosa, swallowing hard. "Or, decided…"

Her normal expression of confidence fell away to reveal a fear Eliza had not yet seen.

The possibility they'd intentionally left them in the boarding room washed over Eliza like a glass of cold water poured atop her head. They had a way out through the passage in the closet, but no one else knew that. Her mind began to swim, jumping through scenarios. *They think we helped Bridget. They think we're crazy, too. They think we're dangerous. They'll send us away… or keep us locked here all day for the rest of our time.*

The sound of the key in the lock was a welcome relief until the door opened to reveal a ward assistant with a tray of breakfast.

"Good morning, ladies. Miss Trill has decided that you are to be confined to your room while she investigates what happened at dinner last night," she said in a loud voice.

She placed the tray on Lila Grace's empty bed, then closed the door, remaining inside with the girls. Her voice was hushed, her face serious. "You're Bridget's friends," she said. It was a statement rather than a question. "I'm Dot. She's my friend, too."

Eliza's heart jumped and she stood, eager to hear what Dot had to say. "Is she alright?"

Dot shook her head somberly. "I don't know. I only saw her for a moment before they took her away. Sounds like they sent her to an asylum, but I know her. She must have been fakin' it."

"Same place as Lila Grace?" asked Rosa, hopeful.

Dot shrugged. "All I know is they aren't coming back. And I don't mean to scare you, but you need to know. No one is safe in this place."

She backed away from the tray, motioning for them to eat.

"You take care now," she said and closed the door. They heard the lock click back into place.

The rest of the day came and went with no other visitors. Not even another tray of food. When darkness fell, the girls had lost hope of dinner and had had to use the washing basin in their room to relieve themselves. They'd emptied it out the window like medieval maids, making room for whatever else they had the urge to do.

"When we are finished here," said Rosa, through gritted teeth, "I'm bringing down the fire of hell on Trill.

Eliza felt her fury, but she was too tired to waste energy on yelling about it. They knew they had a way out, but couldn't risk using the closet tunnel in the daylight. Not when another ward assistant, or Miss Trill for that matter, might come to check on them. But no one came. No one.

They waited until later, after the grandfather clock in the foyer struck midnight. It was a muted sound, but with ears to the door, and the holding of breath, they could hear it echo up the stairs and down the hall.

"Let's go," said Rosa. "First stop, bathroom. Second stop, pantry."

"Third stop," said Eliza, not quite as confident. "Figure out what's going on. Let's head to the library through the passage and hope Miss Trill is there. Maybe we'll hear or see something—anything."

But she wasn't there upon their arrival. There was no sign of Miss Trill or any of her workers. In fact, the house was so quiet Eliza was afraid to move in the walls, afraid to creak a board or rub up against sides in the wrong way. So, they waited. And waited.

When their legs had cramped and their patience had run out, the girls were about to return to their room when they heard a thudding. It came from behind the opening to the stairwell. It was loud, like something was being thrown down the stairs. The thuds were followed by a mumbling of sorts, a muted conversation between two ward assistants, but this time they were not on a cigarette break.

"This is ridiculous," said one voice as it became clearer. "If this is the kind of work Trill wants us to do, she needs to do it herself."

"I know. I didn't sign up for this," said another voice.

Sounds of struggling and physical effort bled through the wall, the grunts and heaving and exasperated breathing in a jumble of base notes.

"We're going to need more than the two of us to do this," said one.

"I need some air. Let's stop and catch our breath, check in with the others and see who we can get to help," said the other.

"Yes, good plan. This isn't working."

Their voices trailed off into nothing. There was an opening and closing of a door. And then there was silence.

Rosa was about to open the panel to the hallway when Eliza placed her hand on her friend's arm. "Wait, I don't think we should..."

But Rosa shook her head. "No, I have to look. I want to know what they were moving." Her voice held a knowing in the dark and Eliza fell silent.

The panel cracked open slowly, letting electric light into the passage, enough for them to see a bundle on the stairs. It was long and white—well, whitish. And what at first appeared to be knotted sheets, darkened with use, took on the grotesque form of a human body. A mummy—cold and frozen on the stairs.

Eliza's breath caught in her throat, and her mind went to the worst possible idea. She blinked, shook her head, denied the potential, because it was too horrible to believe. A soundless "no" escaped her lips.

Rosa pushed the panel open, scampering down to the wrapped body, pulling and prying at it in a desperate attempt to see its face. Eliza took a breath and gathered her courage, then followed. Together, they tugged and pulled, pulled and tugged, until the sheets finally came loose.

The light hair was the only thing that looked human to Eliza's eyes. The face was pallid with a bluish tint. The eyes were half closed and stared into nothing. The jaw hung open in a perpetual scream. Rosa pulled the sheet over the face quickly, squeezing her eyes shut to erase the image.

"Mary," she whispered, her voice breaking with emotion.

Eliza stumbled backward up the stairs, jumped into the passage, shaking and trying to contain her revulsion. She was able to maintain control until Rosa was beside her, shutting the panel. And then the contents of her stomach were on the floor, the taste of the buttered rolls they'd stolen from the pantry rank with digestion in her nose. And the Rosa followed suit, coughing up her food and sobbing in between gasps. The girls were on their hands and knees until their stomachs were emptied.

And when they had finished retching, they became aware

of eyes staring at them through the grate.

"Who goes there!" boomed Miss Trill's voice, filling the passage with a furious phantasm. The thuds followed, slamming against the library wall.

Panic exploded into Eliza's chest, pushing her body into action. She rose and ran, feeling in front of her in the dark. Then Rosa was able to click the flashlight on. There was no point in keeping it dark now.

Trill knew.

They ran. They balanced their rounded bellies and ran. Back to the heart of the labyrinth beneath the house. The place where the passages split into many—like their possible fates. There was no going back now. All that awaited them was torture. And perhaps death. Just like Mary.

Good God, please don't let that have happened to Bridget or Lila Grace, thought Eliza, though she had no breath for words.

They needed to decide which way to go next, but time was running out. Did Miss Trill know of these passages underground? Surely not. Surely. They would have been discovered on their night adventures.

Without discussion, they both sprang for the tunnel to the cemetery. What they would do then was beyond either of their comprehension. They just knew they needed to get out.

Eliza felt ill. She tried to run straight but swayed in the dark. She said nothing to Rosa, who was ahead of her, leading the way with Bridget's torch.

It might have been the lack of food for most of the day or the fact she'd thrown up everything they'd stolen from the pantry. It might be the fast pace at which they ran, panic pushing them forward and away from the threat. Or perhaps there was some foul gas down in the passages, contaminating the air and her body.

By the time they emerged into the night air and the cemetery gate came into view, Eliza had not thought—not for one moment—about the *muló*. They had no plans to seek it out again; why would they? Yet, there they stood, two friends on the precipice of what should be hallowed ground, and she thought of their supernatural foe.

Eliza looked to Rosa, standing beside her and staring out into the darkness that lay beyond the gate. Her russet eyes were hesitant, her chest rising and falling in time with Eliza's, her hair swept from her forehead and wet with perspiration. The air hugged them with moisture and smelled like rain, yet none had yet fallen.

Rosa glanced behind them, turned off the flashlight. "I don't know how close they are," she said. "But if Trill gets behind that library wall, she'll be into the tunnels. They'll discover all our secrets."

"But she won't have a key, right?" asked Eliza.

"She shouldn't, but we can't be sure," said Rosa. "We should assume she's coming."

Rosa looked back out into the sea of headstones, rising and falling with the land in ominous hills. And the stream must be on the other side—the one they saw from the cliff. Eliza didn't need to ask what Rosa was thinking. She was one with her friend, their thoughts like harmony braided together. But one question lingered.

"Rosa," Eliza began. "Can it get us? I mean, physically? The m—"

"Don't say it!" said Rosa. "Don't give it power."

Eliza clasped her mouth tight, not wanting anything to emerge, even by accident.

"There's no rule to measure this kind of thing. But we can't go back. We could follow the walls of the house to the front, but that's a likely place they'll look for us."

"I wish we had your Grandmama's amulet," said Eliza. She wanted to curse herself for not taking it with them. But how could she have known tonight's adventure would lead to this?

As they stood contemplating, they heard voices in the distance. They seemed to come from the tunnel. Rosa's eyes grew wider. She looked to Eliza and nodded. "We can do this. Together."

Hand in hand, they proceeded under the arch of the gate, through the hinged door they swung ever-so-carefully, and into the place where the dead slept.

Chapter 28

Beneath Eliza's feet, the ground was soft and plush with grass that tickled her ankles. The night was alive with bugs and creatures that sought refuge under the moon. Mosquitoes were hungry, drawing blood from their victims, and she worried whether the *muló* could smell it. She resisted the urge to slap at her skin and walked as gently as she could upon the earth. Maybe if they were quiet, they could pass undetected.

The headstones glowed pale blue-white under the almost full moon, rows of shark teeth in an open mouth. They dotted the horizon in waves of jagged fangs, then crested a hill and dropped off into a ravine that sank beneath trees. This was where the dead stopped.

The girls looked down into the darkness, at first a black hole ready to swallow them both. But as they ventured forth, their eyes adjusted and they could see patterns of trees, young and old, reaching out from the sharp decline of the land.

Rosa stepped forward gingerly, but her foot slid out from under her, breaking her connection to Eliza. She caught herself on a branch, pulled herself back up to safety. And though Eliza wanted the comfort of her friend's hand returned to hers, they needed them free to navigate the steep hill.

"Turn your feet sideways," said Eliza, recalling the hikes

she used to take with her father, back when he was mostly kind. "You can get low to the ground, too. Use the trees to brace your body."

It was usually Eliza who followed Rosa's lead, but the tides had shifted. It was Eliza's turn to coach her friend. So, they proceeded, slowly, carefully, gently as the night. They blended into the landscape, though the trees began to sway more; the wind had woken. It grabbed at their hair and slapped their faces, tugging their clothing with unseen hands.

By the time they reached the water, their confidence had grown, even in the face of the hungry wind. They had made it this far with no sign of their pursuers or the *muló*. The moon was on their side.

"Which way now?" whispered Eliza. She lifted her face to the sky and thought of Hecate, Greek goddess of the moon. She recalled her Ancient History class during junior year, and it had been her silent delight that she chose the mythical Goddess on purpose. Eliza wasn't a cheater, but she'd been able to see what was on the slip before she picked it out of Sr. Catherine's fishbowl. She'd earned an A on that project, but she'd never told her teacher, an Ursuline sister, that she secretly wished Hecate was real. If God was a woman, maybe the world might be different. And now she thought so more than ever; maybe if Hecate was in charge, pregnancy would be seen as a blessing no matter the circumstance.

"Look," said Rosa, probably louder than she meant to. Eliza shrank from the sound and looked about her, hoping the *muló* hadn't heard. Satisfied there was no sudden apparition of a wolf gnashing its teeth, Eliza followed her friend's arm.

What appeared to be the cliff they had sat upon days before loomed above them just ahead.

"If that's our cliff," said Rosa. "The chapel isn't far. At least we have some direction."

"Yes, the chapel," said Eliza.

"Wait, I didn't mean we should go there. I just meant now we know where we are," said Rosa.

"I think…" began Eliza, knowing she had not shared her dream with Rosa. "Remember the space Bridget showed us? Behind the alter?"

Rosa nodded in the moonlight.

"I think I know where it goes," said Eliza.

"Not back to the house?" asked Rosa. "How do you know?"

"I don't," said Eliza. "Not for sure. I had a dream. Another one of Hattie."

"Liza, we can't afford to make this decision based on a dream," said Rosa.

Eliza gulped and couldn't disagree. "Alright. So where then?"

"I think we should cross the river," said Rosa. "Try to climb up the other side."

The plan sounded sensible enough, so Eliza put up no argument, but there was a nagging voice at the back of her mind objecting.

The water was ice on Eliza's toes, so much colder than she thought it would be. During daylight, the summer sun had to reach through pines and maples to kiss its surface, and then it was gone, rushing down the way toward the great Lake Erie. In the dark, any heat it had gathered dissipated. Its shallowness was a mirage, too, for it only took several steps for her to be up to her thighs in water. The current pulled at her, threatening to knock her off balance.

It was then that Eliza's foot slipped on a rock, the moss there offering no grip. She fell forward, catching herself on the rocks beneath the surface, her stomach dipping into the stream. And then Rosa stumbled, too, falling even deeper into the cold liquid, then drifting downstream toward Eliza.

Eliza moved before she had time to think, reaching out to grab her friend's hand, pulling her toward the bank. The two sat there for a moment, dazed and drenched, catching their breath. And as the cold sank into their skin, they realized they had lost the flashlight.

"Not one of my best ideas," said Rosa, her elbows on her knees, head resting in her hands.

"At least we got out. That could have gone worse," said Eliza. She breathed, in and out, in and out. Listened to the rushing water, and for any signs of people or ghosts. There was nothing. "Toward the chapel?"

Rosa nodded and slowly rose. She was limping, favoring her left ankle. "Damnit," she said. This was going to slow them down.

As they followed the water toward the chapel, the wind became angrier, chilling their soaked skin even more. Eliza shivered as she watched it push trees this way and that, bending bows and blowing leaves so they could see the underside in the moonlight. Eliza remembered her grandmother saying it always meant rain when that happened. But it was no secret the sky was about to open, for a hush had fallen over the night creatures and the smell in the air foretold a downpour.

"We need to get up the side before the rain comes," said Eliza. "It will be too slippery if we wait."

"I know," said Rosa. "I'm just looking for a place."

And as luck would have it, as they turned with the bend in the stream, a small waterfall came into view. The surrounding land was more graded, less severe.

As if by some grace, the clouds that had been making their way across the sky parted. The moon's rays shone on the falling water, its beauty a secret tucked into the world behind the house of horrors. As Eliza scanned the banks, her eyes fell upon what appeared to be stone stairs. They were ancient—overgrown and cracked in some places. But they would serve the girls' purpose.

It was when they were halfway up the steps that the smell emerged. Its odor hung in the air like garlic and onions, but not as sweet. Not even the wind erased its trace. Eliza froze.

In the shadows, there was movement. When she saw a black creature with the white stripe down its back, Eliza held her breath. And when it started creeping toward them, she screamed. She didn't mean to—it just happened.

And everything spilled before them with a sense of dread that lit their legs on fire.

The scream was like a clarion call for the *muló,* or so it seemed. He may have smelled them or sensed their fear, but whatever alerted him drew him near. They were already running up the stairs and away from the skunk, but a cold chill crept over Eliza's shoulders, pushing her forward. Faster, more careless. She pushed Rosa up the stairs, shoved her friend forward. Branches smacked them in the face. Vines seemed to crawl in their path in search of ankles. And even the stairs appeared to move beneath them.

The growl was low under the wind. It echoed around Eliza's head, crawled into her ears. She batted at the air, trying to guard her face, gasping for breath. Her legs felt wobbly, unsure, but she ran nonetheless.

When they crested the top of the ravine, the line of trees broke and they were on a cliff, above the clearing that led to the chapel. The stone was jagged but sloped downward. They had no time to think, no time to speak. Rosa sat on her bottom and slid. Eliza crouched after her, and with one last glance behind her, plunged down the sloping face of the cliff.

They left the gnashing of teeth behind them as they slid, the jagged rocks cutting their skin here and there. And when they finally reached the bottom, they did not wait to see what was next.

Rosa grabbed Eliza's arm, yanked her forward through the clearing. She ran despite her limp.

"The chapel!" Eliza screamed. They threw open the doors and rushed inside, slamming them behind. And they fell against the doors, exhaustion overtaking them. They breathed amidst sobs, shaking and holding onto each other for comfort.

They remained that way for a good long while until their breath calmed and their hearts stopped racing. Their embrace was one of sisterhood, safe and secure, and they only parted when nothing banged on the doors after them. It was a good thing, too, for their energy was spent.

After they had gathered some strength, Rosa moved to the altar to look for candles. She knew they were there; they had discovered them while cleaning the structure weeks before. They had even lit one on a rainy afternoon, when they had still been with the others.

In the light of the flame, Rosa's eyes widened as she looked at Eliza.

"Your arm," she said, pointing.

The scratch was deep, leaking red onto her white nightshift and drooping open like a mouth. As soon as Eliza realized it was there, it began to sting. Prior, she had not even felt it.

"A branch maybe," she said, wincing at the depth of it.

"Or the m—you know," said Rosa.

"What does that mean?" said Eliza, wanting to roll her eyes like she didn't believe it. But she did—she did believe it could have been the *muló*. "Just a scratch or some kind of tainted venom?"

Rosa pursed her lips, looked down. She was withholding information.

"Tell me!" said Eliza.

"I'm not sure. It's just legend, you know," said Rosa. "It's not a good omen, I'll tell you that."

And it's not the first time it's happened, thought Eliza, recalling the scratch from that last time, by the gate in the night. She shook her head. "We can't go back out there," she said. "What if it has a taste for me now?"

"It didn't need that to chase us," said Rosa. "It would be dangerous even if it didn't scratch you. Or bite you?"

"It doesn't look like a bite," said Eliza, turning her arm to examine it more.

"So, the passage behind the alter?" said Rosa. "Or wait it out here until dawn. The way I see it, those are our options."

Eliza gulped. She thought of Hattie. The dream. The sisters escaping with a candle—an uncanny reflection of their current circumstances. A doubling Freud would seize upon. "Let's try the tunnel. See how far it goes. We don't even know if it's viable."

"And worse-case scenario, we turn around and come back up here," said Rosa.

Eliza didn't want to say it, but this was a likely place Trill would check. It's part of the property with which they are familiar. That's no secret. Unless the chapel had already been examined. Eliza crossed her fingers and hoped beyond hope that was the case.

Chapter 29

The stone staircase curved downward at a terrible angle. The candlelight revealed a tight coil at the center of the spiral, so if they walked too close, their feet would slip out from under them. So, they hugged the edge of the stairs and followed them down, down into the dark.

It was when they reached the bottom and the path flattened out that they heard the thunder from above. It echoed through the ground in a bass tone grumble, bringing with it an ominous air. But so far, the tunnel seemed as solid as those under the house, a fact for which Eliza was grateful.

They had walked for less than five minutes when the tunnel split into two and the girls paused, considering which way to go.

Rosa pointed left. "That seems to lead back to the house," she said.

"Yes," said Eliza. "Let's take the other one."

As they walked with Rosa leading the way, Eliza felt a chill up her spine, like someone—or some*thing*—was closing in on them. Trill or the *muló*, or some new threat? Was it her intuition warning her or her imagination? She couldn't tell anymore. Fear had clouded her judgment.

Eliza tugged at the haphazard bandage Rosa had made

from her nightgown hem. It stuck to the wound on her arm and itched. Yet she dare not scratch it and anger the injury.

"Stairs," said Rosa, quickening her pace.

There were only three of them, but they still felt like progress. The girls walked down the crude stone steps to another leg of the tunnel—this one offered darker dirt into which their feet sank. Eliza examined the sides of the tunnel as they walked and could see where water may have settled at one point, leaving a ring around the edge. She recalled the ring she'd leave in the bathtub as a child on especially dirty days—the ones she spent playing outside with friends barefoot in high summer.

And then it dawned on her she could hear water dripping. Not a slight trickle either, but running water—like a stream.

When they reached the place where the water was thick, she had already been imagining the worst—a dark pit of stagnant liquid that reeked, filled with growing things. But what they found only smelled like earth and seemed to be rather fresh, with water spilling into a small pool from the sides.

The girls exchanged glances in the firelight.

"Rain from above," said Rosa. "It has to be."

"So, what happens if it keeps raining?" asked Eliza, the panic rising in her chest. She examined the growing surface and the shrinking lip of the pool.

"Well, let's get across now so we don't find out," said Rosa.

Eliza stood frozen in place. Her legs began to shake. "But what if we can't get far on the other side? What if we have to turn back?" The walls seemed to close in on her, the water rushing faster, faster. She almost heard it whisper her name. *Eliza...*

Her breath came more quickly. She couldn't gasp enough

in. She grew hungry for more. But the more she inhaled, the tighter her throat became. It cinched like the tunnel, closing in. Strangling her. She was floating, floating away. The edges of her eyes dimmed and she sank to the earth.

"Hey!" said Rosa. Her face was close to Eliza's now, her dark eyes round and concerned. The candlelight reflected in them like an old-fashioned painting.

Rosa took Eliza's hand. "Liza, you're alright. We're alright. We just need to get across the water. One-two-three. Easy as pie."

"One-two-three," repeated Eliza, trying to focus on Rosa's fingers.

"You're hyperventilating. Breathe with me, slowly," said Rosa. "In…. Out…"

Eliza obeyed, breathing in time with Rosa. Slowly, her sense of balance returned, and she was able to stand. "But what if—"

"No!" said Rosa. "Don't let your mind go there. We're doing this. Together. We're getting across this pool if I have to drag you myself."

Despite the seriousness of what she had experienced, Eliza almost laughed at Rosa's determination. Or maybe she wanted to cry. It was hard to tell.

So, she swallowed her feelings, and all they threatened to do to her, and followed Rosa across the water, stepping on the stones that stuck out enough to help them reach the other side. She prayed they weren't slippery. She hadn't even asked Rosa if she knew how to swim. And while Eliza knew how, there was something about a pool with an endless bottom. It could have been two feet or twenty.

No, she thought. *Don't think about it. Just move.*

She was a woman on a trapeze, arms out to the side, feet placed carefully. Not too quickly, not too carelessly. She stepped, waited for her foot to be sure, shifted her weight. Then again, realizing only when she had reached the other side that Rosa held the candle the whole time.

She exhaled a shaky breath, then permitted a smile to grace her face. But Rosa wasn't smiling. She was looking at her funny. She was looking at her with concern.

"What?" said Eliza.

"Your nightgown," said Rosa.

And Eliza looked down to see the bloodstain, dark and deep and growing.

When she lifted her shift, it revealed red streams running down her inner thighs. They were trickles, like the beginning of a rainstorm, dripping slowly, steadily.

"Oh, my God," said Eliza.

It wasn't like her to take the Lord's name in vain. The nuns at St. Ann's had scared her out of that habit years ago. But it felt appropriate now. "The baby? Or me?" she said.

Rosa shook her head. "Either way, we need to get you some help."

The tears came quickly as Eliza grasped the possibilities. They were underground, and who knows how far away from help? If Trill caught them, it was likely not help she would get. She knew what they had to do—keep going.

"Let's walk," said Eliza. "Let's hope there's another end to this tunnel, and it's not somewhere Trill knows about."

She shoved away the image of Trill waiting in the dark, ready to spring a trap. The girls walked arm in arm, as the width of the tunnel would allow. Eliza left a red trail behind them in the dirt, marking their steps with bits of herself. When they reached the gate that stretched from floor to ceiling, the panic set in again.

Rosa pulled the key from beneath her nightgown, its string still tied around her neck.

"Please let this work," she said. With a deep breath, she slipped the key—the one that had led them to all the secrets in the home—into the hole. With a turn of her wrist, the lock budged. It resisted, old and rusted, but it moved, little by little.

As the key had been for the last few months, it was again their savior.

There was something final that fell upon them as they closed the gate behind and ventured forth. Trill could not reach them now, unless she had a matching key or headed them off at the destination, but Eliza rejected the possibilities. They would not let Trill win.

The tunnel sloped upward, and the dirt shifted from black to a tan, gravely brown. The candle was now half as tall as it had been when they'd first lit it. Eliza kept her eyes on the light, bobbing up and down in Rosa's hand as they walked. It threw shadows on the wall, contorted reflections of Rosa's silhouette, maybe echoes of who she had been in another life. But it was also the beacon guiding them to hope. They just had to keep moving.

Eliza's chest burned with a longing for fresh air, for the night sky, for a feeling of safety. Her legs were so heavy beneath her, as if her ankles had weights around them. Her knees threatened to crumple, wobbling with every few steps. The air was thick in her lungs, and she tried to breathe deeper, harder, to make it stick there.

Rosa's shadow peeked back at her, wild hair flowing in an unseen breeze. And she wondered what her own shadow was doing. She tried to catch it out of the corner of her eye, but as soon as she turned her head, it was gone, a blur against the jagged face of the rocks. It was chased into crevices, where it tucked in to haunt the tunnels forevermore.

"Rosa?" Eliza said, stars appearing in her periphery. She fell to the side and caught herself on the rock wall. The world became hazy, a blend of light and dark, reality and shadow, swirling together as she fell forward and everything became quiet.

When Hattie opened her eyes, Rebecca appeared flushed in the candlelight, her face contorted with worry.

"Hattie? Hattie-Hen?" cried Rebecca. She lightly tapped Hattie's cheeks, trying to rouse her from the spot where she'd collapsed in the tunnel.

She placed a hand to her head and sat with her sister's help. The pain came in waves along with the nausea. "Oh," was all she could muster.

"Tell me," said Rebecca, her pale blue eyes imploring. "What is it? What can I do?" She was crouched down beside Hattie, her breath quickened.

"I'm hungry," said Hattie. "Or, it may be... the baby."

Rebecca's eyes widened, and her lips parted in shock. Hattie could see her sister working it out. "But... Michael's been gone for..." Her eyes narrowed. "His father. He touched you? He did this to you?"

Hattie was silent, but it was all the confirmation Rebecca needed. She stood, a huffing, small girl preparing for a fight. "How dare that monster do this? What a wretch. A thief of your womanhood. A traitor to his own son!" She spat as she yelled, paced back and forth.

Hattie breathed calmly, slowly, feeling her stomach tighten and then relax. Tighten, relax. It was too soon for the baby, she knew. Only six months. She was protective of this little life, no matter the pain that brought it about. There was no need for the child to suffer. She would love it with her whole heart. She already did.

Rebecca was turned away from Hattie, staring into the darkness from whence they had come. Her shoulders rose heavily as she struggled to control her temper. It had always been this way with her, docile for most of the time, but heaven look out if the scales tipped in another direction. She was a torrent of thunder and lightning unleashed.

"You coward! Ratbag!" she screamed into the shadows. "Shame on you!" Her voice echoed down the passage, drawing out the fury in her small body. Her clenched fists shook by her sides.

"Bec, let it go," Hattie said, her voice a gentle whisper. "It's done."

Rebecca turned to face her sister, the candlelight drawing her features upward, making them more severe. Her lip shook. Her eyes were red, brimming with tears she refused to let fall. "I shouldn't have let you come. Not alone."

"*So, you could meet the same fate?*" Hattie said.

"*But I was warned, Hattie-Hen,*" said Rebecca. She cast her eyes downward, a look of shame masking her face. "*Pauline said—*"

"*Rebecca! Mother said you were no longer to see her!*"

Rebecca's lips pursed, sealing her words inside. She swallowed them. Several moments passed with only her heavy breath between them. "*Mother is mistaken. She attends church with all of the others who simply leave to sin again. I love the Lord, Hattie. I do. But what if there's more?*"

"*This is not the time, Rebecca. We need to save ourselves right now. Help me up,*" said Hattie, holding the wall for support as she tried to stand.

Rebecca rushed to her side. "*Of course, forgive me,*" she said. "*You are devoted. Your faith is strong.*"

"*Do not place me on a pedestal, sister,*" said Hattie, now sure on her feet. She paused. "*I don't deny your freedom to question. I've questioned as well. But Pauline's ideas. Her practices. I've heard things… Disturbing things. That's all I'll say on the matter for now.*"

Rebecca held Hattie's arm, steadying her as they walked, seeking the end of the tunnel. "*Very well,*" Rebecca said. "*I admire your willingness to accept God's will.*" Her eyes moved to Hattie's stomach, then to her face. "*But know this. I will not be so forgiving, dear sister, when it comes to your tormentor.*" The bite in her voice sent chills down Hattie's spine. "*There are ways to deal with men like that only a goddess might understand. And that is all I will say on the matter for now.*"

"Rebecca?" said Eliza.

Rosa heard the name from behind her and stopped in her tracks. "What did you say?" she asked, but the words hung in the air as she turned to find Eliza falling to the ground. She braced herself on the wall and then slid down. Rosa caught her before her head hit the path. Her body was limp and her eyes flickered under their lids.

She had seen the red streaks down her friend's legs become heavier, more crimson as they walked. But they pushed ahead despite this because what else were they to do? And now the time for a decision had come.

Rosa knew this was a possibility—that she might have to make a hard call if Eliza could not go on. The thought of leaving her friend in the tunnel had plagued her since they crossed the pond. But there was nothing to be done about it now. Both of their survival depended upon Rosa's two legs to reach the end— and come back with help.

Maybe it was better this way, with Eliza fainted and unaware of the darkness that would fall upon her. Rosa would have to take the candle to find her way, and there was nothing to leave for her friend.

"Liza Lie," she said, though her friend could not hear her. She pushed the words out in a shaky voice. "I'll be back for you. I promise."

Rosa kissed her friend on the forehead and positioned her as best she could on the cold dirt floor. She choked back tears as she turned to face the black hole alone.

Rosa was beyond exhausted. She was hungry, wet, and cold. She was limping. But now she had a new mission. She had to save Eliza's life.

Her friend's face burned in her mind and she pushed her legs faster, faster. Her womb was starting to cramp, and she wondered if she might meet the same fate. But she dare not look down at her own legs. For if she found red there, it might be the end for them. If she fell, too, before reaching the end of the tunnel, they might both be lost to the earth forever.

It was hard to tell how long it took Rosa to reach the stairs. It might have been only thirty minutes, but it felt like hours. The more distance she put between Eliza and herself felt like a growing betrayal.

Up, up she climbed, in a spiral, like the one they had descended beneath the chapel. The candlelight flickered, the wax dripped on the holder, and she had to be careful to hold it away from her gasping breath.

And then there was a door. It loomed before her with all the possibility she could imagine, a portal into the world above. But when her hand turned the knob, there was no response. She looked for a keyhole, but there was none. She turned the knob this way and that, shoved the door with her shoulder, kicked at it. But it stood like a stone guardian, not allowing her to pass.

At her wit's end, Rosa's temper finally got the better of her. "Help!" she screamed. "Help!" She pounded on the door with her fists. "Can anyone hear me?" She bumped at it with her hips. And when everything else was tired and sore, she kicked at the door with her legs. One after the other.

It became a rhythm. Pound, pound, kick. Scream. Over and over, she banged, cried out, until her hands were bruised and her throat raw.

But then there was a noise.

It was a scurry at first, then grew into a gait.

"Help!" Her throat ached with each noise, but she could not let up now.

The voice came like a cool drink on a hot summer day. "Is someone in there?"

"Yes! Help me! Please!" said Rosa, and the tears overtook her.

It had taken an axe for the women behind the door to reach Rosa. But they hacked and chopped, traded turns, until the hole was big enough for her to crawl through. They were dark women, still clad in nightclothes, though the morning light was making its way through the windows in what appeared to be a basement.

They lifted Rosa up, and their eyes grew wide as they saw her round belly.

"I don't know how you got in there or what you're runnin' from," said the tallest of the women. It was her strong hands that birthed Rosa back into the world. "But we have you now."

"My friend," said Rosa. She could taste the blood in her mouth. Was it from the screaming? "You have to help her. She's still in there."

It wasn't until she was being led up the stairs that she noticed some of the women helping her were pregnant, too.

Chapter 30

When Eliza returned to the world, it was bright, even with her eyes still closed. Rebecca's face dissipated; the memory of her voice echoed down an otherworldly tunnel. And when Eliza's lids lifted, she saw a white ceiling—plain, like a blank canvas ready for color. Her mouth was dry. All she wanted was water, but the veils of sleep threatened to pull her back into their realm.

She tried to form words, but they were slow to come to her lips. A sound escaped—a kind of groan that felt foreign to her.

"Liza?" Rosa's voice held both concern and excitement. And then it was louder. "She's awake!"

There was a rush around her. Dark, beautiful faces with soft and nurturing eyes looked down on her like angels. *Was this a dream? Was she dead?*

"Welcome back," one woman said, her hand gentle upon Eliza's forehead. "You had quite an adventure, I hear."

Eliza tried to nod, but everything hurt.

"Rosa tells me Eliza's your name. I'm Nurse Wendy," she said, her voice rich and buttery. "We're going to take care of you now. You're safe."

You're safe. The words echoed in Eliza's mind, tingled all the way to her fingertips. There were a thousand questions floating inside her, but the most urgent one had been answered.

"I'll leave you two to talk," Nurse Wendy said, nodding to Rosa. And then added in a lower tone, "You want to have that talk, or you want me to do it?"

Rosa swallowed; emotion clear upon her face. "I'll do it. Thank you, Wendy."

As the nurse left, closing the door behind her, a hush fell over the room. Rosa took Eliza's hand.

"How's my Dandelion Girl?" said Rosa.

Eliza smiled, her heart fluttering at the term of endearment and its connection to the other girls. It symbolized her time at the home, arriving there like a weed, floating on the wind without direction. It was Lila Grace, she thought, who had suggested perhaps she was more like a lion—filled with secret courage in the guise of a flower. The sadness rose to her throat in a sudden surge. *Lila Grace. Bridget.*

"Where are we?" asked Eliza.

"End of the line," said Rosa. "The tunnel led here, to a house some miles away from the chapel. Seems this was the next station on the Underground Railroad."

"So, it was true, then. That's what those tunnels were?" asked Eliza. She tried to focus on Rosa's large brown eyes, but the edges were still hazy.

"That's what they tell me here," said Rosa.

"And where is *here*, exactly?" asked Eliza.

"Believe it or not, it's another unwed mother's home," said Rosa.

Eliza's eyes narrowed. "What? A different one?"

"For colored women," said Rosa.

"Huh," said Eliza, for that's all she could think of to say. So many women, so many babies… such a judgmental world.

"Why they bother separating us is beyond me," said Rosa,

rolling her eyes.

"How long have I been…" asked Eliza, not finishing her thought. Not needing to.

"You passed out in the tunnels," said Rosa. She gulped and added in a softer tone, "I had to leave you there."

Eliza's eyes grew wide at the thought. "In the dark?" she asked.

Rosa nodded and rushed into her apology. "I'm sorry. I didn't know what else to do." She squeezed Eliza's hand harder.

"And Trill?" asked Eliza.

"I don't know. We called the police. A detective should be here to talk to us soon. Nurse Wendy said they take their time responding to anything from this neighborhood," said Rosa. "But, Liza, there is something else."

Eliza just looked at her friend, waiting. Rosa couldn't meet her eyes. When they finally lifted, Eliza saw tears. Eliza squeezed her hand.

"What is it?" asked Eliza, then held her breath.

"You remember bleeding?" Rosa asked.

Eliza nodded. Nausea crawled up from her stomach. "I lost the baby, didn't I?"

Rose exhaled slowly, nodded her head. "Yeah, you did."

Eliza's glance moved to her belly. She placed her free hand there. "But it feels like I'm still pregnant." She felt disconnected somehow, like everything they had just lived through had happened to someone else.

Rosa licked her lips. "I know. That's because—" She exhaled a shaky breath. "You've still got to deliver it."

It. The baby had become an *it*.

Eliza was two people then. One who felt a sudden rush of relief. Her fate had changed. And yet… she had started to imagine this little one who might love her always. Someone she could share all the beautiful things about the world with and protect from all the ugliness, too. But that image was just a dream. And now it was fading.

The pain hit her chest with a thud and dragged her insides down toward her feet.

Rosa sat with her in the silence. The tears fell down Eliza's face in long drags, leaving trails of wetness and salt, of dreams that were not to be. But there was hope, too, for her future was not yet written. She looked out the window, into the gray sky that still warned of rain and sadness.

"Well," whispered Eliza. "Maybe we didn't escape the *muló* after all."

There was a knock on the door.

Nurse Wendy entered reverently. "You alright?" She looked back and forth between the girls. None of the nurses were like this at the other place, Eliza thought. None of them.

"We're alright," said Rosa. "As alright as we can be."

Nurse Wendy pulled up a chair from the side of the room, sat beside Rosa and looked into Eliza's eyes. She could almost feel the warmth radiating from this woman—a nurturing she had always wished for from her own mother. And she'd found it in this place of strangers.

"This is going to be the hardest thing you have ever done," said Nurse Wendy. "But you're not doing it alone. You've got your friend here. And you've got us."

And it *was* the hardest thing she had ever done, in some ways, that is. It was the final culmination of the cocoon she had been living in for the last several months—a home run by a sadistic woman who held no warmth in her heart. Haunted by a beast, once the soul of a wicked man whose hatred for young women had tied him to the earth. Baby bones of forgotten children, at least one who had been placed there with loving hands and some who would never be found.

But there was beauty, too. The birth of friendships like Eliza had never known. Secrets and stories, adventures and intrigue. Tales of resilience and the courage to protect others. A sense of family that would set the bar for all relationships she sought thereafter. A sisterhood of blood and tears and survival.

These truths revealed themselves as Eliza floated between dreaming and consciousness in the hours after the birth of her dead child. *It.* But the child would not be *It* for long. She just had to find the right name for the baby bones that would never be forgotten.

When Eliza woke fully, hours after the traumatic delivery, Rosa was asleep in the chair beside her bed. She'd remained with her the whole time—a constant companion even through the shadows and pain of this loss. In the midst of her broken heart, where the tendrils of hope sought rich soil, Eliza felt a rush of gratitude for this lovely friend in her life. 'Thank you' would never be enough.

In the silence, Eliza thought back to the first game of Questions and Commands they had all played together. She couldn't remember the question exactly, but it was something about discovering another flower within yourself.

Dandelion Girl. The name had once captured all the shame she felt. A weed to be plucked, tossed aside to make way for the perennials and annuals people cultivated. She once would have done anything to shed the ugly flower that haunted her with its terrible leaves. But something had shifted in her—

through her friendships, fleeing from a wolf spirit in the night, birthing a child she had never wanted to begin with. She had begun to see the bloom with new eyes.

Dandelion Girl! The roar of the lion, the shedding of the mane, the wishes not as mere pieces scattered to the wind but possibilities for the future. There was power in those seeds and she had so many to sow. She *was* the collection of wishes. And she was the wind upon which they would be carried. She just had to decide which way to blow.

The hum of the wind picked up outside, acknowledging her newfound power. Leaves tapped against the window, dancing in time upon their branches. And when they stood still, something alighted upon a branch. Something familiar.

Eliza rose from the bed, though she was under orders not to do so. But this—this felt more important in the moment.

She moved slowly, carefully, placing her naked feet on the cold floor one at a time, shifting her weight with intention. As the space closed between her and the window, the creature came more fully into view. The sparrow peered in through the pane, tilting its head this way and that. Then it let out a lilting song and sounded like *hello*.

"Thank you, Hattie," Eliza whispered.

And just like that, the sparrow was gone. Had she even been there at all? Eliza placed her hands on the glass, a sheer veil separating her from the other side.

"Liza?" Rosa's voice came from behind her. "What are you doing? Lie back down."

Eliza turned to see her friend rushing to help her back to bed, taking her arm and guiding her back to safety.

"I've named the baby," Eliza said, pulling the covers back over her legs. "Fae."

Rosa sank back into her seat, placed her hands on her belly. She nodded. "How do you know she was a girl?" she asked. "You weren't even aware when…"

Eliza shrugged. "I just know."

"Fae," said Rosa, nodding. "From the fairy realm."

"Too magical for a body to hold," said Eliza, her throat tight with emotion. But sharing the name with Rosa brought a sense of relief, and she knew it was right.

"I love it," said Rosa.

Chapter 31

It was on the fourth day they had been at the unwed mothers home for colored women that Eliza and Rosa ventured onto the first floor of the house. Eliza was well enough to walk and though Rosa was coming upon the end of her pregnancy, the nurses said walking would be good for both of them.

Neither of the women was ready to go outside. The mere idea of this filled Eliza with dread. For even though the police had come, and they had divulged everything (well, almost everything, save ghosts in the walls or the *muló* or the mystic hand), Trill had not faced any charges. In fact, there had been no follow-up at all. Nothing from the police and not a word from Trill or her associates. Even their parents questioned their honesty. It was as if it had never happened at all. As if their suffering and fear meant nothing. They were invisible.

"How can such abuses go unpunished?" asked Rosa, her face filled with outrage as they made their way down the stairs.

"Maybe they think we're hysterical women—not reliable, over-exaggerating," said Eliza. In her gut, she felt this was truly the case.

"But what about Bridget? Lila Grace? *Mary,* for God's sake?" said Rosa.

"This isn't over," said Eliza. "We just need some time to

rest."

"Yes, figure out our next step," said Rosa. "And if the police won't listen to us, I think I know someone who will."

"Who's that?" asked Eliza, as her feet finally touched down on the wooden foyer of the first floor. She helped Rosa down the last step.

"My neighbor, Thelma. I've babysat for her children before. She promotes women's rights. Her husband is a reporter for the Cleveland Press. Maybe we can get her to bend his ear," said Rosa. She swiped at a loose curl that kissed her forehead.

"Rosa, look," said Eliza. Her eyes had drifted into a room beyond the foyer, where a portrait hung on the wall. The faces were familiar, even in the dim light. "What it the world…" she said.

The women walked arm in arm into the library, with its curtains drawn and flames crackling in the fireplace. Books hugged the walls from floor to ceiling and a wooden piano stood quietly in a far corner. The portrait of two white women was a focal point of the room, just above the fireplace, with a set of armchairs facing it.

The dark-haired woman on the left was clad in a green dress, simple and demure. Her eyes echoed the color and held a quiet confidence. The other woman had light hair and pale eyes full of impetus; her dress was blue and buttoned up to her neck, though it did nothing to mask her bravado. They held hands and sat beside one another in a sisterly embrace.

"Hattie," whispered Eliza. "And Rebecca." She turned to Rosa, whose eyes were wide, studying the faces.

"Amazing," said Eliza. "They're who I saw. *Exactly* who I saw."

"But what are they doing *here*?" asked Rosa.

The floor creaked under Nurse Wendy's feet as she approached them from behind. "Our benefactress and her sister," she said.

Eliza reddened, wondering if she had heard… if she knew about the dreams. She raised her eyes hesitantly, but Nurse Wendy was fully focused on the painting.

"The story goes," said Nurse Wendy, her voice like velvet. "That the Webb sisters escaped from a nearby house, came in through the door in the basement, just as you did."

As Nurse Wendy spoke, Eliza noticed for the first time the trinkets on the mantle. A lit candle surrounded by dried flowers, feathers, rocks and coins. They were scattered like offerings beneath the portrait.

"Harriet Webb Prescott, the dark-haired one," said Nurse Wendy. "Had lived in the house with her husband, Michael Prescott. She was an abolitionist. Worked with wealthy like-minded people to construct the Underground Railroad in these parts. But after her husband was killed in the war—the Civil War—his father came back to claim the property. Abused her, locked her away like something you hear in a storybook. When her sister, Rebecca Webb, stopped receiving her letters, she came to find her. And they got out."

Eliza took a shaky breath, emotion filling her chest. Everything she had seen—it *had* been real. Hattie and Rebecca—they'd come for the girls in the house. They'd come to lead them out. The truth of it wanted to leap off her tongue, but she dare not speak it. She wanted Nurse Wendy to like her, and heaven only knows what she might think if she knew… Accuse her of witchcraft, shun her out of fear.

"What happened to them?" asked Rosa. "After."

Nurse Wendy's eyes fell upon the women, dark pools that

felt like an embrace. The corners of her mouth turned up a touch. "They met my great grandmother." She gestured behind them, to the opposite side of the room.

The painting was equally as grand as the one of Hattie and Rebecca—a striking woman clad in scarlet with fabric wrapped around her head. Her skin was tan—not white, not colored, but somewhere in between. Her features were strong and beautiful at the same time, with dark eyes that had seen much. They knew much. Eliza walked closer, closer, drawn in by the magic that seemed to swirl around her.

Several candles burned in tribute to her as well, with even more dried flowers and coins. There were also small slips of paper with writing on them. *Prayers?* Eliza wondered.

"Mama Zo," said Nurse Wendy, "was a most powerful woman. My mama said she learned her craft from Marie Catherine Laveau, the Voodoo Priestess in N'Orleans. Mama Zo was a free woman in Louisiana. Married and came north to help others."

"Priestess?" asked Eliza. She had only ever heard of male Catholic priests.

"A master of magical arts—a teacher, a healer," said Nurse Wendy. "And a midwife." She let the words hang in the air, sink into Eliza. "She had the sight. Like you."

Eliza's mouth opened in surprise. "How did you—"

"And like me," said Nurse Wendy, smiling with her eyes.

Eliza's gaze went to the cross that hung around Nurse Wendy's neck, and she tried to make sense of how all these things could be true. How they could all fit in the same picture.

"One thing about white people—white families—I have noticed," said Nurse Wendy. "They think about things as separate. They see the world of the living and the world of the dead as two different things. But this rule is fiction. It doesn't exist."

"You sound like my Grandmama," said Rosa, edging closer to Nurse Wendy.

"Probably a wise woman," said Nurse Wendy, her laughter filling the room, hugging them with its vibration. As it dissipated, she took another breath. "Mama Zo was a healer. But you cross her, and her teeth would come out."

"When she met the Webb sisters, she found kindred spirits," said Nurse Wendy. "But Mama Zo was both the dark and light wrapped into one. The sisters…" she gestured to the other painting. "Were like two halves—reflections, but not the same. Harriet was a healer—graceful, kind, gentle. Mama Zo taught her midwifery. Rebecca was a warrior—a protector, and sometimes this meant revenge."

Nurse Wendy walked back toward the sisters, her words swirling around Eliza and Rosa, drawing them back in time.

"While Harriet was content to walk away from her abuser, Rebecca was not. She returned to the Prescott property under the guise of a maid. The only one who knew what she looked like was no longer at the home, so there was no one to reveal her secret. The master of the house had never laid eyes upon her. The story goes that she sought her revenge on the Prescott Senior, then she disappeared, never to be seen in these parts again.

"Well, by anyone outside of this house, anyway," said Nurse Wendy. "I was told she did come to visit her sister every once in a while, but Rebecca returned to New York. And had some other adventures. Harriet stayed here mostly, in this house, by Mama Zo's side. Even to her last days."

"They were friends," said Eliza.

"Yes," said Nurse Wendy. "The best of friends."

"Nurse Wendy?" said Eliza. "Thank you."

"We're grateful for your help," said Rosa.

"When you do the right thing, knowing that is thank you enough," said Nurse Wendy. "Maybe one day, you help someone else."

With that, she left the two women to reflect in the silence, under the watchful eyes of the guardian spirits.

On the sixth day, Rosa went into labor. It was a long process—20 hours—and filled with moments of fear and triumph. Eliza was by her side the whole time, holding her hand, saying encouraging things, swallowing the sadness that would rise up without warning, like she had to purge some spoiled food in her gut. But she breathed through it; like Rosa giving birth to a child, so Eliza released her pain. She turned each time to her friend, loyal beyond measure, and committed again to standing with her through this—no matter what. And in the early hours of morning, before the sun peeked over the horizon, Rosa's little girl was born.

Chapter 32

It was in the haze of sleep deprivation, in the wake of the tension of a laborious birth, and after Rosa had slipped into a restful sleep with the baby by her side, that Eliza ventured out of doors.

Overcome with gratitude for her friend and the pain of having lost her own baby, Eliza sank to her knees on the grass in the home's backyard. The blades were soft beneath her, tickling her legs and itching as they mixed with her sweat. She imagined she was sinking into the ground with a dandelion's roots, being hugged by motherly tendrils deep beneath the soil. The ground hummed beneath her, the bosom of life witnessing the tumult of emotion inside. There was also something she did not expect—a longing to hold on to this time that felt like it was slipping between her fingers.

The journey was coming to an end. There was nothing she could do to stop it. It was the way of life, graduating from institutions and moving on to what society expected. But her life had taken a whimsical adventure over the past several months, tugging her this way and that. When she had entered the home, all hope for a normal life, one with a loving husband and respectable house in the suburbs, had been shattered. She was tainted—a single, unwed mother who would carry shame wherever she went.

But now the slate had been wiped clean. Suddenly. Unexpectedly. The trajectory of her life had shifted again, and possibility loomed before her in an overwhelming apex that she had yet to crest. She knew not what lay on the other side.

But she knew she would never look at her parents in the same way. For all her life, they had told her they loved her. But did love glare at you with judgmental eyes? Did love drop you off at a strange place to battle with demons alone? What they had for her was expectation. And perhaps there was love there, too, for she did love them truly, though the more secret parts of her wanted to yank back that love like a rug out from under a set of beautiful China. China that had no cracks or flaws. China that lied. It deserved to be smashed into tiny pieces and crunched under her feet.

Eliza breathed. She breathed deeply. She let tears flow and thoughts come and go while she was held by the unwavering earth beneath her knees. And she prayed, not to the conception of God that her parents had presented, but to the force of being she had always felt there. She had no need to name it, call it He or She, say specific words that reflected a strict dogma. She simply felt a communion with what she thought an unwavering parent might offer—unconditional love.

Eliza's shoulders dropped. She sank further into the earth, lying down upon its soft surface, running her hands over the blades of grass and spots of clover. She rolled onto her back and looked up into the trees that swayed above her, sweeping back and forth across the morning sky like giant paint brushes. She placed her hands on her flat stomach, absent of the life that had been growing there. It was foreign, a distant memory of an older version of herself. The flatness felt empty.

A white butterfly danced in the wind, fluttering its wings

in time with her heartbeat. Bees buzzed by, paying her no mind, and songbirds piped tunes that wove in and out of each other. The world kept on turning despite her heart hanging in suspension.

The sound of a clearing throat pulled Eliza out of her reverie. She sat up, the world spinning until she was upright.

The woman stood on the steps at the back of the home, her uniform crisp and clean, and for a moment, Eliza's body stiffened. It was a uniform of the previous place—the one with Trill. Eliza was on her feet and backing away before she knew what she was doing, looking around for matching uniforms, for arms reaching out to grab her. But none came. It was just the one woman—her dark face and eyes not vicious, but soft. Caring.

"Eliza, right?" she said. "I'm Dot, you remember?"

Eliza nodded, reorienting herself to the memory of the kind ward assistant—the one who had helped Bridget. It was strange to see her here, in this new place that had become her solace.

"Are you here to take us back?" Eliza asked. Her whole body was rigid, ready to run at the slightest hint of threat.

Dot's face relaxed into a smile. It was a kind one, if holding something back. "No, ma'am. They don't know I'm here."

Eliza nodded, tried to calm her pounding heart.

Dot stepped forward. "I wanted to work here, at this home, but there were no more jobs. My sister—she's Edna—the large assistant with the birthmark here." She touched the right side of her face and the memory of the woman came into Eliza's mind.

"Yes, I know Edna. She's kind," said Eliza.

Dot smiled, nodded. "Mm hm. She said two white girls

came up through the tunnels, like something from an old tale. Thought it might be you since you and the other one came up missing."

Eliza took a step forward, realizing she was being rude. Years of coaching had been lost to her, and she struggled to remember the rules for this sort of engagement.

"Have you been offered a drink? Some water?" asked Eliza, awkwardness rising to her face, warming it.

"I'll only be a moment. Have to get to work," Dot said. "For now, anyway. I come to tell you about your friends. I know where they sent Bridget and the other one…"

"Lila Grace?" said Eliza, her heart jumping. "Are they alright?"

Dot shook her head warily. "I don't know. The files say they went to the Cleveland State Hospital. Both of them. Lila first, then Bridget after. I heard Miss Trill talking about it. Said they'd never get out, that they deserved no better."

A lump formed in Eliza's throat, and a heaviness grew in her stomach. "The hospital—but isn't that to help them?"

"You would think that, yes," said Dot. "But… I don't think so."

The air hung around Eliza in a heavy blanket. The world felt like too much. What could she do?

Dot took a deep breath, like she was about to make a confession. "I'm going after them," she said, with such a strength it lifted Eliza out of the sinking veils that caught her in a spider's web. "I'm going in to help them. It's not right, sending people to suffer."

"Wh—How?" said Eliza, words losing their sense in her mouth.

Dot raised her eyebrows. "There's an advantage to being

a colored worker, a cleaner. You can be invisible." She motioned Eliza to come into the house, eager to tell her more. Hadn't Eliza just been lamenting her own invisibility? She felt her perceptions shifting, considering Dot's words.

As Dot disappeared into the home, Eliza followed, leaving the imprint of her body on the grass behind. She turned around to glance at the sky one more time, hoping to catch a glimpse of the white butterfly. It was then she sensed a shift in the air, a feeling of eyes upon her.

It was as if someone—something—stretched out its intention to surround her, hold her, strangle her. And she stood for a moment, captivated, scanning the trees for movement. Her ears perked up, listening past the rush of wind, and noticed the birds had fallen silent. There was a predator lurking there. A hint of musk on the breeze.

The *muló* was waiting. Perhaps it always would be. But for now, Eliza had to focus on her friends. She had to step forward with courage and run through the night, if that's what it took.

With determination, Eliza stomped her foot. She glared into the trees. She dared the *muló* to jump. And there was nothing. For in the sunshine, shadows scatter. It would have to wait until a dark night fell. For now, Eliza shone in the light.

Epilogue – The Trill Diaries

August 15, 1948.
Father,

I beseech you grant me forgiveness. A blasphemy occurred on the steps of your house—an affront to your order of love and marriage. The violation is so wicked and contemptuous it has poisoned the very ground upon which the home stands. The offenders have been relocated and will receive both punishment and treatment; they will repent for what they have done. I will ensure this is carried out swiftly and without mercy until they renounce their ways. On my name as a Christian woman, I declare this will be done.

Your devout servant,
Christine Trill

August 16, 1948
Father,

I have seen your sign! The bird alighted on your steps as I groveled before them, begging your forgiveness. Only you would have such power to relieve my despair.

I will go. I will oversee their correction myself. I am to continue your work at Cleveland State Hospital, righting the minds of your humble people—and subduing those who are not yet humbled.

I remain your devout servant,
Christine Trill

About the Author

Mary Carroll Leoson is a Pushcart Nominee and Affiliate Member of the Horror Writers Association who specializes in literary and historical horror fiction. Her writing has been featured in publications such as *The Lost Librarian's Grave* Anthology, Castabout's *Halloween Anthology*, *Free Spirit Historic Tales Anthology*, *Twisted Vine Literary Journal*, *Coffin Bell Journal*, and *Untoward Magazine*. Leoson holds a Doctor of Arts in English Pedagogy & Literature, an MFA in Fiction, an MA in English, and an MS in Psychology. When she's not writing about ghosts or co-hosting the podcast *Exhuming the Bones* (Ohio Chapter of the Horror Writers Association), she teaches creative writing, literature, film, composition, and psychology at the college level. She lives on the shores of Lake Erie with her husband and two very spoiled dogs. You can learn more at www.maryleoson.com.

Acknowledgements

I would like to acknowledge these wonderful writers and professionals who have all been involved in various aspects of fostering this book into existence: Tim McWhorter, Lee Murray, Megan E. Hart, Meghan Wagner, Beverly Bambury, and Brooklyn Ann.

Thank you to my family and friends for your unwavering support. These amazing individuals deserve much more than a note of acknowledgement, and I hope I tell them that enough: Ed Leoson, Korinne Courtwright, Becky Swersky, Finnian Burnett, Jeffery Buckner-Rodas, Kelly Griffiths, David Williams, Amanda Rabuck, Laura Kunchik, Diane Mull, and the Carrolls (Kim, Gene, Jamie, Brendan, and Phil).

Thank you to my colleagues in the Horror Writers' Association and the NEOMFA, especially Christopher Barzak and Imad Rahman.

I would be remiss if I did not also mention my dogs, whose tail wagging and desperate pleas for attention often interrupt my writing time, but always fill me back up with just the right amount of spirit to sit down at the keyboard again: Samwise the Golden and Penny the Chocolate Lab Mix.

A sneak peek at Book #2...

Of

Monarchs

And

Songbirds

Chapter 1

August, 1948.
Eliza Kendall– Dandelion Girl.

Eliza examined her old scrapbook, a collection of things that belonged to a disconnected past. Scraps of notes passed between friends. Candy wrappers from the drive-in. Ticket stubs from Euclid Beach Park. A pressed rose that Michael had given to her—just before… Photographs in gray hues that stared back, her own gaze like a stranger's. Had she ever been that girl? Happy. Filled with dreams. Hopeful. She gulped down her feelings, turned the page.

> *Dear Future*, the letter began. *When I am 25, I will be happily married with one child and another on the way. We'll live in the suburbs, not too far from my parents, but just far enough for some independence. When I envision my husband, I see someone tall and strong, though I can't quite see his face…*

The lump grew tighter in Eliza's throat. She shut her eyes, cursing the tears that squeezed out the corners. They dripped in long trails, spilled onto her new pink dress—the one her mother had bought for her homecoming. Pink blush. Not white—her mother would never buy her white again. But pink was close—white with a dash of red that pulled it toward passion. Muted passion. Murdered passion.

Eliza's future had been stolen. Damn the day she ever laid eyes on Michael. Anger should spill in first, but it didn't. Instead, there was a dull ache and a longing for the person she had thought he was. But that boy was just an illusion.

Through swollen eyes, she looked around her childhood room, baby blue walls she'd painted with her mother at 10. Her name hanging from the ceiling in puffy stitched letters, each one spinning of its own accord. The bedspread she sat upon, embroidered with daisies. And the gilded framed mirror that hung on the wall. The one that had been her grandmother's and was fit for a princess. Those were the things of a little girl. An innocent maiden. A fool.

And she was no longer a fool.

She sat there for a long time, considering this odd place. It was familiar yet strange, like she had become some other person in her time away. She had shed skin that now belonged to a memory—held that other girl to the standards of a proper young lady. It hadn't been enough to keep this version of Eliza in check. Shame swelled within her for a moment, pushing on her organs, thumping on her heart, but it was joined by bitterness that crept up through her throat and tickled her tongue. It wanted to speak.

As Eliza sat with these things, the sun fell lower in the sky, spilling light in through the window and bathing her in a halo of gold. She thought of her friends, like fairies in the mist somewhere, lost to time. Rosa, with her confident smile, fiery Bridget and her crass words, and complicated Lila Grace, one moment sweet, the next like a devil in waiting. Her sisters. Her soulmates.

Where were they now? The only one she knew for certain was Rosa, who had quietly gotten married in front of a judge and was preparing to move to base with Matteo and their new baby girl. They still had yet to learn where. Eliza had been the only non-family member to witness the union. Their age difference was not lost on Eliza then. With only a year between them, Eliza almost 17 and Rosa at 18, it was an ocean. Rosa was a wife and a mother now. An adult. The chasm separating them was painful.

And Bridget and Lila Grace were out there somewhere. Locked up. Going through God knows what. What she wouldn't give to see them. Talk to them. Hug them.

Eliza let out a long, shaky sigh. There was nothing to do but let it be. And look forward to Rosa's next letter. Maybe a phone call. A quick hug before departure if she was lucky. What would she do without Rosa, with her mischief and wild laughter?

Emptiness nuzzled into Eliza's stomach.

If Bridget was here, she'd have some well-crafted swears to give the pain life. Shouting them out the window was tempting. If Lila Grace had a say, she'd tell Eliza to be a behave. Accept her parents' help and their rules. And then seek retribution quietly from the inside, so they'd never know it was her.

Could Bridget and Lila Grace see the setting sun? Breath the fresh air? Had they found one another? Eliza shuddered. *We always have the sky*, she whispered, looking out the window, shielding her eyes from the sun and examining the treetops that hung like lace against a pale blue backdrop. She hoped they remembered—all of them. They must.

She had never been to an asylum, knew little of what it meant save for "crazy." But she was barraged with horrific images—screams and bound hands and feelings of terror that twisted her stomach. She breathed through the nausea that rose and then subsided.

And then the thought of Ms. Trill seeped in, a smoky lingering that smelled of betrayal. It was her fault. She's the reason for her friends' suffering. She's the reason they were torn from one another. Anger burned in Eliza's chest. Notions of revenge crept up the back of her neck. And when she looked into the gilded framed mirror, she didn't see herself.

Eliza's light blonde hair had turned a shade darker, and her cornflower eyes became water, an eerie pale blue-green. It was Rebecca, Hattie's sister, that stared back at her, held her gaze from within the mirror, a ring of flame behind her head. Was the setting sun deceiving her? Eliza blinked. Then blinked again. But Rebecca didn't disappear. She sat, waiting.

The hum emerged from somewhere dark, rising into the air like tendrils, wrapping its vibration around Eliza. Intertwined voices held notes that hugged each other, leaned toward discord, then resolved. The music was compelling. Beautiful. Haunting. And calling to her.

Eliza rose from her seat on the embroidered bedspread, leaving daisies in her wake, spilling the scrapbook onto the floor. Memories scattered, tumbled underneath the bed and into the corners of the room. But Eliza could not look away from Rebecca.

The reflection drew her closer, bidding her forth to the veil between them. The smell of rosemary tickled her nose, followed by a tangy citrus. The light shifted in the periphery as shadows grew long. The hum became louder, and lines drew Rebecca's face downward. Her skin sagged, age softening her edges. She was an old woman now, with pale eyes nested in wrinkles, emanating power. Her hands rested upon a walking stick, calmly folded. Here lips did not move, but Eliza heard Rebecca's thoughts.

What does a lion do?

Eliza knew the answer. Roar, she thought.

Say it.

Eliza's lips parted. "Roar," she whispered, moving closer, her breath fogging the mirror.

Louder.

"Roar," she said.

I know you're angry. I can feel it.

"Yes," said Eliza.

Show me.

Eliza needed no words. Images of her friends swam between them—Rosa's soulful eyes, Bridget's sassy comebacks, Lila Grace's tears. All of them laughing, connected. All of them sharing fears and hopes and dreams. Holding onto each other, trusting in their friendship. And this bond being torn from her. Followed by emptiness. And silence.

Then a burst of emotion.

Running, running through the tunnels, over graves and through the rain. Falling into darkness. Losing the child that had been growing within her. The disdain on her parents' faces before, and the shame she felt in their presence now.

And then there was Trill. Her empty eyes. Her spiteful words. The destruction she caused. The pain. Eliza's fists tightened. Her teeth bit down. And she began to shake.

Burn, Trill. Burn.

In that moment, Rebecca's face shifted in the mirror, contorted into fury. She raised the walking stick and slammed the tip into the ground, the sound echoing through Eliza's room.

Roar!

And Eliza screamed. It was a scream of fury and anguish. Her soul was on fire and needed to escape. All the rage was eating her alive. She sucked in air again and shrieked. Louder, higher, angrier. It was the sound of wrath.

But she was not alone. The sisters were all around her. The hum of a hundred voices wrapped around her cries and lifted them to the sky, where surely God heard it. He had to. *She* had to.

Eliza sank to the floor, surrounded by pieces of shattered glass.

www.ingramcontent.com/pod-product-compliance
Lightning Source LLC
Chambersburg PA
CBHW061529210726
48287CB00006B/1887